BERRIED TO THE HILT

A GRAY WHALE INN MYSTERY

BERRIED TO THE HILT

KAREN MACINERNEY

WHEELER
CHIVERS

This Large Print edition is published by Wheeler Publishing, Waterville, Maine, USA and by AudioGO Ltd, Bath, England.
Wheeler Publishing, a part of Gale, Cengage Learning.
Copyright © 2010 by Karen MacInerney.
The moral right of the author has been asserted.

LIBRARY OF CONGRESS CATALOGING-IN-PUBLICATION DATA

MacInerney, Karen, 1970–
    Berried to the hilt : a Gray Whale Inn mystery / by Karen MacInerney.
        p. cm. — (Wheeler Publishing large print cozy mystery)
    ISBN-13: 978-1-4104-3182-0 (pbk.)
    ISBN-10: 1-4104-3182-7 (pbk.)
    1. Bed and breakfast accommodations—Maine—Fiction. 2. Murder—Investigation—Fiction. 3. Cranberry Isles (Me. : Islands)—Fiction. 4. Maine—Fiction. 5. Large type books. I. Title.
PS3613.A27254B47 2011
813'.6—dc22   2010046348

BRITISH LIBRARY CATALOGUING-IN-PUBLICATION DATA AVAILABLE

Published in 2011 in the U.S. by arrangement with Midnight Ink, an imprint of Llewellyn Publications, Woodbury, MN 55125-2989 USA.
Published in 2011 in the U.K. by arrangement with Llewellyn Worldwide Ltd.

U.K. Hardcover: 978 1 445 83616 4 (Chivers Large Print)
U.K. Softcover: 978 1 445 83617 1 (Camden Large Print)

Printed in the United States of America
1 2 3 4 5 6 7 15 14 13 12 11

Dedicated with love to the memory of
Merrie Leigh Orton MacInerney

ACKNOWLEDGMENTS

Thank yous, as always, go first to my family — Eric, Abby, and Ian — for all their love and support; also to Dave and Carol Swartz, and Ed and Dorothy MacInerney. I am so lucky to have my extended family so close! Thanks also to Bethann and Beau Eccles, my adopted family; my wonderful nieces and nephews on both sides; to my sister, Lisa, and her family; and to my fabulous grandmother, Marian Quinton (and Nora Bestwick).

Many thanks to my agent Jessica Faust, who is there for me at every plot turn. I cannot say enough good things about the fabulous Midnight Ink team — particularly Terri Bischoff, whose support, (and willingness to wait a few months when things got hectic) has been amazing. Thanks also to Connie Hill, editor extraordinaire, for finding my mistakes and making me look good, and Ellen Dahl, whose cover concepts rock.

I also want to give a shout-out to Thea Eaton, here in Austin, for all of her help with the web page.

And a big thank you to all those supportive friends out there — particularly Dana Lehman, J. Jaye Smith, Jessica Park, Austin Mystery Writers, and all my friends at the Westbank Library and my local coffee shop and bookstore. Thanks also to all of the wonderful readers who take the time to tell me you enjoyed the books; I couldn't do it without you!

ONE

"What were you thinking?"

It was a question I had often asked myself over the last few years, ever since I quit my job, sold my house, and plunked down my life savings on the gray-shingled inn on Cranberry Island, Maine. As gorgeous as the locale was — after more than a decade in sun-baked Texas, I was still awed by the beauty of the mountains across the water, their granite shoulders now swathed in the brilliant golds and russets of early October — starting a bed and breakfast had been fraught with challenges.

But Charlene wasn't referring to my decision to gamble my life savings on a house on an island. Nor was she talking about my recent transition from bed-and-breakfast to full-service inn, which, even with help, was turning out to be a more-than-full-time job.

"I don't know," I said, switching the phone to the other ear and stepping out of my steamy kitchen onto the back porch. A welcome gust of cool fall air swept over me, and I took a deep breath of it before continuing. "I guess it sounded like a good idea at the time."

A month ago, Tom Lockhart, the Cranberry Island selectman and head of the lobster co-op, had asked me to judge the annual cranberry bake-off. Flattered to be included, I had said yes, thinking it was a wonderful way to become more involved with the community.

I was right about the involvement in the community. But I got the "wonderful" part all wrong.

"Natalie, you're doomed," Charlene said. "It doesn't matter who you give the prizes to; everyone else will accuse you of playing favorites. Ten years from now, they still won't have forgiven you."

"But the entries are anonymous!" I protested. "I won't know whose is whose!"

"We live on an island of under a hundred people, Natalie. Do you really think you won't recognize Claudette's sugarless cranberry pie?"

I puckered involuntarily at the mention of the infamous pie, realizing that Charlene was right as usual. As Cranberry Island's postmistress and general store owner, she was the arbiter of all things island. She and I had hit it off almost immediately, and now I couldn't imagine life without my impeccably dressed, bubbly friend.

"So what do I do?"

"I don't know. Maybe you could ask John to drop something on your head — something heavy enough to put you in the hospital for a few days. It might be easier."

Despite my dire situation, I couldn't help feeling a little tingle at the mention of my neighbor — and now fiancé — John. I held up my left hand; the sapphire stone of the engagement ring sparkled in the light. We hadn't set a date for the wedding yet — I'd been too busy with the transition to lunch and dinner service to do much other than sleep — but we were thinking maybe early spring, before the tourist season began. "I can't go into the hospital," I said. "I've got a business to run."

"Then we'll have to come up with a strategy," she said.

"I've got a novel idea. How about I taste all the dishes and give the best one the award?" I asked.

"You're so naïve," she said. "I'll think about it and get back to you. I've got to get down to the dock for a delivery. Talk to you later!"

And then she was gone.

I hung up the phone and shaded my eyes, squinting into the distance. Sure enough, the *Island Princess* was puttering over from the mainland, leaving a pearly wake in the dark blue water as it hauled tourists, groceries, and mail to the island. Unless you had a boat, the only way on and off Cranberry Island was the mail boat, which made stops only a couple of times a day. Today's load would not include a large grocery order for me, since my four guests would be departing the next day, leaving only one room booked for the weekend. The mortgage, unfortunately, didn't care how many rooms were occupied; it still needed to be paid.

And then there was the bake-off to worry about.

I turned reluctantly from the sweeping view, my eyes lingering only briefly on John's carriage house, which was just down the hill from the inn. I knew he had gone to Mount Desert Island in his skiff, *Mooncatcher,* to stock up on paints for the toy boats he sold at Island Artists. Like many on the island, he was a jack-of-all-trades: island deputy, artist, craftsman, and now part-time chef at the inn. The barn next to the small house functioned as his workshop, and would continue to — but to increase our income we had talked about renting out the carriage house once we were married. *Married.* Just the word was enough to send tingles through me.

The buzzer sounded as I opened the oven door, releasing the warm, yeasty scent of fresh rolls. Lunch was lobster salad, which I'd prepared a half hour ago and was already in the fridge, along with rolls, a lightly dressed green salad, and a cookie. I pulled the tray of golden cloverleaf rolls from the oven and put them on a rack to cool, then grabbed the flour and sugar from the pantry and set to work making my favorite gingersnap recipe. The recipe for the gingery cookies was a gift from an old friend, and a perfect accompaniment to the crisp fall air. The afternoon sun slanted through the old mullioned windows, making the yellow walls glow, and the antique pine floors creaked under my feet as I creamed the butter and sugar, then cracked an egg into the bowl. A few minutes later, as I scooped the stiff dough into balls and rolled them in sugar, I found myself smiling with contentment. So what if I didn't have any bookings for the next few weeks? So what if I was about to commit social suicide at the bake-off?

Maybe I'd run a fall special, I thought, rolling another round ball in the sugar. I could e-mail my former guests and advertise a special weekend getaway. Even if I got only one or two takers, it would still be better than an empty inn.

As the smell of fresh-baked rolls mingled with the smell of ginger from the cookies I'd slid into the oven, I glanced out the window at the dark green pines at the end of the driveway. The copper-tinged blueberry bushes made a gorgeous autumnal carpet at their feet, and a white gull hovered overhead. As mercurial as the business of owning an inn was, I couldn't think of anywhere I'd rather be.

I had just finished cleaning up from lunch when John burst through the kitchen door, adding his familiar woodsy scent to the already intoxicating aroma. His sandy hair was windblown, his tanned face ruddy. Biscuit, my well-fed ginger tabby, glanced up from her perch on the radiator, then settled back down. I, on the other hand, felt my heart pick up its pace a bit.

"Did you get everything you needed?" I asked as he came up and wrapped his arms around me, kissing the top of my head.

"They were out of the green paint until next week," he said. "But I heard some exciting news in Northeast Harbor," he said.

"They've canceled the bake-off?" I asked. I was still shaking off the dream I'd had the night before — the one that had half the women in the island chasing after me with cranberry-stained butter knives. I'd just locked myself into the town library when the alarm went off, allowing me to escape.

"You wish," he said, laughing. "Adam got a diver friend of his to clear up some tangled pots out by Deadman's Shoal." Adam Thrackton was a lobsterman — and also the beau of my niece, Gwen, who helped me manage the inn.

"I thought they just cut the lines and had done with them," I said.

"Usually they do, but this time there were about a dozen of them tangled up, and Adam didn't want to lose them. Anyway, you'll never guess what they found."

"Please tell me it's not a body," I said, feeling my stomach turn over. We'd had more than enough of those on the island recently; I wasn't sure I could handle another.

"A sunken ship," he said, his green eyes gleaming.

I shivered, thinking of the boats that occasionally disappeared in winter's brutal storms. "That's almost as bad. How recent?"

"That's the thing," he said. "They think it's one of the old wooden sailing ships, from a couple hundred years ago. Eleazer thinks it might even be the *Black Marguerite*."

Eleazer, the island's shipwright — and my dear friend — was something of an expert on sailing ships.

"What's the *Black Marguerite*?" I asked.

"The *Black Marguerite* belonged to Davey Blue, the pirate who used to operate off this part of the coast; he was supposedly in love with a woman who lived in the area. He and the *Marguerite* vanished sometime during the eighteenth century."

"There were people living here then?" I asked.

"Not many, but some. Some people say Smuggler's Cove was Davey Blue's hideout," John said. He was referring to a cove just a little way down the coast from the inn. It had a treacherous entry that was completely hidden at high tide.

"Why not call it Pirate's Cove?" I asked.

"Sounds like a mini golf course."

I laughed. "So, why do they think it might have been his ship? I've never heard of pirates prowling the Maine coast."

"He didn't prowl here, but he came from here, and returned often. He was supposed

16

to be shipping out to the Caribbean, but he never made it, apparently. The legend is that it went down in a storm almost as soon as it shipped out, but it's never been found."

John gave me another squeeze and released me. "Smells like gingersnaps in here." The gingersnap recipe I'd gotten from my old friend Rhonda Shield, who worked at my favorite Austin library and was an amazing cook, was one of John's favorites. I called the cookies "Me-Maw's Gingersnaps," after Rhonda's grandmother, who passed the recipe down to her. Just the smell of them in the kitchen made me think fondly of Rhonda's ready smile. Plus, they had an autumn tang that went well with the weather. "Mind if I sample a few?" he asked.

"Go ahead," I said. He walked over and plucked three warm cookies from the cooling rack, making appreciative noises as he bit into the first one. Like my niece, Gwen, he could plow through half a jar and not gain an ounce. "How can they tell whether it's the *Black Marguerite*?" I asked as he groaned in ecstasy.

When he'd finished the cookie, he licked the crumbs from his fingers, then answered my question. "I don't know. Apparently they're calling in a bunch of experts to see what they can find." He opened his mouth to insert a second cookie, then paused. "You know, we've got a few mooring lines off the inn's dock. If we moved the skiffs over, they could stay here and tie up right outside. Business is kind of slow right now."

"As in dead," I said. I had a few rooms occupied now, but with the exception of one booking — a woman named Cherry Price, who was arriving from New York that afternoon — the next two months were not looking good.

"And it would help fund the wedding," John added. He had barely finished his sentence when there was a knock at the kitchen door. Adam stood on the back porch, an expectant smile on his face.

"Hi, Natalie," he said when I opened the door and invited him inside. It was obvious why Gwen was taken with Adam — with a shock of dark hair that contrasted with his light eyes, he was a handsome man, and he was gifted with an outgoing personality and a great sense of humor that made him excellent company. In jeans and a heavy wool sweater, he looked more like the college kid he used to be than the lobsterman he now was. The two were a good match, I thought, with a twinge of misgiving. What would happen if Gwen went back to UCLA? Would the couple survive?

"Is Gwen ready to go?" Adam asked.

"I thought she was going to do some painting this afternoon!"

"She is," he said, and winked. "Scenes at sea."

I laughed. "John tells me you've had some excitement the last few days. I just found out about it, but evidently all the island's abuzz with your discovery!" Except, I realized, Charlene. Maybe I'd get to fill *her* in on the local gossip, for the first — and probably the last — time.

"It was pretty amazing," he said. "I was with Evan Sorenson — he just got back into town a few weeks ago, and is thinking of getting into lobstering." Evan, who was selectwoman Ingrid Sorenson's son, was back from a stint in rehab, I knew. I was glad to hear he was moving forward — away from the drug addiction that had almost destroyed his life. "Ingrid asked me to hire him for a few weeks. He was out with me — he was helping with the winch. Anyway, we were having trouble pulling up one of the traps — I thought we were going to have to cut the line — when finally it comes up with this huge timber attached to it."

"How did a timber get in the trap?" I asked.

"It wasn't actually in the trap," he said. "It was tangled in the line; I'm surprised the rope didn't break."

"I've heard of that happening from time to time," John said, "but it's rare. How did you know it belonged to a ship, instead of just being part of an old pier?"

"It was too far out to be part of a pier. Plus, it was curved," he said. "That's what made me suspicious. I wasn't sure, so I called a friend of mine who does dive tours out on Mount Desert Island."

"What did he find?"

"It was murky, but he located several more timbers — they were jumbled up, and spread around down there, but because of how they were grouped, he said he was pretty sure it was one of the old sailing ships."

"What else did he find?" John asked Adam.

"He spotted an anchor sticking out of the sand, and something that looks like a cannon, but nothing he could bring up."

"Cannons? Maybe it is the pirate ship!"

"That's why I called the university," Adam said. "They should be here today."

"Do you think it could be Davey Blue's ship?" I asked.

"If it is, and there was treasure aboard,

maybe Gwen's mom won't be so worried about my chosen career," he said with a lopsided grin.

"I hadn't thought about that," I said. "It sure would make things easier. Would the treasure be yours if you found it?"

He shrugged. "I majored in political science, not law. From what I've read, though, I think it depends on where the find is, and who owned the ship originally. There's a chance, though."

"What would you do with it?"

"I'd want it in a museum, of course," he said. "First, though, let's find out what it is."

"Wise man," John said.

Adam looked at me. "I'm hoping you'll get some business out of it — when I called the university, I told them about the inn."

"I appreciate the plug," I said, and gestured to the cookies cooling on the rack. I might have to make another batch if I kept getting visitors. "Help yourself," I told him.

"Thanks." He scooped up three and grunted appreciatively as he bit into the first gingery cookie. Rhonda's cookies had made another convert.

"I wonder what they'll find," I said, gazing out the window at the blue water.

"Could be Selfridge's ship," John said.

"Or Davey Blue's," Adam put in optimistically. "We'll just have to wait and see!"

Gwen came down the stairs, her dark curly hair pulled up in a loose bun, the canvas bag I knew held her art supplies slung over a slender shoulder. Her face glowed when she looked at Adam. "You're early!"

"You're late," he said, grinning at her. The two exchanged a quick kiss, and stood with their arms around each other. They'd been together more than a year, but they were both still smitten. "It sounds like Adam's filled you in on the news," she said, glancing at the cooling cookies. "Oooh. Rhonda's gingersnaps. Can you spare a few?"

"Of course," I said. Next time, I'd have to make a double batch. Or maybe even triple. "Gwen — how come you didn't tell me about the ship Adam found?"

"You were asleep when I got home, Aunt Nat!"

"Next time, wake me up!"

Gwen made herself a small stack of cookies and turned back to me. "It is pretty cool, isn't it? Wait until I tell my mother!"

I shifted from one foot to the other, wishing she hadn't brought up my sister Bridget. I had no idea what would happen when Gwen's mother found out that the boyfriend

22

she thought was a shipping magnate — a misunderstanding I'd accidentally fostered and never got around to dispelling — was a lobsterman.

Gwen had come out to spend the summer with me a few seasons ago — largely to escape her mother's company for the summer — and ended up postponing her degree to stay on the island. She lived at the inn with me and helped me manage the place. A gifted artist, she also studied art with Fernand LaChaise, a well-known painter with a studio on the island. But I knew Adam was the real reason she stayed. Adam had a Princeton degree to his name — or at least he did, before he tipped it overboard — but his lobsterman credentials were not going to hold much weight with my sister Bridget.

"It'll work out fine," Gwen said, reading my mind.

"I hope so."

"You're the one who told her Adam was in shipping," she reminded me, slipping on a jacket and grabbing her bag of art supplies.

"Maybe a promise of free lobstergrams will win her over," Adam suggested lightly.

Gwen shot him a skeptical look. "Clearly you haven't met my mother," she said.

23

"I haven't, but I'm looking forward to it," he said. "I think."

Gwen shouldered her bag and finished the last cookie. "Anyway, it sounds like you have all the news on the ship. I promise you'll be the first to know if I find out anything else."

"Thanks," I said. "I'm looking forward to having a scoop for Charlene for a change of pace."

"I wouldn't count on it," John said.

"She didn't know about it this morning!"

"That was hours ago," Gwen said.

"True," I admitted.

"Anyway," Gwen said. "I'm headed out to work on the boat for a few hours — I'll be back to help with dinner."

"Thanks," I said, the mystery of sunken ships eclipsed, at least for a few minutes, by the details of running the inn. "John's cooking, but if you could help with serving, that would be great. Marge is taking care of the rooms, so we're set."

Marge O'Leary had been my enemy when I arrived on the island, and I'd sworn I'd never hire her to help me. That was before I discovered she had spent years in an abusive relationship, fearing for her life. In fact, Marge and I had both almost died at her husband's hands.

Once he was in jail, however, and Marge

24

was able to live without fear, she had blossomed — and had quickly become my right-hand woman. She kept the inn in tiptop condition, cleaning rooms and readying them for guests, leaving me to handle the business side of things — and the food. Even now, I could hear the vacuum droning in the distance.

"If we find out anything else, you'll be the first to know." Adam opened the door for Gwen, letting in a gust of chilly wind.

Gwen paused, turning back to me. "There is one thing I forgot to tell you."

"What?" I asked, expecting another tidbit about the sunken boat.

"They've started a pool down at the co-op."

"A pool?" I asked, perplexed. "Why would the lobster co-op need a swimming pool?"

"As in gambling," she clarified, while Adam laughed. "They're betting on who you're going to pick to win the bake-off."

"Please tell me you're joking," I said.

"Who's got the best odds so far?" John asked with a grin.

"Don't tell me," I said, holding up my hands. "I don't want to know."

"I don't envy you," Gwen said, shaking her head. "They couldn't pay me to take that job."

Adam followed her out the door, both of them off for a day's work. A moment later, after coming over to give me one more kiss — and a hug that left me warm all over — John disappeared to his workshop, leaving me alone in the kitchen with Biscuit.

The phone rang as I pulled out the corn-meal for cornbread, and I answered it on the second ring.

"Cherry Price speaking," announced the voice on the other end of the line. "I just wanted to confirm that I'll be arriving this afternoon."

"I've got you in the Crow's Nest," I said. "Will you be staying to dinner?"

"I'm looking forward to it."

"Likewise," I said. She seemed like a delightful woman — and her name was familiar, too, somehow. I had barely hung up when the phone rang again. It was an islander I'd barely spoken to, asking how I felt about cranberries in fruitcake.

How had I ever let Tom talk me into do-ing the bake-off?

TWO

"So, Adam thinks it might be Davey Blue's ship?" Charlene asked as she poured me a cup of coffee from behind the counter of the Cranberry Island Store that afternoon. I'd broken the news about the ship to her yesterday, and she'd been calling me every half hour since for updates.

Leaving Gwen in charge of lunch clean-up, I'd headed down to the store with a batch of muffins for Charlene to sell at the counter. I was planning to enjoy a bit of the gorgeous fall weather before my new guests checked in that afternoon. Adam's recommendation had worked; I now had five additional rooms booked. Fortunately, I had plenty of supplies in the freezer, but was expecting an additional shipment of ingredients from the mainland that afternoon.

The sun was shining and the breeze off the water was mild, but chilly enough to make me thankful for my jacket. The fall

27

colors were stunning, the leaves scattered like red and orange jewels across the russet blueberry patches and the straw-colored grass.

By the time I arrived at the homey little store, with its rockers on the front porch, a wall of old-fashioned post office boxes behind the counter, and shelves stocked with everything from peanut butter to fishing line, I was ready for a cup of coffee and a pleasant chat. Which was a good thing, because that was exactly what Charlene had in mind for me.

Charlene's store was often referred to as the island's living room, and the front part of the old wood-frame building was outfitted with several squishy couches and a few chairs. After transferring the muffins to the bakery case she kept by the register, I eased myself into the chair closest to the window, feeling refreshed and relaxed — until I spotted the big red flyer taped to the window. In huge block letters, were the words "Annual Cranberry Bake-Off!"

I tore my eyes away from it as Charlene handed me a cup of coffee and sat down across from me. The sequins on her lavender sweater sparkled in the afternoon light that poured in through the mullioned front window as she crossed her legs and looked at me expectantly.

I told Charlene — again — what Adam had told me about the wreck. "Adam told the marine archaeologists about the inn, and they booked five rooms — so hopefully, I'll have more to tell you soon," I said. "What are the islanders saying?"

"That they found gold," she said.

"If they have, I haven't heard about it," I said.

"Some of the guys are saying it's probably worth millions of dollars — a sunken treasure. And they're already arguing over whose it is; there have been a lot of boats out on Deadman's Shoal, using fishing nets to try and find the site."

"You're kidding me," I said. "Have they pulled up anything?"

"No, but one of them put a hole in his boat and two of them have lost their gear."

"Serves them right," I said. "No divers, though, I hope."

She shook her head. "Nobody's got gear but Diver Bob, and he won't do it — he doesn't want to disturb the site further." She sipped her coffee. "So, will Adam get the booty?"

"It depends on how far off the coast it is, I think. And what ship it is."

"It's amazing that no one's found it over

all these years — it must have been down there a couple of centuries, and nobody knew," Charlene said, shaking her head. "There's always been a rumor that Smuggler's Cove was a pirate hideout; maybe there was something to it!"

"How can they figure out whose ship it was?" I asked.

Charlene shrugged. "Eleazer told me they can tell lots of things just based on what they find in the wreckage. Plates, glasses, cannons — all kinds of stuff. I heard there are marine archaeologists coming in from around the country to investigate it."

"Two are coming in from Portland, and they're staying at the inn," I said. "The other three said they were from a marine research company out of Florida." Which was strange; Adam had only mentioned getting in touch with the University of Maine. I'd ask him next time I saw him. "Maybe you can use your charm to get the details out of them."

"Are any of them cute?" she asked.

I laughed. "I have no idea — and besides, two of them are women."

"That still leaves three. What was your first impression?"

"The man I talked to sounded . . . well, like a normal person. But we only talked on the phone. You'll have to come by and find out for yourself!"

"I may do that." She took a sip of coffee and looked sidelong at me over the rim of her mug. "So. Any progress on the local front? Made any big decisions?"

"If you're talking about the bake-off, I've decided I'm just going to give the award to the best dish," I said primly.

She shrugged. "I think you're crazy, but have it your way."

"Why?" I asked, leaning forward despite myself. "Did you think of a better plan?"

"Other than John beaning you with a two-by-four and putting you in the hospital for a few days?" She shook her head. "Not yet. But I still think it's not a bad idea."

I arrived home to a nervous-looking Emmeline Hoyle, carrying a heavy tray with a tea towel draped over it. Her dark eyes looked nervous in her round face, and I noticed she was wearing her Sunday clothes — in this case, a long straight skirt and a red wool sweater that years of her excellent cooking had made a bit snug.

"Hi, Emmeline," I said warily. Emmeline was one of my favorite people on the island, and normally I would be delighted to see her, but I knew she was also a top contender for bake-off champion, having taken home the title for three of the last five years.

"Good morning, Natalie. How are you?"

"Great," I said, eyeing the tray. "What's under the towel?"

"I brought a few things for you to try," she said, whipping off the floral towel to reveal three plates laden with cranberry-studded breads, cookies, and even something that looked like a steamed pudding.

"But the bake-off doesn't start till Saturday!"

"I only get one entry," she said, "so I thought I'd find out which one you thought I should submit."

I shook my head. "I can't, Emmeline. You know I'd love to be able to help, but people might think I was playing favorites."

Emmeline's lips tightened into a thin line. "I wasn't asking you to cheat. I just wanted your opinion."

"I know, Emmeline. I wish I could help."

"I understand," she said in a tone of voice that said just the opposite. She nodded sharply and turned away, walking up the hill from the house. The sixty-something woman had carried that tray over a mile to get here. With a rush of guilt, I realized she would have to carry it home, too.

"Wait a moment," I said.

She whipped around and looked at me with hope in her eyes.

"Why don't you leave the tray with me? I've got several guests coming in today; I'll let them try everything, and I'll set up a little comment box." I smiled at her. "That way, I've got snacks for my guests, and you can get feedback, but nobody will be able to say I rigged the contest."

"You'd do that for me?"

"Absolutely," I said. "I'll just put up a little sign explaining that you're taste-testing for the bake-off, and that you'd love their opinions."

"Oh, Natalie, that's wonderful! I'm baking you a batch of my banana bread when I get home," she said.

"That would be lovely," I said, taking the heavy tray from her, "but why don't you wait until after the bake-off!"

"Do you think?" she asked.

"I insist," I said. My stomach gurgled as I breathed in the sweet aroma of Emmeline's creations. The streusel cake looked particularly appealing. I hadn't eaten for hours . . . would it hurt if I took one little bite?

"I'll drop by tomorrow to pick up the results," she said, reaching out to squeeze my arm.

"Do you want to come in for a cup of

tea?" I asked.

"No, no . . . wouldn't want anyone to accuse us of impropriety," she said, and I was relieved to see the familiar twinkle back in her eyes.

"I'll see you tomorrow then," I said, and carried the tray into the inn, pleased with my ingenuity.

The first set of archaeologists arrived at the kitchen door, surprising me. Most of my guests arrived at the front door, not the back. There were two of them: a tall, lean man with graying hair and a worried look, and a younger, cheerful-looking woman with curly, bright red hair and freckles. Both wore jeans and windbreakers; as the woman put her hand up to shade her eyes, the sunlight flashed off the face of her huge, utilitarian looking watch. She clearly didn't go in for delicate accessories, I thought.

"Welcome!" I said, opening the door to them. "I see you found the mooring lines!"

"Saved us the long walk from the pier," said the younger archaeologist. "Plus the fees to the harbormaster. I'm Molly O'Cleary," she said, extending a hand. "And this is my colleague Carl Morgenstern," she said, nodding her head toward her partner. "We've got a reservation. At least I hope we do, or we'll be sleeping in the wheelhouse!"

"Not to worry," I said. "I've reserved two rooms for you. Please come in."

They followed me through the kitchen into the dining room. As we passed Emmeline's tray, Molly lingered for a moment. "Looks delicious," she said. "I'm starving."

"You're welcome to some," I said.

"Let's get checked in first," said Carl. "Then you can gorge."

"It's fuel for all our hard work," she said, snagging a piece of cake and following me to the front desk.

They didn't have much to carry; each of them had a small suitcase, and it didn't take long to check in and put their bags in their rooms. Emmeline's samples enticed them to linger in the dining room when they came back down, and I served them coffee as they helped themselves from the tray.

"What is this?" Molly asked as she took a bite of Emmeline's steamed pudding.

I told her, and explained the theory behind the tray of goodies — and my role in the contest. "If you have a favorite," I told them, "don't tell me; write a note to Emmeline." I pointed to the mason jar and the stack of index cards I'd set up for comments.

"A woman with morals," Carl said. "I like that."

"So," I said. "You're here to investigate the shipwreck?"

Carl glanced at Molly, and I saw something pass between them before he answered. "That's why we're here," he said.

"You're not the only ones," I said.

Carl looked startled. "We're not?"

"I've got another couple of archaeologists coming in today."

"Oh, really?" Carl spoke, but both seemed suddenly wary. "Who?"

"They're with a company called Iliad," I said.

Molly sighed and shook her head. "They're not really archaeologists, I'm afraid. They're treasure hunters."

"Do you know who called them?" Carl asked.

I shrugged. "All I know is that they booked three rooms."

"I knew they'd find out about this," Carl said, radiating anger.

Molly laid a hand on his arm. "Calm down, Carl. They weren't the ones who found it, and we don't even know how many miles offshore it is. Don't jump to conclusions."

"If they manage to pillage this one . . ."

"We'll do everything we can," she said, soothingly.

"What's wrong?" I asked.

Molly sighed again. "We've had dealings with Iliad before. There was a shipwreck — a Spanish galleon from the 1600s — and they took over the entire thing. We didn't even get a chance to map it, and then all of the artifacts . . ." She snapped her fingers. "Gone. Sold for profit."

"That's terrible," I said. "How can they do that?"

"It all depends on who finds the ship — and where it is," Molly told me. "If it's within Maine territorial waters, then it may be under the state's jurisdiction. If not, well . . . the law can be fluid."

"Too fluid, if you ask me," Carl said, and I could hear the passion in his gravelly voice. "They're destroying our cultural heritage! These shipwrecks — they're snapshots of another time, preserved under the waves for centuries . . . and then, in a period of a few weeks, some guy who's out for a quick buck can take the whole thing apart and sell it for profit." He smiled grimly. "Every age has its pirates," he said.

"Do you think it's a pirate ship, then?" I asked.

"It could be," Molly said. "The location is right; records indicate the *Black Marguerite* was along the coast when it disappeared.

There's long been speculation that Davey Blue had a lady friend in this neck of the woods."

"How long ago was it?" I asked.

"Mid-seventeenth century," Molly said. "It would be an amazing find. The biggest since the *Whydah*."

"What's the *Whydah*?" I asked.

"It was originally a slave ship out of England, but it was attacked by the pirate 'Black Sam' Bellamy and became his flagship. It went down off Cape Cod in 1717 — he was actually headed toward Maine when it sank — and was only recovered about twenty-five years ago."

"I had no idea Maine was such a pirate destination," I said.

"Even pirates need vacations," joked Molly.

"There was another captain whose ship disappeared," I said. "He used to own this house, in fact — he built it for his wife. His name was Jonah Selfridge. One of his descendants, Murray Selfridge, lives on the island."

Jonah Selfridge had built a beautiful house, but I'd learned last fall the he wasn't exactly a nice guy. The room was still haunted by one of his victims.

"Do you know what his ship was called?"

I shrugged. "No idea, unfortunately."

"What was the time period?"

"Somewhere in the early to mid-eighteen hundreds, if I remember correctly. Matilda Jenkins is the town historian — she could tell you tons more than I could."

Carl looked at Molly. "Could be good news. Not as old, but at least there might be less profit in it, so we wouldn't have to fight Iliad as much."

"Depends on the cargo," Molly said. She turned back to me. "Do you know what he was trading?"

"Again, you'll have to ask Matilda," I said. "How can you tell which ship is which, anyway?"

"It's not easy," she admitted. "Sometimes, if we can find an old image or the specifications of the ship we suspect it is, we can identify it by size and shape, or by something unique to the ship — like a figurehead, if it's been preserved." She took a bite of Emmeline's streusel cake before continuing. It did look delicious; I had to restrain myself from grabbing a slice too. "It also depends on how broken up it is," Molly said after she'd finished her bite. "Sometimes, they are almost intact, and sometimes, they're in pieces."

"What do you do if you don't have an image to go by?"

"We look at the artifacts. There are often features — the ship's size, the number and make of the cannons, the ship's bell, if we're lucky — that can positively identify the vessel. If not . . ." She shrugged. "We'll see what puzzle pieces we can find and try to put them together!"

"Sounds like exciting work!"

"It is," Molly said. "But it's slow going. Measuring, mapping; and many times, if things weren't immediately covered in sand or mud, metal artifacts — and anything close to them — are buried in concretions."

"What's a concretion?"

"Concretions form when the metal rusts, and all kinds of things — shells, debris — stick to it, forming a hard layer around the object." Molly took another bite of Emmeline's pudding and swallowed before continuing. "We X-ray them to see what's inside, and then we have to carefully chip the artifacts out. We usually have conservators to help us . . . the process takes days."

"Wow. And you have to dive down and get this stuff, right? That water's about 50 degrees!"

"We prefer to use submersibles, but our biggest research vessel — and the university's submersible — is booked for another month. Usually, researchers can't even take the smaller ones out without a captain, but Carl has logged enough hours they're making an exception, and allowing him to be the captain."

"It's not that big a boat. But not to have access to the bigger vessel . . . rotten luck, really," Carl said.

"It's much less expensive this way," Molly reminded him. "And at least this site is shallow enough that we can dive!"

I shivered. "That water is freezing!"

"We use dry suits," Molly said, "so it's not that bad. But yes — it's a lot of work." She grinned at me. "Which means we'll be staying here for a while, most likely."

Which was good news for my bottom line, for sure.

"Maybe. It depends on *Iliad,*" Carl said grimly. He was taut, like a bowstring full of barely leashed energy.

"Don't be such a pessimist, Carl. I'm sure we'll have better luck this time." Molly took a last sip of her coffee and glanced at her watch. I'd never seen a woman wear such a clunky piece before; it looked like it weighed ten pounds. "It's pretty calm out there, and it's still daylight. What do you say we go and have a look?"

"Thought you'd never ask," Carl said,

pushing his barely touched plate away and standing up quickly.

"Let me know what you find out," I said, leading them back through the kitchen to the back door.

Molly turned back. "That reminds me — how do we get in touch with the historian?"

"Her name is Matilda Jenkins. You can find her in the museum — the only brick building down by the main pier."

"Thanks," she said, giving me a sunny smile. She was a likeable young woman, a huge contrast to her brooding partner, Carl. "And tell your friend I liked the pudding the best!"

I watched the archaeologists head out in their research vessel, a small boat named the *Ira B* that Molly told me they frequently used for student expeditions. They had barely vanished around the point before the doorbell rang. I reluctantly went to answer it, hoping it wasn't another would-be bake-off winner trying to bribe me with baked goods.

Three people stood at the front door, two men and a woman. All three were dressed in jeans and blue windbreakers with a logo — *Iliad* — stitched on the breast pocket.

"I'm Gerald McIntire," said the oldest of the trio, who I guessed to be in his late forties. "I believe we have reservations?"

"Of course," I said, opening the door wider so the trio could file in. Gerald McIntire was the university archaeologists' archenemy. He didn't look like a pirate, I thought. He was tall and stocky, with a bit of a spare tire, but his baby cheeks and light blue eyes, fringed with short blond lashes, gave him an innocent look. "You're here because of the wreck, right?" I asked.

"Right," he said, wheeling his case behind him. He was pink from exertion, and puffing. "Long walk from the pier," he said.

"I wish I'd known when you were coming! I would have picked you up!"

"No worries," he said. "The suitcase rolls. Besides, I needed the exercise."

I glanced at my watch. "The mail boat doesn't come for another hour, so I assume you have a boat. Did you leave it down at the main pier?"

"We did."

"I've got mooring lines out back you can tie up to if you want. There's going to be another boat docked there, too, but unless you came in a cruise ship, there should be plenty of room."

"Thank you," he said, and turned to the other two. "This is Frank Goertz, my partner, and Audrey Hammonds, our primary archaeologist. We'll have more crew coming soon; our main research vessels are down in the Caribbean at the moment, on other excavations. We're doing a preliminary review of the site." He grinned. "If this is what I think it is, we'll be back with the big guns in the spring."

"Big guns?"

"One of our two biggest vessels — they both have submersibles, and we'll be able to map the site — even pull up cannons, if we find any." I could see the excitement in his pale eyes. "I've been looking for Davey Blue's ship my whole life; wouldn't want to miss a chance to find her!"

"I hope you find what you're looking for," I said politely.

"I'm kind of glad we don't have the *Nibelung* here," the other man said, his eyes roaming around the antique furniture, plush peach-colored rug, and sparkling windows looking out over the water. "This sure beats a six-foot cabin."

I laughed. "I certainly hope so!"

I shook hands with Audrey and Frank; both of them had firm handshakes, and their skin was warm and calloused. She was wiry and fit-looking, with a weathered face, probably in her early thirties. The man was equally wiry, but much taller, about the same age as Gerald. Despite his cheerful assessment of their lodging, there were worry lines etched into his tanned brow. "Let's get checked in, and we'll go back and move the *Lorelei*," Gerald said with an easy air of authority. As they finished the paperwork and I handed them the keys, he asked, "Is the other boat yours?"

"Actually, no. A couple of marine archaeologists from the University of Maine came up in it today. Carl Morgenstern and Molly O'Cleary," I said, watching his expression. "They're currently out investigating the wreck."

"Ah," he said, smiling back at me and not looking at all concerned about the potential of academics horning in on his turf. Either he was a good actor, or he didn't view them as much of a threat. "It's going to be a regular get-together, then," he said, glancing at Audrey, who smiled back at him. "Just like old times."

"I hope you'll enjoy your stay," I said neutrally. If there was any truth to what Carl had said earlier, I hoped it would be significantly better than old times.

Unfortunately, that wasn't how it worked out.

THREE

I had just finished early dinner prep and was thinking about heading down to the store when there was a rap at the kitchen door. I looked over at it with trepidation; three islanders had already come by bearing food gifts that afternoon, offering me sneak peeks of their recipes or inquiring as to my culinary preferences. I had offered them the same deal as I had Emmeline, and now had four trays of food offerings in the dining room — including Maude Peters' cranberry pickle chutney, which smelled as bad as it sounded.

I was relieved to see Eleazer White smiling through the glass panes, even if he was carrying what looked like one of his wife's infamous cranberry pies. I liked Claudette immensely, but had never been a fan of her pie.

I hurried to the door. "Come in, come in!" Eli's bright eyes and weathered face always cheered me up.

"Brought you a pie," he said. "She made it special; she even put sugar in it!"

"Thank you," I said. "Unfortunately, I can't eat it, but I'll ask the guests what they think."

"I told Claudette it was best not to bring it — said folks might think she was trying to stack the odds."

"I wouldn't worry. The whole island is guilty of that." I led him into the dining room and showed him the array of cranberry-related food items. "I've got a jar for comment cards, and I'll send the feedback to Claudette."

"May I?" he asked, indicating Emmeline's streusel cake. It looked tempting to me, too; it had been harder to resist than I expected.

"Be my guest," I said.

He picked a large piece and took a bite. "Claudette's got some competition this year," he said, surveying the spread as he chewed. "What is that?" he asked, pointing to the chutney.

I told him.

He shuddered theatrically. "Who's the bright bulb who came up with that one?"

"Maude Peters," I said. "At least it's creative," I offered.

"That's one word." He finished off the

47

cake in one big bite, swallowing it almost whole. "Good cake," he said with an approving nod. "But I didn't come to jaw about baked goods. I hear some of the folks from the university are staying here."

"They are," I said.

"Good," he said, and reached down and drew a sword. I involuntarily took a step back.

"Eleazer . . ."

"She's a beauty, isn't she?" he asked, cradling the sword. The hilt was worked in cracked leather and silver, and the blade was filigreed. "It's a cutlass, I believe from the eighteenth century. I was hoping they could take a look at her," he said, holding it up in the light. "It's a family heirloom. I don't know where my grandfather got it, but the legend is it belonged to the old pirate himself."

"Davey Blue?" I asked.

Eleazer nodded, a twinkle in his eye.

"Unfortunately, they're not here right now," I said. "They went out to the wreck site. Do you want to leave it here?" I asked. "I'll be sure to ask them."

"Nah," he said, re-sheathing the cutlass — which was a relief, to be honest. It wasn't that I didn't trust Eleazer — I was just happier without weapons being waved about.

"I'll bring it by another time. In the mean-time, I've got the skiff out back; want to go look at the wreck site?"

"I wouldn't think there's much to see," I said. "It's underwater."

"Yes, but don't you want to know where it is? Besides, the archaeologists are out there. You never know what they'll find!"

I glanced at my watch. I'd done most of the prep for dinner; if I made it back in two hours, there would be plenty of time to fin-ish getting ready. And since two of my guests were presumably out at the wreck site, I wouldn't have to worry about them showing up and me not being at the inn.

"Why not?" I asked. I slid the wrapped pan of scallops into the refrigerator and grabbed my jacket and gloves. "Let me just get a thermos of hot cider to take with us. It's cold out there!"

"Mind if I take a few of your goodies to munch on?"

"Go ahead," I said. I knew Claudette kept him on a tight diet at home; this was a real treat for him. As he selected a few choice morsels, I headed back to the kitchen and fixed us two thermoses of cider and a few cookies for myself. Then I left a note for John and followed Eleazer outside.

The fall air was bracing, and I shoved my

gloved hands into my pockets as I followed Eleazer down the walkway to the dock, my bag of goodies bumping against my hip. The grass had turned the pale yellow I'd always thought of as winter wheat, and across the dark blue water, the pink granite mountains glowed in the afternoon sun.

I clambered after him into his skiff, watching with admiration as he deftly untied the ropes and pushed us away from the dock. The process took maybe twenty seconds. He was a waterman through and through; he moved with a graceful economy that I envied. I was getting the hang of my own skiff, the *Little Marian,* which Eleazer had found for me not long after I moved to the island, but I would never handle her with Eli's skill.

"You'll get it, lass," he said when I told him how much I envied his boatmanship. "Just takes practice, that's all."

I turned to watch the island as we pulled away. The gray-shingled inn nestled into the hillside, its mullioned windows gleaming in the sun. A few orange and gold chrysanthemums bloomed in the window boxes, not yet felled by the frost; behind the inn, tall pine trees stood on the gentle rise of the hill, as they had for hundreds of years.

The inn receded as we moved farther out,

and I turned my gaze to the lighthouse out on Cranberry Point. It had recently been renovated, and its fresh white paint was bright and clean against the weathered granite. A gust of wind blew over us, and I shivered, remembering the body that had been found in a hidden subterranean room during the renovation; the bones had moldered there undiscovered for over a hundred years. And now we were going out to see the remains of a ship that had lain hidden under the waves for centuries. How many more secrets did the island hold? I wondered. And how many ghosts?

"Haven't heard a word about the ghost ship in years," Eleazer told me, speaking loudly to be heard over the thrum of the engine and the rush of the wind. The skin on my arms prickled at the coincidence.

"I didn't know there was one."

"Ghosts all over the place in this part of the world," he went on. "Out at your inn, the old lighthouse . . . even the store."

"That's one I haven't heard about!"

"Hasn't done much since Nelda moved on." Nelda was Charlene's great aunt, and it was from her that Charlene had taken over the store several years ago. "I think Nelda just stacked the shelves wrong; cans of tuna kept falling down all over the place."

"I can't believe Charlene never told me about it!" I said. I'd have to grill her on it when I got back. "She didn't tell me about the ghost ship, either. This place sure has a lot of spooks!"

"Most places that have been around a while do," he said. "The story of the ghost ship's been around for years and years. My granddaddy used to tell me it was the ghost of Davey Blue, looking for his lady love and his lost treasure."

"That's the pirate who disappeared a couple of hundred years ago, right?"

"One of New England's first pirates," he said. "Round about the 1630s, give or take a few years."

"Was he from Maine?"

"Ayuh," Eleazer said, steering the little skiff out of the path of a lobster boat. He waved at the sternman and waited until they had passed the boat to continue his story. "Davy started out an honest man — a fur trapper, earning a decent living. He didn't go bad until a bunch of French pirates cleaned him out. Stole everything he had."

"What did he do then?"

Eleazer grinned. "Why, he stole a boat and turned pirate himself."

I grinned back. "If you can't beat 'em . . ."

"Exactly," Eleazer said. "Turned out he

had a talent for it. They sent almost half a dozen ships after him over the years, and he slipped away from every one of them. Built up a fortune, before he disappeared."

"What happened?"

"Some say he went back to England, and some say he died in a sword fight." He patted the cutlass at his hip. "This cutlass used to belong to him — at least that's what the story is."

"How did you come by it?"

"I don't know, but it's been in the family as long as I can remember," he said. "When I die, it'll go to the museum. I'm hoping to ask the archaeologists to take a look at it, see if it really did belong to the old pirate. Legend has it that Cranberry Island was one of his favorite places — lots of folks think Smuggler's Cove is where he hid his booty — so it may be my granddad was right."

"I'm confused. If he was supposed to have gone back to England or died in a duel, why do people think the shipwreck might be the *Black Marguerite*?" I asked.

"Ah, that's the thing," he said. "Local rumor is, he came back from pirating to pick up his lady love and stash his loot. Problem was, no sooner did he pick her up to whisk her away than a storm came in, and legend has it the ship went down just off the coast." A pair of seagulls skimmed over the water toward us, then began following the little boat, diving and swooping in the chilly wind. I pulled my jacket closer around me; it was cold out on the water, and the wind bit through even the thickest jackets. "My granddaddy used to tell me stories about Davey Blue," Eleazer continued. "They say he still sails these waters, searching for his lost treasure — and his lost lady love."

"Quite romantic," I said.

"It may sound far-fetched, but they took it mighty serious back when my granddaddy was a lobsterman. They avoided the place — and not just because of the rocks. Used to give Deadman's Shoal a wide berth, even if the lobstering was good." He shook his head, remembering. "Time was, you could net ten-pounders out there regular."

Ten pounds? Forget a pot — you'd need a hot tub to cook them in. "What about now?" I asked.

His eyes glinted with mischief. "Not too many ten-pounders — and couldn't keep 'em if you caught 'em, anyway."

"I'm talking about the ghost ship, Eli — not the lobsters!"

"I know," he said, eyes sparkling. "Just

playing with you." He squinted out over the water, and I followed his gaze to where two boats floated in the distance. "As for Deadman's Shoal? Nobody pays any mind to the oldtimers' stories," he said. "It's still dangerous out there — there are lots of rocks out on Deadman's Shoal, so folks with sense steer clear of it — but no one worries about ghost ships anymore." He gave me a wicked smile. "Till they see one, that is."

I leaned toward him. "Have you seen one?"

He shrugged. "Maybe. Maybe not."

"I sense a story," I said.

He shrugged again, and seemed to debate telling me for a moment. Finally, he said, "I don't tell too many folks about it — some of them think I'm a few crackers shy of a full bag as it is, and I don't want to encourage it, you know?"

"I won't say anything," I said.

"I know you won't," he said with a sharp nod, and a moment later, he began. "It was a foggy night, round about midnight, I'd say. I was fifteen at the time, out with my da, searching for a lobsterman's boat that didn't come back from the fishing grounds. We didn't mean to be out by the shoals — like I said, folks with sense avoided it back then, 'specially at night — but there was a light flickering in the fog, and we headed over to see if it was our missing lobsterman." Eli paused to reach in his pocket and pull out a bite of cake. A hopeful gull swooped overhead; as he stuffed the sweet morsel into his mouth, he batted the bird away with his other hand. "Anyway," he said when he'd swallowed, "there was something there all right, but it weren't no missing lobster boat."

I sat on the edge of my narrow bench, breathless. "What was it?"

"That's the thing," he said. "I don't rightly know what it was. But it was dark, and it was big, and it looked like a ship. My da and I could see her in the fog and hear the waves slapping up against the sides. And the smell . . ."

"What did it smell like?"

"Tar," he said. "Tar, and wet wood, and gunpowder. And something rotten. Dead things," he said quietly; I had to strain to hear him over the sound of the motor. He took a deep breath and looked out to sea. "It smelled like death."

Again, I felt the skin on my arms prickle, and I dug my hands deeper into my pockets. He was quiet a moment before continuing. "My da called out to her, hailing her, you know. But nobody answered."

"Did you see anything on it?"

He shook his head. "Not a soul — or even a sail. It was dark as pitch out there, and foggy to boot. Nothing but the flicker of a lantern, and that could have been a trick of the night, you know. And then, like that" — he snapped his fingers — "she weren't there no more."

"It just disappeared?"

He nodded.

"Even the smell?"

"It hung around for a minute or two, but then it was gone, too."

"Creepy," I said.

"Ayuh," he said, nodding. "That was the strangest night I've ever passed, on water or on land. My da steered out of there quick as anything. I never saw that old boat cut through the water half as fast — even with the fog thick as chowder."

"Did he think it was a ship?"

"To tell you the truth, I don't know," he said. "It seemed best to leave it behind us; we never said a word about it."

"What happened to the lost lobster boat?"

"Turned up the next day," he said.

"Was everyone okay?"

"Ayuh. They just ran out of gas. Looked like total idiots. They were lucky the Coast Guard found 'em drifting south." He chuckled. "They would have been halfway to Florida soon enough."

I gazed at the dark, restless water — beautiful, but deadly. We were heading east of the island, out toward what looked like open water. "Where did Adam and Evan find the wreck?" I asked.

"Funny thing about that," he said, reaching in his pocket for another piece of cake. He looked back at me with shrewd eyes. "It's right smack in the middle of Deadman's Shoal."

I swallowed. "Where you saw the ghost ship."

"If that's what it was," he said, with a half-shrug. There was a faraway look on his craggy face. "Fog can play tricks on a man's mind. And it was a long time ago."

"It's a great story, though."

He looked back at me and winked. "Maybe so. But not one I'd want bandied about, so if you'll keep it close, I'd be much obliged."

"Of course."

He nodded and returned his gaze to the boats, which were drawing closer by the moment. I looked back at Cranberry Island, which had shrunk to a dark gray mass in the distance. "Who was Davy Blue's lady love?" I asked.

"A young lady named Eleanor Kean," he said. "Or at least that's the story."

"Really? She was one of Charlene's ancestors?"

"Unless there was another Kean family on the island, I'm guessing she was."

I chuckled to myself; evidently the Kean women's effect on men ran in the family. Charlene, whose natural beauty was enhanced by her carefully coiffed caramel-colored hair and always-impeccable makeup, had half the lobstermen on the island mooning after her. She hadn't seduced a pirate yet, though — or at least not that I knew of. "So, she's not the only heartbreaker in the family," I said.

"Comes by it honestly, I'd say."

Any further conversation along that vein was tabled till later; we were growing closer to the two boats — and moving into the danger zone.

Eleazer nodded to me. "Head up to the bow and keep an eye out for rocks, will you?"

I'd steered around rocks in my own skiff many a time, but the tale of Deadman's Shoal made me nervous. If a seasoned pirate could get caught by submerged rocks, where did that leave me? "Any tips on what to watch for?" I asked.

"Well, you want to holler if you see anything sticking out of the water, for starters. But sometimes you'll see light patches, or seaweed — you know, you've done it before. If you see something, just yell out 'eleven o'clock' or 'two o'clock', and I'll adjust."

"Got it," I said, and spent the next few minutes staring hard at the inky water, trying to prevent the little skiff from joining the ship on the bottom of the ocean.

Fortunately, Eleazer steered us through the danger zone without incident, and soon we were idling next to the two larger vessels. Evidently we'd come at a bad time; despite Eleazer's friendly hail, the boats' passengers spared us barely a glance. I recognized Molly's curly red hair aboard the *Ira B.* Her partner, Carl, looked completely different, perhaps because he was beet red and his eyes were bulging out of his head.

"You're not going to get this one, Gerald."

"Settle down, Carl," Gerald said from the deck of the *Lorelei.* He oozed an irritating blend of confidence and condescension.

"Just because you have friends in high places doesn't mean the entire ocean belongs to you," Carl fumed.

Eleazer glanced at me. "We came at a bad

time, it seems."

"Jurisdiction quarrel," I said.

His eyebrows went up. "Jurisdiction? It's not just the university out here?"

"That one," I said, pointing to the *Lorelei,* "belongs to a company called Iliad. And that one," I said, gesturing to the smaller, utilitarian-looking *Ira B,* "belongs to the University of Maine."

Eleazer's face hardened. "I've heard of Iliad. Made a mess of a Spanish galleon a few years back. Why are they here?"

"They're hoping to find artifacts and make money selling them, I imagine."

"I'll bet they are — but I'm not going to let them steal that ship." Eleazer looked fierce. "That's our history there under that water. I'll not stand by and watch it pillaged by outsiders."

"I think Carl agrees with you," I said, nodding toward the archaeologist, who was now an unhealthy purplish color and shouting at the top of his lungs. "You're a crook! A vulture!"

The other man turned and issued a few commands to his crew. I gathered they had experienced this kind of thing before, for they seemed utterly unconcerned by the invective being hurled at them by the archaeologist.

"You can't just retrieve artifacts without mapping the site!" Carl yelled as Audrey donned a dry suit and reached for an oxygen tank. "You don't have permission. You're desecrating the site!"

Eleazer stood up in the skiff. One hand, I noted uneasily, was on the hilt of the cutlass. "The man's right," he called to Gerald. "You have no business here. This ship belongs to the people of Maine!"

The man turned to look at Eleazer, while I tried to make myself as small as possible. As much as I might agree with the islander, the man he was haranguing was, unfortunately, my guest. I was distinctly uncomfortable being — quite literally — in the same boat with him.

Gerald, unruffled by Eleazer's and Carl's verbal attacks, surveyed the little skiff; I hunched down in my jacket. "According to the Abandoned Shipwreck Act," he said in a clipped voice, "the wreck does not fall within territorial waters, and is almost certainly not a ship that belonged to the U.S. government. Therefore, it is not the property of the state, and is — as the saying goes — 'fair game'."

"I'm no lawyer, and what you say may be true, but it's still not right, and you know it," Eleazer said. "In any case, you didn't find it. Whatever happened to finders keepers? It should be up to whoever found it in the first place."

"Fortunately, we were, in fact, invited here by the individual who found the ship," Gerald said coolly. "As such, there is no reason for us not to continue our operation. If it is any consolation, you have my assurances that I will do everything to preserve the site," he said.

"Adam Thrackton called you?" Eleazer said, looking stunned.

"No," he said. "Evan Sorenson, the young man who pulled up the timber, contacted us. He specifically requested our presence."

"You're a rotten, dirty liar," Eleazer said. "It was Adam what found that ship, and that's a piece of our heritage you're trying to lay claim to. You're a pirate, plain and simple." There was a menace to his voice that I'd never heard from mild-mannered Eli. "And do you remember what used to happen to pirates?" he hissed. To my horror, he withdrew the cutlass from its scabbard; the blade flashed in the sun.

I blinked, shocked. Everyone on the island knew that as a shipwright, he had a special interest in antique vessels and the stories that went with them — but I never would have imagined him threatening to kill a stranger over a sunken ship. "Eleazer," I said, reaching out to touch his arm. He shook me off.

Gerald looked down at him mildly. "Are you threatening me, Mr . . . ?"

"White," he said. "Eleazer White." He stood for a moment, staring at the man. Then, after turning the cutlass so it caught the light once more, he abruptly jammed it back into its scabbard and started the motor with a sharp jerk. "I'll say naught else. You've been warned."

Before Gerald could respond, Eleazer gunned the motor so hard I almost fell off my bench seat. A moment later the two bobbing boats were behind us, and we were heading full-tilt toward Cranberry Island.

I watched my old friend. His grizzled jaw was set, and the look on his face precluded me from saying anything — including asking the question that interested me the most right now.

Why had Ingrid Sorenson's son betrayed Adam and called a treasure-hunting company?

FOUR

After our brief but stormy visit to the wreck site, Eleazer had dropped me off abruptly, muttering about getting in touch with some people. I'd spent the rest of the afternoon trying to reach Gwen to ask about Evan Sorenson — in between visits from islanders bearing plates of goodies. Evidently word had gotten out that I was leaving the treats out for guests' consumption, and I was regretting my attempt to be kind. After having accepted plates from Emmeline and Claudette, both of whom were my friends, I couldn't turn down everyone else.

The worst came at four in the afternoon, just when I was trying to slip in a quick nap. Biscuit had just curled up beside me when the front doorbell rang. I ran downstairs to answer it, hoping it would be Charlene.

It was Florence Maxwell, wearing a fisherman's yellow rain slicker and holding a big bowl of what looked like mutant gumdrops.

I was instantly wary. Although our exchanges had never been anything but pleasant, Charlene had told me many stories about Florence, none of them flattering. She had always been polite to me, but I knew she had strong opinions of right and wrong, and I had no desire to tangle with her. When Charlene took over the store and decided to add couches and update the offerings, Florence had circulated a petition against it — and had boycotted the store for two years. She was now writing a cookbook, and I knew she coveted the bake-off award to help her find a publisher. If there was even a whiff of impropriety, I was guessing she'd be on the horn with the local paper pronto.

"I heard there was some early judging," Florence told me, proffering the misshapen confections. "I think it may be prohibited in the rules, but I wanted to bring a sample just to make sure I didn't miss out."

"It's not early judging," I said, wishing I'd never let Emmeline drop off her baked goods. "I agreed to put samples out for guests, along with a comment card. I won't be sampling any of them."

"But this way, it won't be anonymous," she pointed out.

I sighed. She was right — but on an island of fewer than one hundred residents, anonymity wasn't much of a commodity anyway. "I understand your concern," I said. "But I have not and will not sample any of the dishes until the judging officially begins. And I assure you," I said, again kicking myself for letting Tom talk me into this, "I will be judging on flavor, presentation, and creativity."

"Hmmph," Florence said. If I had had any interest in bribery, I had several attractive offers to choose from; I had already turned down two offers of free lobster for a year.

"I'll be happy to put your dish out with the others," I said, inviting her in. I placed her crystal bowl on the sideboard beside the other dainties. She scanned them with interest, sizing up the competition. "That cake looks good. I think I'll try a sample."

I smiled thinly. "Might be best to wait for the judging," I suggested.

Florence gave me an appraising look and a short nod. "Well, I'd best be off, then," she said.

"I'll return the bowl next week," I said.

"Thank you," she said gruffly, and squeaked out the front door.

I'd given up on the nap after she left — her visit had been unsettling — and instead gone to the kitchen to mix up a batch of dough. Now, two hours later, as the smell

67

of fresh bread filled the cozy kitchen and I arranged scallops on ovenproof platters, Gwen slipped through the door, her art bag slung over her right shoulder. "How'd the painting go?" I asked.

"Terrific," she said. "The colors are so beautiful this time of year. I lost track of time!"

"I was trying to call, but I couldn't get in touch with you — figured you were out in the boat somewhere, painting *al fresco.*"

She grinned. "*En plein air,* you mean?"

"Exactly," I said.

"I was, and about froze my fingers off, but it was worth it. The light was spectacular today. What were you calling me about?"

"I wanted to ask about Evan Sorenson."

"Who?"

"He's Ingrid's son. The one who was with Adam when he pulled up a timber."

"Oh, yeah. What about him?"

"What do you know about him?" I asked.

"Not much," she said. "I've met him a few times, but that's all. He just got back to the island — he'd been away a few years, off at school, I think."

Rehab, actually, but there was no need to pass that information on.

"Does Adam know him well?"

"Not really," she said. "His mom asked

68

Adam to let him try out lobstering."

"Licenses are awfully hard to get, aren't they?" From everything I knew, licenses were often passed down in families, and the territories that went with them were hard to come by if you were a newcomer. Just a few months back, there had been a murder down the coast — the result of a feud over lobstering territory.

"An uncle of his in Camden is thinking of retiring and passing his license to Evan. He was at school for a couple of years — and, like Adam, decided he preferred a simpler life."

Or had been kicked out of school and had no other options, I thought but didn't say it.

"Anyway," Gwen continued, "when Ingrid asked, Adam agreed to let him help haul traps with him for a couple of weeks."

"Well, apparently he now considers himself the finder of the wreck," I said.

"What do you mean?"

"Evan called in a treasure hunting company. He's laying claim to the find."

Gwen set down her bag with a thud. "But that's not right! All he did was operate the winch. It was Adam's boat and Adam's trap."

"That's not how the Sorensons see it," I

said. "I'll bet you dollars to donuts his mom backs his claim — and the family's got the money to hire big-gun lawyers. When they got back yesterday, Evan called a company named Iliad and told them he found a sunken ship."

"Iliad," she repeated. "I saw that name in the reservation book, didn't I?"

I nodded.

"They're staying here?"

"Yup. And so are the university archaeologists."

She pushed a lock of curly hair behind her ear, looking agitated. "I've got to call Adam," she said. "That jerk. I can't believe Evan double-crossed him that way."

"I'll be curious to hear what he says," I told her. "In the meantime, both the archaeologists and the treasure hunters are having dinner here tonight."

Gwen stared at me. "Together? In our dining room?"

"Not at the same table, I'm guessing. But certainly in the same room."

She gave a short, bitter laugh. "Might not want to put out the steak knives, then."

"Why do you think I'm serving scallops?" I said, only half-joking. After watching Eleazer wave his cutlass around this afternoon, I was thinking a diet of nice, soft food might be just the ticket for a while.

She crossed her arms, still angry. "It seems wrong that these people are going to come in and take over the find. It should be the university's business, not a cash cow for private industry."

"I know," I said, drizzling a ramekin of scallops with melted butter and scattering cracker crumbs over the top.

"Can't somebody — the state, maybe — just tell them to leave?"

"I guess it depends on who 'officially' found it. It may be the only way to resolve that is in court."

"Maybe I should have studied law instead of art," Gwen said.

"There's still time," I said. "Your mother would be delighted." My sister had never forgiven Gwen for choosing to study art instead of something practical, like business. So far, she hadn't pressured Gwen to return to UCLA, but I knew it was coming.

She rolled her eyes. "Never mind, then."

I had sent Gwen out to finish setting the tables and was uncorking a bottle of sauvignon blanc when John walked into the kitchen, bringing the sweet smell of fresh cut wood with him.

"How's my favorite innkeeper?" he asked, wrapping his arms around me.

"Not looking forward to dinner," I said, checking my watch over his shoulder.

"Why not?" he asked, eyeing the scallops hungrily.

"It's been an interesting day," I said. "And I'm afraid my guests are going to start hurling more than invective back and forth."

"What's going on? I've been in my workshop all day with the radio going," he said. "Did something happen?"

I filled him in on everything he'd missed. When I told him about Eleazer's not-so-veiled threat — and Carl's verbal attack — he let out a long, low whistle. "And all of these people are eating dinner in your dining room tonight?"

"Well, everyone but Eleazer," I said. "I wouldn't be surprised if he spent all afternoon in his skiff out at Deadman's Shoal, trying to prevent anyone from Iliad from diving down to the wreck. He's probably home refueling on sugarless pie." Which reminded me of the bake-off, and Florence Maxwell's visit. "Speaking of which, are you sure you don't want to volunteer to help me judge the bakeoff?" I asked.

He stepped back. "I love you, Natalie, but as far as the bake-off is concerned, I'm afraid you're on your own."

I avoided the dining room, focusing instead on plating the food. The ramekins of scallops came out of the oven a beautiful golden brown on top, and the crisp green asparagus made a perfect foil. For the first twenty minutes, I stood poised to go and mediate — but by the time the salad plates came back, I was starting to relax. I retrieved the chocolate mousse from the fridge along with a bowl of freshly whipped cream, feeling relieved at my guests' good manners. Despite their confrontation on the water this afternoon, they seemed able to keep their tempers under control in the dining room.

"How is it in there?" I asked as Gwen brought in the dinner dishes. I was putting the last touch of raspberry drizzle on bowls of chocolate mousse, which I had decorated with little swirls of whipped cream.

"Chilly," she said. "They're still on opposite sides of the room, and I haven't heard a single word."

"I hope they're not terrorizing Cherry," I said.

She was the only guest not on the island to investigate the shipwreck, and had come in on one of the late mailboat runs. "She

73

seems like a nice lady; I'd hate for her to feel uncomfortable."

"She's got her nose in a book," Gwen said.

"Good. That'll distract her. At least they're not at each other's throats," I said, placing a fresh raspberry on each of the bowls.

I had just set the last bowl on a serving tray for Gwen when there was a crash from the dining room.

Gwen and I stared at each other for a split second before both dashing to the swinging door.

I got there first, and froze in the doorway, at a loss for what to do next.

One of my plates lay shattered on the wood floor. A few feet away, Carl stood, murder in his eyes. Molly stood next to him, a restraining arm on his — our eyes met, and I could read fear in hers.

Not good.

"I'll get John," Gwen murmured, and I was thankful for her quick thinking. I didn't know what was about to happen, but the way things were looking, it wouldn't be a bad thing to have the island's deputy on hand.

"Can I help you with something?" I said calmly, addressing Carl. He didn't even hear me. The veins stood out on his forehead; I could see the one by his temple pulsing. He pointed a shaking finger at Gerald. "If you so much as remove one *splinter* from that ship, I will hunt you down personally."

Gerald sat back in his chair, in the relaxed pose of the man who's holding four aces in his hand and knows his opponent has nothing but deuces. "Business is business, Carl. I'm here on authority of the finder, and the wreck is outside of territorial waters." He cut a scallop in half and popped it into his mouth. Carl's chest heaved as Gerald chewed slowly, then swallowed and looked back up at him with a contented smile. "Better luck next time, Carl."

Carl let out a strangled bellow and lunged at him. Molly pulled him back, but he broke free, stumbling over to the treasure hunter's chair and throwing a wild punch that grazed Gerald's chin. Carl fell to the floor, but scrambled to his feet and was about to attack a second time when John dashed past me and into the dining room.

Within seconds, he had the wiry archaeologist's arms pinned behind him, and I could hear my fiancé's low, calm voice telling him to get himself together. Cherry Price gazed at the entire proceedings over the rims of her red reading glasses. She looked more intrigued than afraid, thankfully.

I hurried over to Carl's partner, Molly. "Are you okay?" I asked

Her curly red hair was mussed, and her face was pale, but she was recovering herself. "Yes. Thank you for getting your friend — Carl was really out of control." She reached up and raked her hand through her hair. "I've never seen him so angry," she said. "If he'd been armed . . ." A shiver passed through her.

"But he wasn't, and it's over now," I said, watching John as he led the archaeologist to a chair.

Gerald was still sitting at his table, feeling his chin with his fingers. His two companions sat nearby; while Frank seemed unconcerned, the young woman had fished ice cubes out of Gerald's water glass and was offering them to him, wrapped in a napkin. He waved the impromptu compress away. "I'll be fine," he said. "He barely touched me. Still — it was an assault. If I wanted to, I could press charges."

Personally, I thought he looked awfully unruffled for a man whose life had been threatened just moments before. I wondered if attacks by university archaeologists were a frequent occurrence in his life.

"Oh, please don't, Gerald," said Molly from beside me, addressing Iliad's owner.

"He just has a lot at stake — he didn't mean to hurt you. I'm so sorry he lost his temper."

Gerald? I looked over at Molly, surprised.

A slow, almost rakish smile crossed Gerald's face, and for a moment I could see the energy and drive — and the passion — that drove the treasure-hunter. "It's fortunate for Carl that he has such a charming partner," he said. "The offer of a job is always open, you know, if you're interested . . ."

"I'm not," Molly said, cutting him off. Their eyes met and held for a moment; then she looked away and bent down to pick up shards of the broken plate from the floor.

I hurried to take over for her. "There's no need to pick this up," I said.

"No," she protested. "It's our fault. I'll clean it up — and we'll reimburse you for the dish."

"There's no need for that," I said. They weren't very expensive, and I had more than I would ever use. Still, Molly insisted on paying, and also insisted on helping me pick up the big pieces, only relenting when I told her I'd sweep up the rest.

As I left to retrieve the broom, I glanced at Cherry, who had put down her book and was now jotting down notes in a small, leather-bound book. What was she doing? Keeping a journal? Or was even she some-

77

how involved in the shipwreck?

Phone calls at three a.m. almost never mean good news, and the one that came that night was no exception. John and I bolted upright. He turned on the bedside lamp as I reached for the phone, adrenaline rushing through me.

"Hello?" I said, dispensing with the usual "Gray Whale Inn" greeting.

"Is John at your place?"

"Eleazer! What's wrong?"

"I think I'd best save that for John," he said.

My stomach flipped over as I handed the phone to John. Had another boat failed to come in? The weather was good, but things sometimes happened . . .

My fiancé was fully alert, and there was no trace of sleep in his voice when he spoke. "Eleazer. What's going on?" He was silent for a moment, and I could faintly hear Eli's voice speaking rapidly. I smoothed the comforter nervously. Biscuit opened one eye, then curled up in a tight orange ball and went back to sleep.

"What time did you find him?" John asked, and my stomach did another flip. That didn't sound good at all. "You're sure he's gone?" he continued. Then he let out a short sigh. "I'll meet you at the town pier."

"What's going on?" I asked as he hung up the phone.

"It's Gerald — the guy who runs Iliad," he said, getting out of bed and pulling on his jeans.

"What about him?"

"He's dead," John said. "Eleazer found him out by the wreck site."

"Oh, no," I breathed. I clenched the comforter between my hands. "What happened? Did he drown?"

John shook his head. "Somebody stabbed him in the back."

Murder. And violent murder, at that. "What was Eleazer doing out there at three in the morning?" I asked, dreading the answer. Eleazer had been so angry yesterday; was it possible he had made good on his threat?

"I don't know, Natalie," he said, his face grim. "But I'm sure the investigators will be asking the same question."

He buttoned his shirt and reached for his sweater. Suddenly, my foggy brain registered where he was going. "You're not heading out to the site in a skiff, are you?" It was a couple of miles out to the wreck — far for a small boat, particularly at night.

"I've got to," he said. "First I'll call the

Coast Guard, though. I'm going to meet Eli at the main pier, and we'll go out together."

"Can't you just leave it to them?"

He shook his head and pulled on his wool sweater. "I'm worried about Eli, Nat. I've got to talk to him — and see the body."

I understood. He was going to protect our friend. I didn't like it — Eli was the most skilled boatsman I knew, but that still didn't make it safe — but John was probably right.

"Let me brew you two a thermos of coffee to take with you," I offered. "It'll be cold out on the water, and the caffeine will help."

"There's no time," he said.

"Ten minutes won't change what happened to Gerald," I said. "You can call the Coast Guard just as you're leaving." As I got up and slipped into my bathrobe, a horrible thought occurred to me. "John — what if the murderer is still out there?"

"The thought occurred to me, too, but I'm guessing whoever did it is long gone," he said. We looked at each other for a moment, not wanting to say what both of us feared — that John was about to head out to the wreck in the murderer's boat. "I'm sure it will be fine, Nat. But just in case, I'll take my gun."

Together we went downstairs. John ran down to the carriage house to get a heavy

80

jacket and gloves as I started the coffee, my stomach churning with worry. Gerald might have been unscrupulous — and, at times, I suspected, ruthless — but he didn't deserve to die. I remembered the hatred I'd seen on Eleazer's face out on the water yesterday — and the way his hand had strayed to the hilt of his cutlass. Gerald had been stabbed in the back. Had Eleazer taken matters into his own hands?

The kitchen was filled with the comforting smell of brewing coffee when John returned to the kitchen a few minutes later. As he picked up the phone and relayed the information to the Coast Guard, I filled a small container with muffins and dug a thermos and a few cups out, packing them into a plastic tub. I watched John as I worked; several times, he raked his fingers through his dark blond hair, and his face was grim.

"What did Eleazer do with the body?" I asked when he finally hung up.

"He turned him over," John said, sounding weary, "just to see if there was any hope of saving him. Then he tried to haul him into the boat, but he was too heavy, so he just tied him to the nearest lobster buoy."

"Was the blade still in the wound?"

"No," John said, and looked away.

81

"What's wrong?"

"Nothing," he said.

I stared at him for a long moment. "Was it Eli's cutlass that killed him?"

"I have no idea," he said. "But I'm praying it wasn't."

FIVE

After John left, I debated waking Gerald's colleagues, but decided to wait; a few hours wouldn't make much difference, and at least they'd be well rested.

Audrey was the first one down. I brought out the coffee carafe, but instead of taking her breakfast order, I sat down across from her.

She was an attractive woman, with brown, blunt-cut hair and large, expressive eyes. She had the physique of an athlete, and wore little makeup — just a bit of mascara and some lip gloss. She exuded an aura of healthiness.

"Could I have a bowl of oatmeal this morning?" she asked.

"Audrey," I said. "I've got some bad news."

Her brown eyes fixed on me, looking larger than ever. "What's wrong?"

"It's Gerald," I said. "He died last night."

The color leached from her face. "No," she said. "No." She took a deep breath and closed her eyes. A deep, wracking sob shuddered through her.

"I'm sorry," I said.

After a long, painful moment, she opened her eyes and looked at me. "What happened? Was it a heart attack?" She dashed the table with her palm. "I knew he should have dropped those twenty pounds! I told him again and again . . ."

"It wasn't a heart attack," I said.

She blinked. "What happened, then?"

"I can't give you the details, but the police believe he was murdered."

"Murdered?" She rubbed her eyes with her palm; her mascara was smeared. "Oh, God. I can't believe it. How? Where?"

"They found him near the wreck last night."

"What was he doing out there?" She looked at the window, toward the wreck site. "The *Lorelei*'s gone. The dinghy's gone, too."

I followed her gaze, and realized she was right. The red buoy marking the mooring line bobbed up and down in the waves.

"Why would he go out without me — without us?" she said.

Why would he go out there at all, was the

question I wanted to know. And Eleazer had said nothing about the *Lorelei* being out there — at least not that I'd heard. What exactly had gone on last night?

"Oh, God," she said, lowering her head to her hands. I reached out to comfort her, but at that moment, Frank strode into the room.

He gave me a quizzical look, and Audrey looked up. "You got your wish," she said, tears streaming down her cheeks.

"What do you mean?" he asked, looking puzzled.

"Gerald is dead."

Frank took a step backward. "What? He can't be."

"I'm afraid he is," I confirmed.

"I don't understand," Frank said.

"He's been murdered," Audrey spat. "So you don't have to worry about it any more."

With that, she stood up and stormed out of the room, leaving Frank and me to look at each other.

"I'm sorry for your loss," I said. "Can I get you a cup of coffee or something?"

"A whiskey on the rocks might be a better choice, but it's a bit early," he said, and sat down at the nearest table. "Have the police been notified?"

"They're out at the site now," I said.

"The wreck site?"

"That's where he was found," I said.

He looked out the window. "Where's the *Lorelei*?"

"Gone," I said.

Frank swore, and I disappeared into the kitchen to retrieve the coffee pot. When I returned a few minutes later, Molly and Carl were there too, looking stunned.

"When did this happen?" Carl asked. "And how?"

"I don't know," Frank said, turning to me. "Do you?"

"It happened late last night," I said. "That's all I know. The police are investigating."

"Who found him?" Molly asked.

I swallowed down the lump in my throat. "Eleazer White."

It could have been my imagination, but all three looked relieved.

I had just finished clearing the last of the breakfast things and was wiping down counters when the phone rang. It was Charlene; I was surprised, frankly, that she had waited so long to get in touch. "How come you didn't call?" she demanded when I answered.

"I didn't want to call you at three in the

morning, and I've been doing breakfast service since seven."

"I can't believe you didn't tell me! I heard from Tania when I got to the store this morning."

"Next time I'll call," I promised, feeling very tired. And it was no wonder; I hadn't slept since answering the phone at three.

"So, give me the scoop! I heard it was that Iliad bigshot, and that somebody strangled him on his own boat."

"Not exactly," I said, and glanced over my shoulder to be sure I was alone. "I'll tell you, but only if you promise not to say a word to anyone."

"Scout's honor," she said.

"You're not a scout."

"You know what I mean, Natalie. I promise, mum's the word."

"It was Gerald McIntire — you're right about that. Eli found him floating out by the wreck," I said in a low voice. "He was stabbed."

"With what?"

"I don't know," I said.

"And Eli found him at three in the morning, and called John?"

"Apparently so."

"What was he doing out there in the middle of the night?" she asked. "Unless . . ."

I bit my lip. If Charlene, John, and I had all come to that conclusion about our dear friend, then what would the police think?

"He says he was just guarding the wreck site," I said.

"Sounds fishy to me."

I sighed. "I know."

"What do the police say?"

"John came back at six; they're taking the body to the morgue for an autopsy, and they've been looking for the boat ever since."

"What boat?"

"The *Lorelei.* It's gone missing." I glanced out the window at the satiny surface of the water. Was the *Lorelei* under those shiny waves somewhere?

"Not a good night for Iliad, was it? I hope they had insurance."

"I hadn't thought about that," I said. "The *Lorelei* must be worth a lot of money. I wonder who would get the payout if that boat went down?"

"Worth asking," Charlene said. "Assuming it was insured, that is. It's worth asking anyone who might have a motive, really. I can't stand the thought of Eli going to jail for the rest of his life . . ."

"Don't jump to conclusions," I said.

"I'm not," she said. "I'm just being prepared."

"Like a good scout," I said, automatically.

"Exactly. Hang on a sec, Nat . . ." I could hear a murmur of voices in the background, and Charlene telling someone she'd be right there. "Gotta go. Half the island just walked in for a mug-up. I'll see what the gossip is and call you later."

"Got it."

"You know, there's one good thing about this," she said.

"What?"

"At least everyone will be talking about something other than the bake-off."

I groaned. "Thanks for reminding me."

"Always looking for the silver lining," she said. "Anyway, gotta run. If you hear anything on your end, let me know — day or night!"

"Aye aye, captain."

Despite Charlene's reminder, I finished wiping down the counters in a slightly cheerier mood. I was hoping the police wouldn't arrest Eli. But if they did, I knew Charlene would have the entire island leaping to his defense.

John was on the phone when I knocked on his door twenty minutes later; he waved me in, and I perched on the edge of his oatmeal-colored couch and listened as he finished the conversation. From the GPS coordinates being batted back and forth, I knew he was getting an update on the search for the *Lorelei.*

"Have they found anything?" I asked when he hung up a moment later.

"Some debris out by Deadman's Shoal," he said, "but nothing identifiable — at least not yet."

"The other crew members could probably ID anything they found," I said.

"I'm sure they'll ask them," he said.

"I'm surprised no one's been by the inn to question anyone yet." Unfortunately, I was more than familiar with post-murder procedure on Cranberry Island.

"They've been talking with Eli all morning," John said. "They're out at his house right now."

I suddenly realized I hadn't called Eli's wife, Claudette. She was strong and stoic, but I was sure she was shaken up — particularly with the police at her house. "I need to swing by their house this morning," I said. "But I don't understand; why aren't they questioning Gerald's coworkers — or even Carl? He attacked Gerald last night," I said.

"You need to tell them about it," he said.

"I'll make sure they interview you."

"They've got to look beyond Eli," I said. "Charlene brought up another good point; if the boat was insured, who is the beneficiary, now that Gerald is out of the way?"

He gave me a wry smile. "You and Charlene are good at thinking of ulterior motives, aren't you?"

I sighed. "Unfortunately, I haven't been overly impressed with law enforcement's ability to see beyond the easiest solution."

"Hey," John protested.

"Present company excluded, of course," I said, giving him a peck on the cheek. "I think I'll head over to Claudette's and Eli's now — I've got some time before lunch."

"Send my love, will you?"

"Of course," I said. "If you're lucky, she'll send you some pie."

"Maybe all the excitement will mean she hasn't had a chance to bake," he said.

"Let's hope so," I said. "Keep me posted, okay?"

"Always," he said, with a look that made my insides do a delightful little flip.

I pulled my coat tight around me as I walked down the end of the road to Claudette and Eli's; the wind had freshened since last night, and a flood of gray clouds had extinguished the sun. Muffin and Pudge, the goats Claudette raised for their soft wool, were happily munching on a bed of roses, a block down the road from Claudette's; they had evidently managed to drag the tire she kept them chained to within range of Ingrid Sorenson's prize Souvenir de la Malmaisons. I hauled the tire back to the meadow, but by the time I made it to Eli and Claudette's, they were already tugging it across the road. I made a mental note to stop by Ingrid's and ask about her son Evan; something told me he might somehow be involved with the disappearing *Lorelei*.

There were no cars outside Claudette and Eli's house; either the police had arrived on foot, or had already left. Eleazer's jumble of bleached hulls and burnt-out motors dotted the long grass behind the small, wood house; his workshop had a desolate look to it. I hesitated a moment before knocking.

No one answered. A gust of wind pushed against me and set the two rockers on the porch into motion, and I knocked again. This time, I heard movement behind the door, and a moment later the knob turned, and as the door opened, the familiar faint smell of fried sausage and wet wool wafted out. Claudette's solid figure stood framed in the doorway, her broad shoulders slumped, her face leached of color. "They took him," Claudette said.

"What?"

"They found the cutlass that killed that man. It was Eli's, and his fingerprints were on it." She recited it as if by memory, with no feeling. She must be in shock.

My stomach dropped. "The antique cutlass?" I already knew the answer, but still dreaded to hear it.

She nodded, confirming my worst fear. "He keeps it over the fireplace. Polishes it every week — convinced it's Davey Blue's heirloom." She glanced over her shoulder. "But it's not there now. They found it."

"Where?"

"Near the pier, in a bunch of brambles."

That didn't make sense at all. "He wouldn't just leave that cutlass in a bush!" I said.

"I know," she said, her voice hollow.

"Did he have it with him all day yesterday?"

"I don't know," she said, putting her head in her hands. "I know he had it in the morning, because he was going to talk to the archaeologists about it. I don't know if he had it all day, though. He was back a couple of times, and he could have put it back. I didn't think to look. If only I had . . ." she moaned a little bit, wracked with grief.

"If you didn't see him with it, there's no way to know if he took it with him. And were your doors locked?"

"Never needed to lock them," she said, looking up at me. "It's a small island."

"So if he left it here, anyone could have snuck in and taken it. It was common knowledge on the island where he kept the sword."

"That's true, I guess."

"Did you tell the police that your doors were unlocked — and that Eli kept the cutlass over the fireplace?"

"I didn't think it would matter," she said. "They're convinced he killed that man." She let out a convulsive sob. "I wish they'd never found that ship, Natalie." She reached out and gripped my hand; hers were dry and cold. "I'm afraid it'll be the death of him."

"It's early days, Claudette," I said, squeezing her hand comfortingly. "Does he have a lawyer?"

"Of course not," she said. "Not much call for one on Cranberry Island."

"Well, then, that's the first order of business. Let me talk to Tom Lockhart, see if he knows anyone on the mainland," I said. "Don't worry — I'm sure we'll get all this sorted out," I said in a bright voice that sounded false even to me. "Why don't you come to my place today? I could use some company."

She glanced back. "Well, there are the cats . . ."

"Just toss some food in the bowl and come with me. They'll keep for a few hours."

"And I've got a sweater to finish . . ."

"You can do it at my place," I said. "Come along with me."

She wavered. "Maybe it would be best to get out for a bit," she said. "Clear my head."

"Absolutely it will," I said. "Gather your knitting things and let's go!"

The goats were back at Ingrid's roses as we walked up the road together a few minutes later, Claudette hunched over, a big bag of wool slung over one shoulder. She didn't even look up when I pointed out Muffin and Pudge. I thought I saw the curtains of Ingrid's house twitch as we passed, though.

I'd definitely have to drop by her place later.

It wasn't until late that afternoon that the police finally arrived at the Gray Whale Inn. I had just laid several cod fillets in a pan of milk to poach — I was making Cranberry

Island Cod Cakes for supper — when the bell rang.

"I'm not sure who's here," I told the two officers. "I think McIntire's coworkers are here, but the university folks have been out at the site all day." Probably making hay while the sun shone, I thought. Who knew how long Iliad would be out of the picture? "They're probably quite relieved to have the site to themselves," I said, attempting to drop a hint.

Neither responded, and I wrote down the names and room numbers of the guests, trying to think of a way to convince them the murderer wasn't already in a jail cell. "Have you found the *Lorelei* yet?" I asked.

The detective shook her head. "Still looking," she said.

"I'll bet when you find it, you'll find out who the murderer really was," I said.

"Do you know something about it?" she asked sharply.

"I know that Eleazer White would never have discarded an antique cutlass in a shrub," I said.

"People do strange things in the heat of passion," she said.

"I'm just saying there were lots of folks who didn't like Gerald McIntire. You know he's had a long history with the university

96

archaeologist, Carl Morgenstern? I was out there yesterday, and he had murder in his eyes — and last night he attacked Gerald in my dining room."

"Did I, now?"

I whirled around; behind me stood Carl, who had evidently just come back in. Molly stood beside him, eyeing me with anger and reproach.

Six

"Mr. Morgenstern, I presume?" the detective said smoothly.

"Indeed," he said, still giving me a hard look. "I don't care for slander, Ms. Barnes."

"I'm sorry, but it's a murder investigation," I said, feeling my face burn. "I was telling them what I saw."

"We appreciate your assistance, Ms. Barnes," the detective said briskly, dismissing me. "If we need more of your observations, we'll let you know. In the meantime, is there a place we can go to ask these two folks some questions?"

"You can use the dining room," I said, feeling chastened. I installed them at a table by the window and returned to the kitchen to make a pot of tea. Claudette was sitting by the window, knitting something large and brown.

"Who's here?" she asked, the needles pausing.

"The police," I said. "They're questioning the archaeologists."

She sat up a little straighter. "That's good, isn't it?"

"I hope so," I said, but as I filled the teakettle, I realized I wasn't feeling very hopeful at all. The police already had someone with means, motive, and opportunity. Why look further?

I tossed a tea bag into a teapot and sat down across from Claudette, who had resumed knitting mechanically. Her fingers moved at lightning speed, but her eyes were glazed, unfocused. "Tell me again what happened last night," I said.

She sighed, and the needles slowed slightly. "Well, all this started yesterday, after he went out to the site with you. I've never seen him so angry. He stayed home long enough for a bite to eat, but then he was gone — out to find Tom Lockhart, I think. He talked about going to see the archaeologists about the cutlass, but I don't know if he ever did it. I think after what happened yesterday, he seemed worried mainly about the wreck site."

"Why did he want to see Tom?" I asked, leaning back in my chair.

"For advice, I think." She finished a row and transferred the needles between her hands. It looked like she was working on one side of a sweater, but it was hard to tell. "He wanted to stop *Iliad* from taking over the site."

"How long was he gone?"

"Almost the whole day. He stopped in for dinner, but hardly touched a bite." I knew it wasn't because of Claudette's cooking; her pastries might be terrible, but she made some of the best chowder I'd ever eaten. "He ate maybe three bites of stew, and was out the door again. I told him to let things be, to sleep on it at least, but he was angrier than I've ever seen him." She lowered her needles; the brown wool was slack in her lap. "And now look what he's gone and done . . ."

"He's innocent until proven guilty," I reminded her. "And there were lots of other people who didn't like Gerald McIntire. He had a long list of enemies."

She looked up at me. "Really?"

"Trust me. One of the archaeologists threatened to strangle him over dinner last night," I said. "I'll make sure the investigators don't overlook that fact."

The tension in her doughy features loosened a bit, and I saw a bit of something like hope in her eyes. She picked up her knitting and continued with her row.

"Now. What we need to know is, what did he do with the cutlass?" I crossed my fingers under the table, hoping that Eli hadn't left the house with it last night.

Claudette gave me a sharp look. "What about it?"

"Are you absolutely sure he took it with him that night?"

"I just don't remember," she said.

"But it's possible, isn't it?"

"He was certainly home," she said. "And he usually left it above the mantel."

"But you don't recall exactly," I confirmed.

She shook her head sadly.

It was still worth considering, though. If Eli left the cutlass at home when he went out to see Tom, then anyone else could have come and gotten it. "Did you tell the police he came home — and may have left the cutlass?"

"They didn't ask," she said ruefully.

"You can still tell them," I said. "When I head out, I'll let them know you've got something to add."

"Thank you, Natalie," she said. "Since this happened, I . . . I just haven't thought clearly." She paused. "Wait — I did see it. Because he was polishing it something

101

fierce. I remember him putting it back up there."

"So it was back over the mantel at what time?"

"He was back in at five-thirty, and we had supper at six, so probably by five-fifty or so."

"He went back out after supper?"

She nodded. "Said he was off to do an errand, and then out in the skiff, to patrol the area. I told him not to, and he usually listens, but yesterday . . ." She slumped.

"He didn't take the cutlass, then?"

"I never looked," she said. "Stupid of me." The needles clacked angrily. "It's gone now, that's for sure."

He hadn't taken it right after supper, but that didn't mean he didn't come back and retrieve it. "Were you at home the whole evening?" I asked.

"I went over to Emmeline's after supper," she said. "I brought her a skein of wool I'd dyed for her — kind of a pale gray-blue. We had a couple of cups of tea and talked about all the goings-on. I walked home around 10 o'clock, but Eleazer wasn't back yet."

"Was the cutlass still over the fireplace?"

She gave me a tortured look. "I didn't look. I never thought . . ."

"Don't blame yourself," I said gently,

reaching over to touch her arm. "How were you to know what would happen? And even if it was gone, there was no way to know who took it."

"I suppose you're right," she said, but the anguish in her face didn't ease.

"At least we know that if someone took it, it had to be after six," I said. "And since the door was unlocked, anybody could have gone in and taken it. Assuming it was there."

"That's true," she said.

As Claudette's needles clacked, I thought back to the previous evening. All of the guests had attended dinner, but had any of them left the inn later that evening? I seemed to remember the front door opening and closing a few times, but I had never bothered to see who was coming or going. The bigger question, really, was whether anyone staying at the inn knew where the Whites' house was — or that the cutlass was kept above the mantelpiece. Eleazer might have mentioned it to one of the university archaeologists; but only Eli or Carl could tell me if that had happened, and Eli wasn't available.

The teakettle started whistling, and as I got up to fix the tea, I glanced at the clock. Dinner was coming up, and I needed to know if I was going to have extra mouths to feed — namely, the detectives in my dining room. I added a few cookies to the tray, along with some cups, cream, and milk, and pushed through the door to the dining room.

"He was waving the cutlass around," Audrey was saying as I pushed through the door. "Told Gerald he was nothing better than a pirate. Then he threatened to kill him!" Her eyes were bloodshot, and her face puffy from crying, but her voice was venomous.

I moved quietly, hoping they would continue to talk, but the detectives broke off the interrogation as I set down the tea tray.

"I'm sorry to interrupt, but will you be staying for dinner?" I asked.

"Would that be possible?" asked the younger of the two, a rather nice-looking young man. "We'd be sure to reimburse you for the expense. Not a lot of restaurants on the island."

"Of course," I said, mentally adding two to the tally. I was hoping they'd continue the interrogation as I laid out the tea things, but not another word was spoken until I was back in the kitchen.

I glanced up at the clock; I had two hours before dinner, and I was dying to talk with Tom Lockhart. John, I knew, was going to be busy with the investigation — but since the menu was fairly simple, Gwen would be able to do most of the prep work. I hated to leave Claudette, but I was sure she'd understand.

I made a few phone calls, and within ten minutes, everything was arranged. Gwen, who had just finished cleaning the upstairs rooms, set to work chopping vegetables for the salad, and a few minutes later, Charlene arrived in her battered pickup truck. Visitors were always a bit surprised when Charlene stepped out of the hunk of 1950s-era steel she drove around the island. The truck, whose original color was indeterminable, gave the general impression of a junkyard refugee held together by duct tape. In contrast, Charlene usually looked like she'd stepped out of the pages of a fashion magazine. Today, she wore a hot pink trench coat that hugged her curves, and her hair was swept back in a stylish updo.

"Ready?" she asked.

"Let me just finish loading this container, and we'll be out." I tucked three more frozen cookies into a big plastic tote and snapped the lid shut. Charlene snagged one of the cookies — double chocolate chip, her favorite — and pulled Claudette into a warm hug.

"How are you doing, sweetheart?" she asked.

"I've been better," the older woman said, still looking shell-shocked. She declined my offer of a cookie — despite her bulk, she was a strict advocate of a sugar-free regimen — and let Charlene lead her out to the driveway. In no time at all, the three of us were packed into the truck's front bench seat, jouncing up the road toward town.

The town pier looked as it always did, the weathered dock lined with stacks of lobster pots, the long, low building that housed the island's tourist shops stretched along the wooden walkway. The plate glass windows of Spurrell's Lobster Pound were dark this time of year, but lights still shone in Island Artists, where one of John's driftwood sculptures was on display: a dolphin leaping from the sea. To the left were a few of the brightly painted toy boats he built every winter; they were snapped up by the dozens in summer, by the tourists who day-tripped to the island on the mail boat. In the next window, a sea glass mobile dangled, the gray-blue shards of cloudy glass mirroring the sullen sky.

Charlene dropped me off just past the pier, in front of a low-slung building, its walls covered in colorful, weathered buoys: the Cranberry Island lobster co-op.

"Half the island's in there," she said, "and the other half is at the store, swapping gossip."

"Let me know if you hear anything good."

"Don't I always?"

"And find out anything you can about Ingrid's son," I added.

"You think he might be involved?"

"Evan's the one who called Iliad in the first place," I said.

"So? If he's the one who called them, why would he want to kill Gerald McIntire?"

"I don't know," I said. "But he's mixed up in all of this, and you never know what he might have seen or heard."

"What does Adam think of all of this?" Charlene asked.

"I haven't talked with him yet. Gwen told me he's coming by the inn tonight," I said. "I'll ask him what he knows then."

"Do you really think we can save Eleazer?" Claudette asked, a tremble in her normally authoritative voice.

Charlene and I exchanged swift glances. "We'll do everything we can, sweetheart," Charlene said, reaching over and patting Claudette's broad knee. "Now, let's get to the store and get a cup of coffee. It's cold out there!"

As if on cue, an icy gust swept off the water. Charlene hit the gas, letting out a plume of gasoline-scented exhaust, and the truck roared up the road. I hurried to the door of the co-op, hoping Tom would have good news — or failing that, at least not tell me anything that would incriminate Eleazer further.

The interior of the lobster co-op was dim and smoky, and smelled strongly of fish — not all of it fresh. A half-dozen men were ranged around a rickety table in the corner, all with grave expressions on their weathered faces. They lightened slightly when I produced the cookies. Adam, I noticed, was not among them. "They're still a bit cold, but they'll thaw quickly," I said.

Tom reached for a cookie, and several other lobstermen followed suit; they were disappearing fast, and I received several gruff thanks. "Tom got you in the soup this year, didn't he, young lady?" asked Mac Barefoot, a grizzled old-timer. "Judging the bake-off and all." I knew his wife, Dottie, had passed away twenty years ago, and from all reports, he wasn't much of a cook. At least one person on the island wouldn't hate me when it was done, I thought.

"That's what Charlene tells me," I replied.

"But I'm going to be completely objective. I've got a score sheet I'm using, and the entries are anonymous." In theory, anyway; I doubted there would be multiple cranberry chutney recipes — or sugarless cranberry pie, for that matter.

"Good luck with that," he grunted, obviously thinking the same thing.

Tom rescued me by changing the subject. "I heard the inspectors were over at the inn." He was a tall, well-put-together man, with a natural charisma that had kept him at the helm of the lobster co-op for years.

I nodded. "They're questioning the archaeologists at the inn right now."

"I don't know why they're bothering, since they've already locked up poor Eli," one of the lobstermen said.

"Just because he's been arrested doesn't mean he's guilty," Tom said.

"That's part of what I came to talk to you about," I said, addressing Tom. "We need to find a good defense attorney."

"Already contacted the top attorney in Bangor — she drove in today. The co-op is taking a collection to help Claudette with the costs."

My heart warmed. The islanders were looking after one of their own. "Count me in, too," I said. "I'll tell Claudette when I see her in a few minutes. She's down at the store with Charlene right now. We're trying to keep her spirits up."

"That shipwreck is cursed," someone grumbled.

"Haunted, too," another said. " 'Always stay clear of Deadman's Shoal,' my dad used to tell me. 'Strange things happen out there.' "

"I know it's supposed to be an old wives' tale, but I thought I saw a ship there once," said Mac. After Eleazer's careful admission the other day, I expected the others to scoff, but there was only a tense silence. A few of the lobstermen exchanged cryptic glances as Mac continued. "The fog was just starting to roll in, and though I usually go round the long way so as not to get too close to Deadman's Shoal, I was trying to make port before nightfall."

"What did you see?" I asked.

"Well, I don't really know. It may have been the fog playing tricks on me, but I swear there was a ship out there, reeking of tar. I could just make out the sails on her."

"Was there anyone aboard?" Tom asked.

"Not that I could tell. I cut the engine, went to hail them, warn them off the rocks. I yelled out a few times, but nobody answered."

"Maybe they were below decks," someone suggested.

Mac shrugged. "Maybe. At first I thought it was one of those historical dress-up ships they float sometimes, or the *Margaret Todd,* out of Bar Harbor, gone astray." The *Margaret Todd* was a four-mast schooner popular with the tourists — but as far as I knew, it never went more than a mile from shore, and Deadman's Shoal was three miles out, in the wrong direction. "But it wasn't a schooner," he said. "It was too big for that."

"Could have been a clipper," someone piped up.

"Or a brig. Jonah Selfridge's ship was a brig, wasn't it?"

"Matilda would know. And Eli, of course."

"Can't ask him now, can we?"

"Could have been either," Mac said, shrugging. "I barely got a glimpse of it."

"What did you do?" I asked, anxious to get back on topic, since I had no idea what the difference was between a brig and a clipper, and didn't much care at the moment.

"I tried to get closer, but a big bank of fog rolled in, and the damn thing just up and disappeared."

"Did you try the radio?"

"Ayuh. No answer, and no other boat reported seeing a ship in the area. Had

111

gooseflesh all over me; I've never run my boat so hard, especially not with fog."

"The ghost ship," someone murmured.

"Probably too much rum in your mug," a young lobsterman snorted. There were a few uneasy chuckles, but not much mirth. An uneasy silence descended on the smoky room, punctuated by the howl of the wind off the water and the occasional crackle of static from the weather radio.

"Any word on the *Lorelei* yet?" I asked, looking at Tom. He shook his head.

"Probably went down to the bottom with the *Black Marguerite*," Mac said. "Comes from messing with the dead."

"I doubt it was a ghost who sank a blade into McIntire's back," Tom said.

Mac bristled, and the tension in the room rose. "Stranger things have happened."

"I wasn't discounting your story," Tom said quietly.

"I heard it was Evan who called that Iliad outfit in the first place," I said.

"Double-crossed young Adam, is what he did," said Mac. "It wasn't his place."

"What do you expect from Ingrid's son?" the young lobsterman — his name was Brad, I thought — snorted. "Thinks he's better than the rest of us."

"And short on cash, to boot."

112

"Even with all the Sorensons' money?" I asked.

"His allowance isn't big enough to cover his extracurricular activities."

"Drugs?" Mac asked with a knowing look, which surprised me. I had no idea Evan's addiction was public knowledge; I knew he had been in rehab, but had promised his mother, Ingrid, not to say anything. Then again, in a community the size of Cranberry Island, there aren't many secrets.

"I don't know much about that, but I do know he likes a wager from time to time," Brad said.

"Gambling debts, eh?" Mac asked.

"Ayuh. He's been a regular at a game in Bar Harbor, ever since he got back a couple of months ago. Word is, he's in the hole for 10K, and some folks have started asking him when he's going to pay up."

"A nice bit of pirate treasure would help with paying that off," Mac said.

"That's what I'm thinking," Brad said.

"After all Adam's done for him, too," someone said, shaking his head.

"Addiction can be a harsh taskmaster," Tom said. "But this is all speculation."

"I do know one of ours is locked up just because that outsider came and tried to steal Davey Blue's treasure," Brad said.

"Could be Selfridge's ship," someone suggested.

"Maybe, maybe not. Either way, it ain't theirs to take," Mac said, to grunts of assent. "It belongs to us."

"It's out of our territorial waters," Tom said reasonably. "And most of it will probably end up down at the university in Portland."

"Better than paying off young Evan Sorenson's gambling debts — or funding a rich outsider's retirement home in Florida," Brad said.

"Paying his funeral expenses, more like."

Brad shook his head. "I never thought Eli had it in him," he said. "I know he was crazy about those old ships, but stabbing that treasure hunter in the back . . ."

I felt like I had been punched; the last thing I expected was for the lobstermen to turn against Eli.

SEVEN

"Do you really think Eli killed that man?" I asked, still reeling.

"Not saying the man didn't deserve it, and since I wasn't out on the water that night, I can't say as he did or he didn't," Brad said, shrugging. "But the last time Tom saw him, he was heading out toward Deadman's Shoal in his skiff, wasn't he? And it was his cutlass what did the job."

"Well, if he did kill that man, he was just protecting what's ours," Mac said. "And I can't say as I blame him for it. Should have taken out Evan while he was at it."

"How do you know it was Eli who did it?"

"You saw him last, Tom," Brad said. "When he came by your place last night, spouting all that stuff about modern-day pirates and protecting our heritage. Didn't he have his cutlass on him?"

"No," Tom said. "He didn't."

Hope flared in me. "What time was he there?"

"He showed up at nine," he said. "Lorraine and I sent him home at around eleven — or tried to. I didn't know he would go back out to the wreck site. Madness."

"But he didn't have the cutlass on him," I confirmed.

I was about to heave a sigh of relief when Brad piped up. "Just because he didn't have it with him don't mean it wasn't in his skiff."

"True," someone chimed in.

"Do you really think he'd toss his precious cutlass in the bushes by the dock?" asked Mac.

"If he'd just murdered someone with it, don't you think he'd want to get rid of it?"

"Why not just drop it in the water then?"

The man shrugged. "Folks do funny things in the heat of passion."

"What I want to know is, what was that Iliad guy doing out there in the middle of the night?"

"And what happened to the *Lorelei?*"

I wanted to know all of those things, of course. But my curiosity was also piqued by Evan Sorenson. I knew of him, but I'd never met him; he'd been off the island in college — or rehab — since I arrived a few years ago. Could Gerald McIntire's death have something to do with his gambling debts? Had he cut a deal with Iliad — only to have it revoked?

"Has anyone seen Evan since Gerald McIntire died?" I asked.

"He hasn't shown his face around here, I can tell you that," Brad said.

"Did he know enough to drive a boat?"

"Course he did. He grew up here, didn't he?"

"Then, just maybe, when they find the *Lorelei,* they'll find Evan."

"Better on the *Lorelei* than in Davy Jones' locker," Brad said.

"Who says they're not both there?" Mac suggested, and a brooding silence fell over the co-op.

The talk died down after that, and I left the co-op a few minutes later, deep in thought about Evan Sorenson — and determined to talk to Ingrid about her son. She and I had never gotten along, but my heart went out to her; as much as she loved him, he always seemed to be in trouble. And one death on the island was more than enough.

I stopped by the store; Claudette was holding court in one of Charlene's squishy armchairs, and after I passed the news about the attorney to my two friends, I headed out to Ingrid Sorenson's house. Charlene promised to drop Claudette by after dinner, along with the grocery order that was due on the last mail boat; the plan was to put her up in one of my rooms for the night, so she wouldn't be alone. On the way back to the inn, as promised, I stopped by Claudette's to refill the cats' bowls and check on the goats. I called several times for Muffin and Pudge, but the dynamic duo had evidently moved on to somebody else's garden, and after about fifteen minutes I gave up. My last stop was at Ingrid Sorenson's, but the curtains were closed and nobody answered when I knocked. I'd try again tomorrow.

The sun was an orange ball in the sky by the time I headed down the final hill toward the Gray Whale Inn. The gray-shingled building nestled into the hillside below me, the meadow beneath it sloping gently to the water. The kitchen windows glowed with a warm light, and despite Eleazer's plight — and the recent tragedy — I felt a wave of deep contentment. Just a few years ago, I had taken a big risk and made a stab at reinventing my life. Now I had a growing business, a great relationship with my niece, an island of friends, and plans to be married to a kind, warm — not to mention drop-dead gorgeous — man.

The sense of peace and contentment were short-lived, though; when I stepped into the kitchen, Gwen immediately informed me that the oven had broken.

"I know we're doing the cod cakes in the pan, and I made the patties and put them on a tray in the fridge, but what about the potatoes?" I had told her we would be roasting the potatoes to serve alongside the cod cakes. Despite her creative personality, she had grown up primarily with take-out, and was only able to cook if I left her explicit, step-by-step instructions.

"We'll boil them and serve them with butter and chives," I said. "It's more traditional, anyway." Tonight wasn't a problem, and I could thaw out a batch of banana bread for tomorrow, and do sandwiches for lunch — but things would be much easier if the oven was fixed in time for dinner tomorrow. I'd done cold meals in a pinch before, and even borrowed the kitchen at Spurrell's Lobster Pound, but it was a huge hassle. "At least the stove is still working," I said. "Did you tell John about the oven?"

She nodded. "He took a look at it, but wasn't able to fix it. He made a call to a repairman on Mount Desert Island, but he won't be able to get here until the day after tomorrow."

"That'll take forever — particularly if they need to order parts!"

"That's what John said. He's down in the carriage house now, trying to get someone else."

I smiled. After two years of handling inn crises all by myself, it was nice having someone to share the load with — although after the grueling three a.m. start and hours dealing with the Coast Guard and the police, calling repairmen was the last thing John needed. As soon as I got the potatoes on, I'd run down and check on him. "Let's hope he found someone else," I said to Gwen, "or I'm going to have to borrow someone's oven tomorrow afternoon."

"Just make sure it doesn't belong to someone who's entering the bake-off," Gwen pointed out.

I groaned as I filled a pot with water. She was right. "Cross your fingers that it's fixed by tomorrow night."

In no time at all, I had the new potatoes nestled in a pot of salted water and set Gwen to chopping chives. I checked on the tray of cod cakes in the fridge — the round disks needed only a last dredge in breadcrumbs and a quick sauté in a hot pan — and stepped into the dining room to check on the tables. Gwen had set them perfectly; she was getting more efficient every day. I was about to go back into the kitchen and compliment her when I heard raised voices from the parlor. I edged closer, curious.

"Someone's taken things from the site. I'm telling you — they've been messing with the artifacts." It was Carl, the university archaeologist.

"The weather's been rough these last few days," Molly said soothingly. "You and I both know the bottom changes all the time. I'm sure everything is still there; we'd have seen it if they pulled anything up. Besides, they don't have a boat."

"Not anymore, they don't," he said. "But it's only a matter of time before Iliad sends out a replacement. And if we don't work fast, they'll locate something specific to the ship and make the claim. We've got to ID that ship and lay claim to it before they can get another vessel and dive gear in."

"We're working on it," she said. Then she lowered her voice. "I told you earlier, I think I may have found the ship's bell on my last dive."

"You showed me the photo," he said. "It's hard to tell, with the concretion."

"It's easier to see in person. We'll pull it up as soon as I get the winch fixed," she said. At least I wasn't the only one with mechanical difficulties.

"That'll take too long," he said.

"There's always the lift bag option. I know you don't like to use them, but I can try it tomorrow."

He sighed. "I hate to take the risk, but it may take some time to get that concretion off, so the sooner we get it up, the better."

"I promise I won't drop it," she said.

"We'll have to be sure to map it, too."

"Of course. If the weather cooperates, I'll dive in the morning," she said. "With Gerald and the *Lorelei* out of the way, we have the advantage. We won't lose this one."

"We'd better not, or we'll lose half our funding," he said darkly, and I hurried back toward the kitchen at the sound of footsteps. Fortunately, they were retreating to their rooms, and had no idea I had overheard their conversation.

I found myself wondering about Carl as I threw on a jacket and headed out the kitchen door to check on John. Molly was right; with both Iliad's primary partner and the research vessel out of the picture, the university archaeologists had a clear advantage. Carl had threatened to kill Gerald yesterday — and now, I'd just learned that if he wasn't able to lay claim to this wreck, he was at risk of losing research funds. Had he followed through last night — and scuttled the *Lorelei* for good measure?

I was still musing over what I'd heard as I knocked at the door to John's carriage house. He was on the phone when he answered the door, and I could tell from the conversation that he wasn't talking about my oven.

"You're giving up too quickly," he said pacing back and forth across the antique wood floor, and my heart contracted. He was quiet for a moment, listening, then spoke passionately. "There are so many other possibilities. Have you looked at the life insurance beneficiaries? Or at the history he had with Carl, who threatened to murder him the night he died?"

Quiet again, and I found myself hugging my arms to my chest as I lowered myself to the couch. John listened for a long time, occasionally breaking in with objections; then, shoulders sagging, he finally hung up the phone and lowered himself to the couch beside me, his head in his hands.

"They've closed the investigation?" I asked quietly, afraid to hear the answer, even though I already knew what it was.

He nodded.

"How can they?" I asked. "I just heard

Carl say that if he didn't 'win' this ship-wreck, he'd lose half of his funding. They're racing to identify the wreck before Iliad; there's a good chance they took the boat out of action, too." I told him what else I'd heard Molly and Carl talking about too. "Although I don't know why the ship's bell would be such a big deal."

"The name of the ship is usually engraved on it," he said.

"Aha. I got the impression that the first people to identify the ship in court get to 'own' the wreck."

"But if it belonged to Jonah Selfridge, wouldn't it pass to the family?"

"I don't know," I said. "They seemed to think the first person to claim it in court has rights." I thought about that for a moment. "If that's true, it means Evan Sorenson might be out of luck — I've heard he was trying to lay claim to the wreck. I was at the co-op this afternoon; word is he got in financial trouble gambling, and was trying to use the wreck to buy his way out."

He shook his head. "Poor Ingrid."

"What if Evan confronted Gerald about the money he was expecting and was told there wasn't going to be any? Maybe Evan killed Gerald and took off with the ship."

"It's a theory," John said, skeptically.

"It would explain why the ship disappeared."

"But what about the cutlass?"

"Maybe Evan stole it from Eli's place to make it look like Eli did it. Did they ever confirm it was the cutlass that killed him?"

"Apparently there was a bit of damage to the wound — probably from fish — but it does appear to have been a curved blade."

"So it could have been something else. Did they find any traces of blood on the cutlass?"

"The lab results aren't back yet," he said. "The conversation between Carl and Molly is interesting. Where did you hear it, anyway?"

"They were in the parlor just now; I overheard them when I was in the dining room."

" 'Overheard?' "

"All right, I was eavesdropping. But if we tell the police about it, will that help convince them to look for more suspects?"

"I can try," he said, "but they seem to think they've got a rock-solid case already. Apparently Eleazer said he left the cutlass with the archaeologist, but Carl claims he never laid hands on it — and the only fingerprints on the cutlass are Eli's."

"But Carl had a motive to kill Gerald!" I

protested. "He's not going to tell the police that Eli handed him the cutlass, is he?"

"I know, Natalie. They zeroed in on Eleazer and refuse to look at anyone else." He ran a hand through his sandy hair. "I hate the thought that we're going to have to rely on his defense attorney to save him."

"Tom got him an attorney," I said. "A good one. From Bangor. And the co-op is pitching in to help cover the costs."

"The island is watching out for its own," he said, with a smile. "I hope it's enough."

I put my arm around him and gave his shoulders a hug. "Just because the police have given up, doesn't mean we have to. We've solved a few murders in the past, you know."

"And you almost got yourself killed a couple of times, if I remember correctly." He wrapped his arms around me and squeezed me tight. "I don't want to see Eleazer go to jail for a crime he didn't commit — but there may still be a murderer out there."

"May?" I said quietly. It disturbed me that he wasn't sure about Eli. Then again, Eli had been so angry yesterday morning, I realized I wasn't sure, either.

"We may never know what happened that night," he said. "And I don't want to risk

126

losing you."

"We'll do it together," I said. "Safety in numbers. Besides, I promised Claudette I'd help."

He sighed. "I guess it can't hurt to ask questions."

"Even if we can cast a bit of doubt on the proceedings — don't they have to acquit if there's reasonable doubt?"

He nodded. "It might be a good idea to find out more about Carl Morgenstern," he said.

"I'll see what I can find out from Molly. And in the meantime," I said, anxious to switch topics before he had a change of heart, "thanks for calling repairmen while I was gone."

"That's one thing that went right, at least," he said with a rueful smile. "He'll be out in the morning."

"You're my hero," I said.

"How's Claudette holding up?" he asked. "I heard you brought her back to the inn this afternoon."

"She's at the store with Charlene right now; she'll drop her off here later, along with the groceries, and I'll put her up in the Beach Rose room." I chuckled bitterly. "At least we're getting some bookings out of this fiasco."

"You're a good woman, Natalie Barnes."

"And you're a good man," I said. He opened his arms, and for a moment, I let all of my worries fade away, allowing myself to be enveloped by the scent and feel of him. Then I remembered the potatoes.

"Can't Gwen handle it?" John said when I told him why I had to go.

"Not if I don't want to serve charcoal," I said. "She's great at cleaning rooms and serving, but she's not what I'd call an intuitive cook. Unless I have every step outlined for her, she's a mess," I said.

"Go save your potatoes, then," he said with a last kiss.

"There's plenty, if you're hungry."

"I'll be up in a bit." As I left, he picked up the phone; evidently he wasn't done doing battle for Eli yet.

Neither was I.

Dinner was a surprisingly civil event, although the presence of the two investigators doubtless contributed to the ceasefire between the two camps. The folks from the university were at one end of the dining room, conferring quietly, and the Iliad employees camped out at the farthest table from them. Audrey still looked stricken, but Frank seemed distracted. How had his partner's death affected the firm? I wondered. Was he now first in command?

Between them sat the two investigators, who were set to head back to the mainland that evening, and Cherry Price, who was picking apart her cod cakes with interest. "These are delicious — I love the lemon, and the crisp crust is just right. Did you use shallots in these?"

"No shallots," I said, "but I substituted fresh chives for the dill."

"The lemon sauce is wonderful, too."

"Thank you," I said, smiling. "You sound like you know your cooking."

"It's my job," she said.

"You're a chef?"

"A food writer," she said.

I swallowed hard. "Now I know your name — you write for the *New York Times*!"

She laughed. "You've discovered my secret."

"Are you here to do an article on the inn?" I asked with trepidation. With the number of policemen traipsing in and out, it hadn't been a very relaxing day. "I had nothing to do with the pickled cranberries, by the way — or the gumdrops," I said, pointing at the table with the islanders' cranberry creations. "I'm supposed to judge a bake-off this weekend, and they've been plying me with their wares all week."

"Don't worry," she said, "I read the sign. But the streusel cake is quite good."

I'd pass that on to Emmeline; she'd be thrilled.

"In answer to your question, I am thinking of including the inn in a round-up article of Maine hotspots," she said. "So far, I'm very impressed — everything is top-notch. And it certainly has been exciting!"

"I'm glad you think so — it's been an unusual day."

"I noticed — something about a shipwreck, and somebody dying?"

Glancing over my shoulder at the investigators, who didn't seem to be paying attention anyway, I gave her a synopsis of events, glossing over the fact that the victim had been staying at the inn at the time of his demise.

"Wow. I've heard of bed-and-breakfast murder mysteries, but never attended the real thing," she said. "So we could have a murderer among us?"

"They've already arrested someone," I said, feeling disloyal to Eli for saying it. "But the investigation is ongoing."

"Well. This *will* make an interesting article!" Something in my face made her add, "Don't worry — I won't link the death with

the inn. Although you'd be amazed —
ghosts and grisly deaths do appeal to some
folks."

"Well, we have a ghost too," I said, thinking of the spectral cook who had once appeared in my kitchen.

"Really?"

"I've got to finish up with dinner, but if
you'd like, I can tell you about her after dessert."

"That sounds wonderful," she said. "What
are we having for dessert, anyway?"

Dessert! I realized that with all the brou-
haha, I'd forgotten dessert.

Eight

What was I going to do? I had absolutely nothing planned for dessert . . . and I had a *New York Times* food writer at my table. "It'll be a surprise," I said, not mentioning that it would be a surprise for both of us.

Excusing myself, I hurried back to the kitchen and opened the freezer.

"What's wrong?" Gwen asked. "Did I mess something up?"

"No," I said. "I forgot dessert."

Normally I would serve cookies, but I had just sent my reserves to the co-op. The only thing I could see was my two half-gallons of Blue Bell Homemade Vanilla Ice Cream which John had had shipped up from Texas especially as a treat for me.

"I guess I can make parfaits," I said, feeling a pang for the loss of my favorite ice cream. I kept waiting for it to be available in Maine, but the brand had only gotten as far as North Carolina — I had a while to wait.

"No way," Gwen said, closing the freezer. "You're not digging into the Blue Bell. Not when we've got a whole tray of goodies in the next room."

"You mean the samples for the bake-off?"

"Absolutely," she said.

"Not the cranberry pickle chutney, though. Or the gumdrops."

"Think streusel cake and pudding," she said.

"You're brilliant, Gwen."

"You can thank me by doing dinner clean-up," she said.

"Done."

She retrieved the trays from the next room, and ten minutes later, we put the finishing touches — including a very small scoop of my beloved Blue Bell ice cream and a dab of cranberry preserves — on each plate.

"Cranberry Island Medley," she dubbed it. "We'll tell them to fill out comment cards and pop them in the jar."

"Perfect," I said, and ferried the first tray of plates out into the dining room. I hoped Gwen never went back to California; I'd be lost without her.

I had just put the last dish into the dishwasher — the dessert, thankfully, had been a hit with everyone, including the food writer — when the phone rang.

"Gray Whale Inn," I said as I picked up the phone. I gazed out the window at the lights sparkling on the mainland, beyond the dark stretch of water behind the inn.

It was Charlene. "I'm on my way over with Claudette and your groceries," she said.

"I'll put her up in the Beach Rose room," I said. "Thanks for staying with her this afternoon."

"I was poking around online today, and found out some interesting things about our recently deceased treasure hunter."

I leaned back against the wall. "Oh, yeah?"

"He got engaged last week," she said as if she were imparting an incredibly juicy detail.

I didn't catch the relevance. "Well, it's got to be terrible news for his fiancée," I said, "but how does that help with Eli?"

"It's all about motive, Nat."

"Why would someone kill him because he was engaged?"

"That woman he's down here with. What's

her name?"

"Audrey?"

"That's the one."

"What about her?"

"Well, someone saw the two of them kissing on the stern of the *Lorelei,*" she said.

Interesting. She had seemed upset the other day — was that just because of her boss's death, or because he had lied to her? Although if she was involved with him and he'd died, of course she'd be upset. "How was your informant able to spot that?" I asked.

"He was out hauling traps, and was watching the wreck site as they cruised by. It's big news right now, and everyone on this island's got binoculars, Nat."

"Still — it doesn't make sense. If they were kissing, why would she kill him?"

"Jealousy!"

"I still don't see it."

"Maybe she didn't know," Charlene suggested. "Maybe she found out last night, and killed him in a crime of passion."

That didn't explain the cutlass and the missing research boat, but it was still a potential lead. "I guess it's worth checking out," I said.

"Of course it's worth checking out. Anything's worth checking out. Anyway, I'll be

over in a few minutes. Got any more cookies for me?"

"Gave the last of them to the co-op this
afternoon, and the oven's broken," I said.

"You're having a rotten week!"

"Did I mention there's a food writer from
the *New York Times* here?"

"I wouldn't bother playing the lottery, if I
were you."

"No kidding. See you in a few, then."

We slept the entire night through, which
was a nice change of pace, but Claudette
was already up and sitting alone in the darkness when I padded downstairs to start the
coffee. I heard the soft clack of her knitting
needles before I saw her. She was dressed
in a shapeless, oatmeal-colored dress, and
dark circles ringed her eyes.

"Did you get any sleep?" I asked as I filled
the grinder with several scoops of fragrant
French Roast coffee. The rich, dark smell
was comforting.

"Not really," she said. The sweater had
been replaced by a scarf, which trailed over
her knee to puddle on the floor beside her.
Had she been up all night working on it?
"The room was lovely, but I just kept thinking of poor Eli, all locked up and alone."
Tears filled her eyes. "Eli's no spring

136

chicken, Natalie. If they put him in prison, he may never be able to come home again," she whispered.

"Don't think that way," I said as I pulsed the grinder, trying to sound optimistic. "We've got a couple of leads we're looking into, and Tom's found Eli a top-notch attorney." I poured the ground coffee into the maker, started it, and walked over to put my arm around Claudette, who was wiping tears from her cheeks.

"An attorney. Does that mean they're going to charge him?" she asked.

"I don't know yet," I said.

She took a deep, shuddering breath. "I'm taking the mail boat over to see him this morning," she said. "Emmeline is going with me."

"Good," I said. "Give him our love, will you?" Then I thought of something. "And will you ask him a question for me?"

"Of course," she said.

"I know the police have already talked to him, but I think they might have missed something. Ask him whom he gave the cutlass to, when, and where. And any details he can remember that might help prove it."

"You think he gave it to someone?"

"John told me he claimed . . . I mean, said he gave it to Carl Morgenstern, the archaeologist from the university." I kicked myself for the poor choice of words, but Claudette evidently didn't notice.

A fire stirred in her eyes, the first since Eli was arrested, and I was reminded that when roused, she could be a formidable opponent. "That university archaeologist hated Gerald, didn't he? Eli told me. So maybe the archaeologist killed him, and set up my poor Eli."

"It's a possibility," I said cautiously.

"If he set up my husband," she said, "I'll kill the man myself."

"Easy, Claudette," I said. "Let's find out as much as we can, quietly. If it's true, we don't want him to be alerted that we know until we have a way to prove it."

"You're right," she said, the knitting needles picking up speed. "If I find out when they met, maybe I can find someone who saw them together. Nothing happens on this island without somebody noticing it."

That was the second time I'd heard that in the last twenty-four hours. "It's worth asking around," I said. "I'll see if Charlene heard anything. She usually knows everything that happens." Happy to see Claudette a little less bleak, I busied myself getting the morning's breakfast ready. As I

138

pulled the last loaf of frozen banana bread out of the freezer and retrieved a carton of eggs from the refrigerator, I prayed Claudette would find out something we could use to prove Eleazer had handed over the cutlass. And that the oven would be fixed before tomorrow morning. As much as I enjoyed the occasional Entenmann's Danish, I didn't want to be reduced to serving it for breakfast — particularly not with a *Times* food writer in the dining room.

Since the oven was broken, the lunch menu was lobster rolls and cold salad, which Gwen assured me she could handle with aplomb.

"The lobster salad is in the fridge," I said, "and I defrosted the rolls this morning. You can serve some sliced cantaloupe on the side."

"So I just put the lobster salad in the rolls, make the salad . . ."

"The dressing's already made and in the fridge," I reminded her.

". . . and plate it," she finished.

"Exactly," I said. "I don't know how many guests you'll have — the Iliad party should be here, since I think they're waiting on another boat to arrive, but I'm guessing the university folks will be diving at the wreck site." Attempting to retrieve what they hoped was the ship's bell, if last night's conversation was anything to go on.

"Is Marge taking care of the rooms?"

"She's already done with half of them." I could hear the washer going, with the first load of towels. "I'm going into town to see if anyone saw anything the night Gerald McIntire died," I said. "Eli said he gave the cutlass to Carl, but Carl claims he didn't."

"You think Carl might have killed Gerald with it?"

I shrugged. "I'm also curious to find out what happened to Evan Sorenson. Have you heard anything more about him?"

Gwen shook her head. "Nothing. He just kind of vanished."

"Along with the *Lorelei*," I pointed out.

Gwen's arched eyebrows rose questioningly. "You think?"

I sighed. "I don't know. But anything we can come up with that points toward someone other than Eli —"

"Good luck, Aunt Nat."

"Thanks. I'm afraid we'll need it."

My first stop was the store. I could have called, but with all the excitement on the island over the last few days, I knew Charlene would likely have a full house — and I wanted to talk with as many people as possible.

Despite the stormy events of the last week, it was a beautiful autumn day, with a robin's-egg blue sky dotted with puffy white clouds. The blueberry bushes were a rich russet color, and orange and red maples flamed at intervals among the dark green spruce and pine trees. The wind off the water was bracing, scented with the tang of salt and autumn leaves, with a hint of pine from the evergreens.

I glanced out at the blue water, which was dotted with whitecaps. How was the university expedition going? I'd read up a bit on Iliad the night before, and I could understand why Carl felt such animosity toward the organization. Some treasure-hunting companies were relatively good about preserving the sites they explored, but Iliad appeared to have a more mercenary approach to the business of salvaging shipwrecks. And the university had lost to Iliad not once, but twice — both times because Iliad had brought an identifiable artifact to court before them. No wonder Molly and Carl were so intent on getting that ship's bell up and identified; if they didn't, Iliad might beat them to the punch a third time. Would Carl be willing to kill to prevent it?

But why kill Gerald McIntire when scuttling his boat would be enough to buy a few days' time?

And where the heck was Evan Sorenson — and the *Lorelei*?

In what seemed like no time at all, Charlene's store came into view. The rose bushes along the front porch still had a few brave blooms on them, but most of the leaves had yellowed and fluttered to the ground. The rockers on the porch were empty today — it was a tad brisk for sitting on the porch — but the mullioned windows, as always, were papered with notices. I ignored the ones advertising the bake-off and pushed through the front door, the bell above the door announcing my arrival.

As expected, the place was full, primarily of lobstermen's wives and old-timers, and tongues were wagging. They were until I walked in, anyway. A dozen pairs of curious eyes locked onto me as I stepped inside. Charlene sat on her stool behind the counter; across from her was Matilda Jenkins, the town historian.

"Any news?" Charlene called over to me.

"I was hoping you'd have some," I said, shaking my head. The patrons quickly decided I had nothing new to add to the gossip mill, and the buzz of voices resumed.

Charlene poured me a cup of coffee as I pulled up the stool next to Matilda.

"Matilda's been researching Davey Blue," Charlene told me.

"I heard he dated one of your ancestors," I said to Charlene.

"That's the most likely scenario," Matilda said, running a hand through her close-cropped white hair. Her eyes shone with excitement behind her glasses.

"What did you find out?" I asked.

"Well, it was a long time ago, and with pirate ships, there aren't a lot of records."

"I guess not," I said.

"But from what I've been able to find out, his ship was last recorded in the Portland area in late April of 1631. There's no record of it after that," she said.

"So he was in Maine," I said. "How did you connect him with Charlene's great-great-great-great-aunt, or whatever she is?"

"Cranberry Island is an unusual place — and a wonderful place to be a historian. Because so many families have been here for so long, a lot of the history has stayed with the families — and on the island itself."

"Like family bibles?" I asked.

"Bibles, photos . . . even diaries." She gave me a pointed look; I had managed to lose an important diary not too long ago, and

143

she still hadn't forgiven me. "We also have correspondence that folks have donated for preservation. The Kean family was particularly prolific," she said, looking at Charlene.

"My grandmother kept trunks of letters up in her attic. When she died, we gave them to the museum," Charlene explained.

"And some of them went back to the seventeenth century. Incredibly well preserved, too; I'm hoping to install a special storage case for them, to prevent further degradation."

"Was there anything in them about Davey Blue?" I asked.

"Not specifically," she said. "There's a legend on the island that one of the Kean girls got mixed up with a pirate, but it wasn't until a few years ago, when Charlene donated materials she found in the attic, that we found any indication there might be truth to the story."

I knew Charlene's family had donated many old documents to the museum, but had never heard anything about Davey Blue. "Did she write to him?" I asked, wondering how exactly one sent a letter to a pirate — and how, if so, it would have ended up in Charlene's grandmother's attic.

"Nothing so direct, I'm afraid. But there

are two letters from a series, written by Genevieve Kean to her sister Felicity in Portland, that may indicate a connection. Genevieve lived in a house right by the pier, not too far from where the museum is, but the house was torn down a long time ago — probably in the 1700s. That's when the other islands were settled; Cranberry Island was the first, and there were only three families here in the beginning."

"No wonder the Kean girls were frustrated with their options," Charlene said, her eyes sparkling as she sipped her coffee.

"What was in the letters?" I asked, trying to gently guide Matilda back to the topic of Davey Blue.

Matilda sighed. "They're a wonderful record of early life on Cranberry Island. Absolutely amazing. All kinds of things — the fishing, the weather conditions, the difficulty in procuring goods from the mainland, particularly in winter. Did you know some of the islanders slept with their bread in their beds, to keep it from freezing?"

"Tell her about Eleanor," Charlene said, impatiently.

Matilda smiled. "You'll have to come down and see them," she said. "There were two letters in particular that caught my interest," she said. "Your ancestor had a beautiful hand — and a wonderful way with words."

"What did she say?" I asked.

"Genevieve was a typical mother, I guess," Matilda said, chuckling. "She was having trouble with her third daughter, an impulsive seventeen-year-old beauty named Eleanor. Evidently Eleanor was not delighted with her marital prospects on the island, although one of the Selfridges was courting her."

"See? The women in my family have always had taste," Charlene said.

Matilda let the comment pass; as the Selfridges had been the primary museum benefactors, I could understand the conflict of interest. "As I was saying," she said, "Genevieve was hoping for a match with one of the Selfridge boys. But Eleanor was not enamored of the young man in question, especially after meeting an unsavory gentleman who had taken shelter from a storm in the harbor."

"A pirate?"

"Genevieve doesn't say," Matilda said, "but she certainly was not impressed by the man. In her opinion, he was an 'ill-mannered and lawless man who styles himself a sea captain,' " she quoted from memory. "She never mentions his name, unfortunately. The timing is right, though."

"Girls always do go for bad boys," Charlene said with a sultry smile. "Who wouldn't want to date a pirate captain?"

"So what happened?" I asked.

"Like any good parents, Genevieve and her husband forbade her to see the man, and were much relieved when he and his ship departed."

"Without Eleanor," I said.

"Without Eleanor," Matilda said. "But he returned six months later. His ship never came into the harbor, but was spotted off Cranberry Point."

"That's not far from the inn!" I said.

"Or Smuggler's Cove," Charlene pointed out. Smuggler's Cove was a cove a little ways from the inn; although its entrance was covered at high tide, at low tide, you could just make it inside. There was a large, dry cave inside, with mysterious iron rings embedded in the rock, for tying up boats. No one knew who had put them there, or when. Rumor had it that it had been used by smugglers during Prohibition — and maybe even pirates in earlier times.

"Maybe Eli is right, and it was a pirate hideout," I said.

"We may never know," Matilda said. "I was hoping to ask one of the marine archaeologists to take a look at the cove. I have no idea how old those iron rings are."

"But tell her about Eleanor," Charlene said.

"Ah, yes. Eleanor. Well, the girl just disappeared," Matilda said.

"While the ship was off the coast?" I asked.

She nodded. "She claimed to be going out for a walk, and never returned."

"Probably escaping with her pirate lover," Charlene said.

"The poor woman," I breathed. I couldn't imagine losing a seventeen-year-old daughter like that.

"According to Genevieve's letter — she was very distraught, you could see it in her handwriting — the ship was seen heading out to sea within hours of the girl's disappearance. And then a terrific storm bore down on the island."

"Oh, no," I said.

Matilda looked grim. "Exactly. They never found or heard of the ship again, but several ship's timbers were sighted in the water the following week — along with three dead bodies."

I shuddered. "Not Eleanor's?"

"Not Eleanor's," she said. "But the girl never returned, and her parents eventually had to presume that she had died when the ship — whichever one it was — went down."

"What makes you think it might have been Davey Blue's ship?" I asked.

"We'll never know for sure," Matilda said, "Genevieve never names the captain, or the ship. But I found a reference to the *Black Marguerite* being in the area at the time. I haven't found any supporting evidence for the first visit to the island, but at the time of Eleanor's disappearance, a log from a captain based out of Mount Desert Island mentions a sighting of a ship matching the description of the *Black Marguerite,* cruising the waters about fifty miles south of here."

"And does the timing line up with Eleanor's disappearance?" Charlene asked.

"Yes," Matilda said. "Legend has it the captain was making a run to the Caribbean, but he doesn't appear to have made it. Like I said, the last sighting of the *Black Marguerite* was in Portland, in April of 1631. Three weeks before Genevieve's letter was dated."

"I wish we had more to go on," Charlene said.

"After almost four hundred years, it's amazing we have as much as we do," Matilda pointed out.

I was still dwelling on the girl's disappearance. "How awful, not to know," I said.

There had been one night when Adam's lobster boat hadn't come in — and my niece Gwen had been on it. Charlene and I had spent a long night in the store, huddled over the shortwave radio, praying for news. I could only imagine how I would feel if my seventeen-year-old daughter vanished into thin air.

"Early death was much more common back then," Matilda reminded me. "No penicillin meant the slightest cut could cause fatal blood poisoning. Many young women died in childbirth. And then there were measles, tuberculosis . . . all the diseases modern medicine has made almost obsolete." The historian pushed her glasses up on her nose and gave me a sad smile. "There were many, many tragedies. That's one of the reasons families were so big — to replace the offspring that were lost."

"It must still have been a blow, though."

"Yes," Matilda agreed, a look of regret on her weathered face for the girl who had vanished close to four centuries ago. "It certainly was to Genevieve."

"Was there anything specific that Eleanor had — a locket, a piece of jewelry — that could still be down there?" Charlene asked, twirling a lock of her caramel-colored hair, her blue eyes unusually dreamy. "Something

150

the archaeologists might be able to find and identify her with? If she was on the ship, that is."

Matilda shook her head sadly. "If so, there's no mention of it anywhere. If she had a locket with initials on it, perhaps, but there's no mention of any particular jewelry, and any clothing or paper would long since have been destroyed. History is often like that — trying to put together a jigsaw puzzle when you're missing most of the pieces."

The mention of puzzles made me think of Cranberry Island's more recent tragedy — and the reason I had stopped by the store. "Speaking of puzzles," I said, looking at Matilda, "What do you think of Eli's cutlass being found in the bushes by the pier?"

"I've known Eleazer all my life," she said, "and he treated that artifact like a favorite child. He never would have tossed it into the bushes like that."

"That's what I thought, too," I said. "He says he gave it to Carl Morgenstern, the marine archaeologist, but Carl claims he never met with Eli."

"Did Eli bring it over to the inn?" Charlene asked.

"I don't know," I said. "Claudette's over visiting him right now; I asked her to find out for me. Part of the reason I came down here was to find out if anyone had seen Eli talking with Carl."

"If so, I haven't heard about it," Charlene said, surveying the women chatting in low, excited tones on the couches, "and I think I've heard just about everything there is to hear on the subject of Eli over the last twenty-four hours. Folks have talked about nothing else."

I felt my hopes deflate; Matilda, too, looked worried.

"They're charging him with homicide, then," Matilda said, looking bleak.

I sighed. "That's what John tells me."

"It's ridiculous. I know he was hotheaded about the shipwreck, and angry at *Iliad,* but Eli would never have killed that man!" Charlene said.

"Any word on Evan Sorenson yet?" Matilda asked. Evidently I wasn't the only one who found his disappearance — and the timing of it — suspicious.

Charlene shook her head. "Nope. Nothing on the *Lorelei,* either."

"Do you think Evan might have killed Gerald McIntire?" I asked.

"I don't know him that well, to be honest," Matilda said. "But it is suspicious."

"It's almost like Eleanor's disappearance," Charlene said.

"I hadn't thought about that," I said. "The boat disappearing, and Eleanor . . . it's the same thing, just a few centuries later."

"Poor Ingrid," Matilda said, shaking her head. "I saw her yesterday; she's a wreck. Evan had just gotten back from . . . from a difficult time," she said, "and seemed to be doing so well, too! It's such a pity."

"Do you know if Evan was seeing anyone?" I asked. "Did he have a girlfriend somewhere?"

"I know he went over to Mount Desert Island a lot, but I don't know if he was romantically involved with anyone."

"*I* heard he was getting into poker," Charlene said. "And that he wasn't very good at it." She sighed. "Maybe he tried to follow Davey Blue to the Caribbean, to shake free of his gambling debts."

"I hope that's all it is," said Matilda.

"It's still a felony offense," I reminded her.

Matilda pressed her lips together in a grim smile. "It's better than the alternative."

NINE

The oven repairman still hadn't turned up when I got back to the inn.

"Did he at least call?" I asked Gwen, after ensuring that lunch had gone off without a hitch.

She shook her head. "He was supposed to be here by two," she said. "John left him a message a few minutes ago — he's down in his workshop now."

I sighed. "I guess it's time to put plan B into action."

"What — borrow an oven? Or light a fire in the back yard?"

"No," I said, checking to be sure I still had clams in the pantry and then picking up the phone. "I'm placing an order with Little Notch Bakery." The little bakery in Southwest Harbor made killer pies and bread. I made a quick call, reserving two pies and enough small loaves of sourdough breads to make bread bowls to hold clam

154

chowder. I added an order for two dozen blueberry muffins, as well. It was more expensive than baking everything myself, but it was an emergency situation. And it was a beautiful day for a trip in the skiff. I hoped the cold air would clear my head.

"Could you pick up a few of their cinnamon rolls for me?"

"Done. Need anything else from Southwest Harbor?" I asked.

"I'm running low on a few tubes of paint," she said, "but the best store is in Northeast Harbor. I'll ask Adam to take me over to the mainland later this week."

"How's he doing with everything?" I asked.

She shrugged. "He's angry at Evan, of course — but more worried about him than anything. And Eli." Gwen pulled her sweater tighter around her. "Any word on how he's doing?"

"Claudette's over visiting him today," I said. "I'll ask her when she gets back. Tom found him a good attorney."

"I can't believe Eli would do something like that," she said.

"I'm hoping we can prove he didn't," I said, pulling on a jacket and glancing at my watch. It was three o'clock; if I made it back by five, I'd have plenty of time to get things together for dinner. All I had to do was put together clam chowder and a salad; Little Notch was providing the dessert.

I stepped out the back door a moment later, glad to be heading out on the water for an hour or two. The fresh air and the waves always soothed me — and after the week I'd been having, I needed all the soothing I could get.

I was halfway down the walk to John's workshop — my plan was to see if he wanted to join me for the trip — when a muffled sob reached my ears.

Huddled on a slab of granite near the shore was Audrey, the Iliad archaeologist, her head cradled in her hands.

I hurried down to the water's edge and crouched beside her, gently putting a hand on her back. She jumped as if I'd shocked her.

"Are you okay?" I asked as she wiped furiously at her eyes. Her tanned skin was splotchy from crying.

"Fine," she said, taking a deep breath. "Just upset about Gerald."

"I'm so sorry," I said. "It must be hard losing someone you've spent so much time working with. You must have been very close," I said.

She gave a bitter laugh. "Not as close as

I'd thought." Swiping at her eyes, she took a shuddery breath. "He played me."

"What do you mean?"

"Just what I said. I thought we had something special . . . and then I find out he's engaged to some floozy from California." She stared out at the dark cobalt water. "After everything we've been through together, everything I've done for him — he was a two-timing bastard," she said, her voice charged with fury.

"I'm so sorry," I said, wondering what exactly she'd done for him — and whether she'd found out about his engagement before or after Gerald's death. "Did he tell you?"

"Of course not," she said scornfully. "He was a coward. My sister found the engagement notice and forwarded it to me."

"Before he died?"

Her eyes flicked to me; she reminded me of a spooked horse. "No," she said shortly. "Afterward." She stood up and brushed at her pants. "I've got work to do. Thanks for talking with me, but I really need to get going."

She strode up the hillside quickly, her slender athletic frame buffeted by the wind from the water. Interesting, I thought as I turned back toward the carriage house. Eli and Carl weren't the only two to hold a grudge against Gerald McIntire.

At his workshop, John greeted me with a kiss. "The repairman's running late," he said. "He says he'll be here at four."

"No worries," I said. "I'm headed over to Little Notch to pick up some bread and pies. Want to come with me?"

"I'd love to, but I should probably wait here — in the event the repair guy actually manages to make it over to the island."

"Probably a good idea," I said. "It's a shame, though — I'd love the company."

"So would I," he said with a grin. I watched as he plucked a small, wooden boat from a small fleet and began sanding the edges. The sweet, clean aroma of fresh wood permeated his workshop, and suspended sawdust gleamed in the air where the light from the studio windows streaked across the room. I thought of Audrey, huddled on her rock — and the venom in her voice. "I think I may have another suspect, by the way."

He paused in his sanding. "Who?"

I relayed the conversation I'd had with Audrey down by the water.

"Interesting," he said. "It would be a true crime of passion. And if they'd gone out to the wreck site together . . . she could have killed him and scuttled the vessel."

"How would she have gotten back?" I asked.

"That is a problem," he said. "Unless she had help."

I sighed. "That would indicate planning, though, and it seemed more a crime of passion."

"And we don't even know when she found out about the fiancée," he pointed out.

"Something about her eyes made me think she was lying to me," I said. "But I wish there were a way to confirm when she got the news."

John eyed me sternly. "You're not thinking of breaking into her computer, are you?"

I felt my cheeks flush. He knew me too well.

"It's illegal, Natalie."

"I know," I said.

But I didn't promise not to look.

Normally, I would enjoy a trip in the skiff on a gorgeous day, particularly when it involved a visit to Southwest Harbor and the always delectable-smelling Little Notch Bakery. The little town, with its old clapboard buildings, was as quaint as always. I almost always took the opportunity to window-shop and admire the colorful artwork displayed in the shining plate glass windows, but the charms of Southwest Harbor were lost on me today. Even the beckoning shop windows — not to mention the seductive aroma of baking bread and the rows of gorgeous-looking pastries at the bakery — couldn't distract me from my worries. My mind kept returning to Eleazer.

The young woman behind the counter handed me a box with my order; I tossed in a few sweet rolls and a tasty-looking apple turnover, and stepped back into the tangy fall air, the smell of fresh bread rising from the box in my arms. It was a short walk to the dock, and before I knew it, I was pointing the skiff back toward Cranberry Island.

The wind was fierce on the way back to the inn; dark clouds were tumbling into the blue sky from the north, and I wasn't surprised to see the *Ira B* moored near the dock when the inn came into view. Had the university archaeologists managed to retrieve the ship's bell? I wondered as I moved the box of baked goods to the dock and tied up the *Little Marian.*

At the inn, Gwen was nowhere to be seen, but I could hear the sound of voices in the parlor as I unloaded my haul in the kitchen. John had left a note on the table — the repairman wasn't going to be able to make it until tomorrow morning. I patted myself on the back for the foresight to buy muffins. Instead of the overnight French toast I'd been planning on, I'd serve cheesy scrambled eggs, bacon, and toast, with fresh blueberry muffins alongside.

I glanced at the clock. I needed to start the chowder soon, but I wanted to see if Claudette had made it back — or if the university team had made any new discoveries at the wreck site. Ten minutes wouldn't kill me, I decided — as long as I was efficient.

I slipped through the door to the dining room just as Carl and Molly rounded the corner from the parlor.

"How'd it go today?" I asked.

"Not as well as we'd hoped," Carl said.

"Weather started coming in, and the current got bad, so we called it off for the day," added Molly.

"Did you manage to bring anything up?" I asked.

Molly's sunny smile faded a bit. "We tried, but the lift bags weren't quite big enough, and the current was rough. We're going to get some new bags and give it another shot when there's less wave action."

"So, no luck?" I asked.

"A few concretions," she said. "But nothing identifiable. The dive chilled me to the bone, though — I was thinking of starting a fire, if that's okay."

"You're welcome to," I said. "There's wood and matches next to the fireplace, and newspaper for kindling; I can do it for you if you need me to."

"I've got it," she said, with a wink. "Years of Girl Scouts."

I laughed. "I'll leave you to it, then. But I'm sorry you didn't find anything more helpful today."

"We'll find something soon enough, I'm sure. Once I've warmed up a bit, I'll probably head back to the *Ira B* in a little bit and see what we can do with what we hauled up. Doesn't look like gold or silver bullion, but you never know what you'll find."

"Not that we're looking for gold or silver," Carl cut in reprovingly. "Our concern is the historical value of the ship."

"Of course," Molly said, her freckled face flushing pink. "It's just a lot easier to date a wreck when you've got coins."

"That's true," he said. "But if we get the bell . . ." He glanced at me and trailed off suddenly.

"You found the ship's bell?" I asked.

"We don't know," Molly said, backpedaling.

"How would that help?" I asked.

"It might help identify the ship," she said. "*If* we could find it — and if the information on it hasn't been eroded."

"I've heard metal often ends up rusting into a big chunk if it's been under water for a long time," I said.

Carl nodded. "It's called a concretion; the artifact gets buried in it, along with anything nearby. It can envelop not just the metal, but any object close to it — even leather and wood."

"How do you get it off?"

"Sometimes we chip it off," he said. "We also use electrolysis — putting the metal into a charged, sodium hydroxide solution — to soften up the concretion and preserve the artifact. It can take years, though," he said.

"Gosh. And I thought electrolysis was just to get rid of unwanted hair," I said.

Molly grinned. "Unwanted hair, unwanted rust . . ."

"So, if you manage to track down the bell," I said, "how long do you think it would take to identify it?"

"It would depend on the condition of the bell, and the level of concretion," Carl said. "And whether we're able to locate it." Which I knew they likely had. Why was he

163

being so cagey? "Unless we have the artifact, I'm afraid, there's no way to tell."

I decided to push my luck. "How exactly does someone lay claim to a shipwreck? I thought it was finders keepers, but I understand there may be more involved."

The two exchanged glances, and it was Carl who spoke. "If you find artifacts that can positively identify the ship, you can register the claim in court."

"So you would be able to lay claim to the wreck," I said.

"The university would, yes. It gets dicey if you're talking about naval ships; one of the big treasure hunting companies found a eighteenth-century Spanish ship called the *Merchant Royal.* They pulled up a hundred thousand pounds of gold."

"Wow. No wonder it's big business. Do they get to keep it?"

She shook her head. "They've been fighting about it in court for years, but the court ruled in favor of Spain not too long ago."

"I just hope the Spanish treat the wreck as an archeological site," Carl said, shaking his head. "Of course, everything's been disturbed, so the site's no longer intact . . ."

"They did map it first," Molly pointed out. I was a bit surprised to see her defending a treasure hunter.

"So the company didn't get anything?" I asked.

"Doesn't look like it. They're appealing the decision, of course," Molly said. "But it was a military ship, so even though it sank four hundred years ago, the court ruled that since Spain never officially abandoned the ship, it still belongs to the Spanish government."

"What about this wreck?"

"It's outside of Maine's territorial waters," Molly said, "so it's fair game. If it does turn out to be Davey Blue's ship, then the organization that first files the claim takes home the spoils."

"And if it's the Selfridge ship?"

"That's a bit murkier. It all depends on whether there's still family to claim it — and whether they'd be willing to go to court to defend their right."

"Oh, I'd bet they would," I said, thinking of Murray Selfridge, Cranberry Island's wealthiest resident. I couldn't imagine Murray giving anything up — ever.

"It usually depends on the value of the find," she said. "We'll see."

"I know Adam Thrackton called you in," I said. "If there was anything of value, would he be entitled to a percentage?"

Carl smiled. "Adam is a delightful young

man, and has assured me that his interest in the wreck is purely archeological."

"But if there's gold . . ."

"It all belongs in a museum," Carl said staunchly.

"I think we're putting the cart before the horse here," Molly said. "We've found some concretions, but no coins."

Carl turned to his partner. "We don't know what's in the concretions yet, Molly. And some of them are missing."

"You *think*," she said. "We haven't mapped the site, and you know as well as I do that the sea floor changes constantly. There's no way to be sure."

"But if I'm right, and Iliad has them, they could be putting together a claim on the vessel right now. And we've got nothing."

No wonder Carl was concerned about anyone knowing about the bell — and about hauling it up as soon as possible. If Iliad had indeed pulled artifacts up from the wreck, knowing that their competitor had located the bell might spur Carl and Molly to speed up identifying the artifacts — and making a court claim. Honestly, though — the company had just lost both its top guy and its research vessel. Did Carl really think Illiad was such a threat?

"Iliad is a mess right now," Molly said,

echoing my thoughts. "They've got no ship and no equipment. We've got time."

"I won't sleep until I know we've identified it," he said. "Damn. I wish we had those lift bags now!"

"They'll be here tomorrow," Molly said, patting him on the arm. "One day won't kill us."

"I hope you're right," he said grimly.

TEN

"I'm going to call down to the lab and see when we can get the *Sea Vixen* up," Carl said, excusing himself and heading for the phone.

"What's the *Sea Vixen*?" I asked Molly, who was stretching like a cat.

"She's the lab's biggest vessel — she's got cabins, and can stay out at the site twenty-four hours a day. She's also equipped with a submersible and sonar equipment. The only problem is, she's out on another research project until next week." She grinned at me. "Not that I mind the wonderful food and the comfy beds here."

"Speaking of food, I'd better get the clam chowder going," I said. I turned to go, and Molly headed toward the fireplace. Then I hesitated. "Molly?" I asked.

She turned toward me. "Yes?"

"I don't know if you can answer this, but do you know anything about Audrey Hammonds?"

"What about her?"

"I was wondering about her and Gerald. I understand they were seeing each other. But Gerald had just gotten engaged to another woman."

"I've heard rumors," she said. "Gerald always had a woman on his arm, and had no concerns about mixing business with pleasure. I did an internship with him one summer, years ago, and he rarely slept alone." Something in her tone of voice — and the hint of intimacy I'd seen between Molly and the treasure hunter the night Carl had attacked Gerald — made me wonder if Molly hadn't been one of his companions.

"But you don't know anything about their relationship?" I asked.

Molly smiled, deepening her dimples. "You're wondering if maybe she killed him out of jealousy?"

"Perhaps," I said. "I'm just looking at all the possibilities. A good friend of mine is in jail for the crime right now, and I just can't believe he did it."

"People do crazy things when they feel threatened," she said, shaking her head. "You never know what someone is capable of."

Too true, I thought. But Eleazer wasn't the only one feeling threatened. "What about Gerald's partner — Frank? Was everything smooth between them?"

"There's always been a rivalry between them," she said. "I heard rumors there were some changes in the partnership, and Frank wasn't happy about them. A friend of mine told me it's been pretty tense over there."

"What kinds of changes?"

"I think they were talking about going public with the company. Also, there was talk of investing in a new vessel — apparently Frank wasn't as excited about it as Gerald."

"Did you tell the investigators any of this?"

"I may have mentioned a few things," she said, "but they really didn't ask many questions."

That's what I thought. I'd have to tell John all of this when I saw him. "I have one other question, while we're talking."

Her eyes were wide. "What is it?"

"I meant to ask Carl before he left, but maybe you know. Did Eleazer meet with him at all?"

"What do you mean?"

"Before Gerald died. I understand Eleazer was going to ask Carl to take a look at his cutlass."

"The one he thought belonged to Davey Blue?" she asked. She thought for a moment, then shook her head. "I don't remember him saying anything about it. I'll ask him, though."

"Thanks," I said, and as Molly grabbed a log and laid it on the grate, I headed back to the kitchen to start dinner.

In less than twenty minutes, the cozy kitchen was redolent with the scent of frying bacon, onion, and potatoes. Outside the wind gusted, and the water had turned from cobalt to lead. Clam chowder was perfect for a cold autumn evening meal. A particularly strong gust rattled the windowpanes, and I realized I hadn't heard from Claudette yet. Had she made it back to the island before the bad weather hit?

I made a quick call to Charlene to check on Claudette, but she wasn't at the store, and Tania, who answered the phone, hadn't heard anything. Frustrated, I added some clam juice to the potato-bacon mixture and put a lid on my stockpot. I hated the feeling of helplessness — I had no idea where Claudette was, and couldn't do anything to help poor Eli, who was miles away and behind bars. I hoped the beds weren't too hard on his arthritis.

I pulled off a corner of the apple turnover

I'd bought and sat at the kitchen table to eat it. The flaky pastry and gooey apple filling were wasted on me, though; I was too preoccupied to appreciate them. John had told me I shouldn't snoop. But if Audrey had killed her lover and nobody found out about it, the lives of three innocent people would be ruined: not just Gerald's, but Eli's and Claudette's as well. My heart bled to think of Eli spending the rest of his life behind bars, and Claudette alone in her little clapboard house, her husband's workshop empty.

After approximately two minutes wrestling with my conscience, I got up, grabbed a stack of fresh towels, and headed to the front desk to pick up the skeleton key. I smiled at Molly as I passed; she was curled up on the couch before a crackling fire, trying unsuccessfully to get reception on her Blackberry. Despite my nerves, I smiled to myself; another of Cranberry Island's mixed blessings was the lack of cell phone service.

Audrey's room was upstairs, near the end of the hallway. I knocked, half holding my breath; when no one answered, I unlocked the door and slipped inside, relocking the door behind me.

The room was neat as a pin; either Audrey was a tidy soul, or Marge had outdone herself cleaning again. The desk was annoyingly clear of any debris; there was no laptop to be found, and there was nothing in the drawers, either. I peeked into a dresser drawer, but there was nothing but a neat stack of sweaters. Even the small closet turned up no clues.

I sat down on the edge of the bed, frustrated. The room looked practically unoccupied; the only sign that anyone was checked in was a book on the nightstand. I reached for it, expecting it to be a tome on marine archeology; to my surprise, it was a self-help book called *All the Rules: Time-tested Secrets for Capturing the Heart of Mr. Right.*

I couldn't help but be surprised, particularly when I glanced at the table of contents. "Be a 'Creature Unlike Any Other,' " was one of the rules. How exactly was one supposed to do that? I wondered. "Don't accept a Saturday night date after Wednesday," was another. What was Audrey — sleek, athletic, no-nonsense Audrey, who looked like she could hike a mountain before lunch — doing with a book that seemed aimed at a Southern debutante?

As I set the book back on the nightstand, something caught my eye. It was a photograph tucked between the pages, like a bookmark. The snapshot had been torn into pieces, but taped back together with painstaking care. It was Gerald, on the deck of a boat, smiling broadly, his arm around a beaming Audrey.

I stared at the photo for a moment, then tucked it back between the pages of the book. After a check of the nightstand drawers — again, empty — I retrieved the towels and quietly left the room.

On the way to the staircase, I paused. Carl was another suspect, and was currently down on his boat. What if there was something in his room to prove he had murdered his rival in a fit of passion?

Before I had a chance to think about it too much, I slipped the key into the lock and stepped into Carl's room.

Unlike Audrey's, Carl's room was a mess. Marge had made the bed — the blue and white counterpane was folded neatly at the corners, but the desk was stacked with reference books on sailing ships, bottles — even cannons. Carl was clearly a man obsessed. I did a cursory search, but there was nothing but a jumble of clothing in the drawers of the antique chest and stacks of books everywhere — and not a self-help tome among them. Nor, alas, did I find an empty scabbard, or any other indication that Eli

had relinquished his cutlass to the archaeologist.

I stepped back into the hallway and
glanced at my watch; the chowder didn't
need to be checked for another ten minutes.
Molly was downstairs curled up in front of
the fire, and the skeleton key was in my
hand. A Do Not Disturb sign hung from
Molly's doorknob, which I found odd —
particularly since she was downstairs. Would
it hurt if I took a quick look at her room,
too? I listened for the sound of footsteps,
then slipped inside.

On the neatness spectrum, Molly's room
was right between Audrey's and Carl's; a
few reference books, primarily on sailing
ships, were stacked haphazardly on the
dresser, alongside her clunky digital watch.
There was also a short stack of folders. I
peeked into each of them; they contained
copies of accounts of Davey Blue's battles
and ports of call, along with a few articles
on identifying cannons. I closed the folder
and looked around the room. A pink sweater
was draped over the corner of the made
bed, and the corner of a suitcase peeked
out from under the dust ruffle. I accidentally
kicked it as I rounded the bed, and as I bent
to push it back under, I noticed something
bright orange sticking out beyond the zip-

per. I pulled the suitcase out and flipped up the lid; inside was a pack of neon orange diving lift bags. "Lifts up to 100 pounds" read the label on the outside of the package. The plastic had been opened, and only one remained.

I tucked the bag back into the suitcase and pushed the case under the bed, confused. Carl had said they were out of lift bags, and Molly had told him more were coming tomorrow. Why hadn't she used this one? Was the size wrong?

I did a quick check of the rest of the room — loosely folded clothes in the bureau, a few jackets hanging in the closet. Nothing out of the ordinary.

The bathroom, on the other hand, held a few surprises. Next to the toilet was a jug of something that looked like white vinegar; I opened the lid and took a sniff, but it didn't smell like anything. Beside it were stacked several large plastic tubs. After pausing to listen for the sound of footsteps, I pried the lids back and peeked inside. Two were empty, but the third contained some kind of metal screen material and a car battery with wires attached to it. What the heck was it?

And why was it stored in her room, instead of the research vessel? When she'd checked in, she certainly hadn't lugged all of this stuff up here. All she had brought up from the boat was a small suitcase. When had she transferred everything else to her room?

I took another whiff of the liquid in the jug, but couldn't smell anything. Was it water? And if so, why would she store it in jugs? Hoping I hadn't just inhaled poisonous fumes, I retrieved my towels and crept out of the room, wondering what the heck I had just seen. As I locked the door behind me, there were footsteps on the stairs. It was Molly.

"Warmed up already?"

"Working on it," she said. "Is everything okay up here?"

"Just checking to make sure everyone has enough towels," I said. Smiling, I walked down the hall and turned down the stairs, glancing over as I headed down the stairs. Molly was bent over, picking up the "Do Not Disturb" sign from the floor. I must have knocked it off when I closed the door. I pretended I hadn't noticed and kept moving down the staircase.

The potatoes were just beginning to become tender when I made it back to the kitchen with my stack of clean towels, and I set to work adding cream, milk, and the clams to the pot on the stove. I then took the beautiful rounds of sourdough bread and sliced a 'bowl' in the middle of each and whipped up a Dijon vinaigrette for the salad.

All the while, though, I was thinking about what I had seen in the rooms upstairs. Audrey was clearly upset with Gerald, but break-ups happened all the time. And while she'd torn up the picture of them as a couple, she'd also taped it back together. Had she been hurt and angry enough to kill him in a fit of passion? And if so, why do it in the middle of the night, out at the wreck site? Besides, assuming the *Lorelei*'s disappearance was linked with Gerald's death, why get rid of the boat? It didn't make sense. Carl and Molly were the only ones who benefited from the vessel's disappearance — unless Evan, of course, had taken it. I didn't know whether a crew of one would be sufficient to handle a boat of that size, and made a mental note to ask John when I saw him.

And then there was the paraphernalia in Molly's room. I was curious about the stuff in her bathroom, of course, but even more curious about why they were waiting for a delivery of lift bags when there was already a lift bag in her suitcase. I also found it strange that she would keep equipment hid-

178

den in her bathroom, rather than on the research vessel. Was she doing something she didn't want her partner to find out about? I hadn't seen any artifacts, though. What was she up to?

ELEVEN

Gwen had the evening off, so I set the tables myself, lighting candles at each of them. The smell of clam chowder permeated the entire downstairs — a warm, comforting aroma — and I found myself looking forward to the reactions of my guests. I crossed my fingers the *Times* writer wasn't a fan of Manhattan-style chowder.

Rain began to lash the windows as I put the finishing touches on the tables. I had just lit the last candle when I heard the sound of a car bumping down the driveway. I extinguished the match and hurried back through the door to the kitchen, where I peered through the window.

It was Charlene's truck. I shrugged my jacket on, grabbed an umbrella, and hurried out to help Claudette from the truck. The older woman looked stricken. Charlene caught my eye as I reached out a hand to help her out, struggling to hold onto the

180

umbrella with my left hand. The visit to Eli must have been a difficult one.

When we'd installed Claudette in the kitchen with a cup of tea, I drew Charlene into the dining room. "What happened?" I asked.

She shook her head. "It was so upsetting to her — she's convinced he'll never come back to the island again."

"Did she ask about the cutlass?"

"He says he came by late, but no one was here, so he left it at the front desk at the inn, with a note on it."

"I never saw it," I said. "Who was it addressed to?"

"He said he left it for Professor Morgenstern," Charlene said. "Oh, Eli. Why couldn't he just have held onto the darned thing?"

"The police believe he did," I pointed out.

"And I would too, if I didn't know him as well as I do. The whole story sounds fishy."

"Did he mention if he left the scabbard?"

"He says he left both the cutlass and the scabbard here."

"Well, then, that's something," I said. Assuming he was telling the truth, a little voice inside me pointed out. I quickly quieted it. "If we find the scabbard . . ."

"I assume you've checked the rooms?" she asked.

"I have," I said. "Except for Gerald's," I said.

"Is it still cordoned off?"

"No," I said. "But everything has been taken to the lab. From what John told me, the investigators didn't find anything — certainly not a scabbard."

"It was worth asking," she said.

I glanced at my watch. "I'd better get going. Dinner's in ten minutes."

"What are we having?" she asked.

"Clam chowder and pie from Little Notch Bakery."

"Mmm," she said. "Do you have enough?"

"You may have to skip the bread bowl, but I've got plenty of everything else."

"Count me in then," she said.

"Let's go check on Claudette first," I said. "And the chowder."

Claudette was sitting where we left her, her tea untouched, tears streaking down her pale cheeks. Charlene slid into the chair beside her and gave her fleshy shoulders a quick hug. "It'll be okay, sweetheart. We'll have dinner together, and then you can get some sleep."

"But Eli . . ."

"He's strong, Claudette. He'll be okay.

And he'll sleep better knowing that you're being strong."

My heart ached for my friend, and I was glad Charlene was on hand to comfort her. I busied myself plating salads, and was adding cherry tomatoes to each plate when John appeared at the back door.

He greeted Claudette and Charlene, his voice strained; I could tell his efforts had not gone as well as he'd hoped. I abandoned the tomatoes and crossed the kitchen to give him a hug. The smell of him and the strength of his arms around me was a comfort — and underscored once more what Claudette must be going through.

"Any luck?" I murmured into his ear, already knowing the answer.

"No," he said.

"I've got some new information that might help," I said.

He released me, and gently grasped my shoulders, looking me in the eye. "None of this information came from illegal trespassing, did it?"

"I happened to notice a few things while cleaning the rooms," I said primly.

He cocked an eyebrow. "I thought Marge was in charge of the rooms today."

"She was," I said. "I was just doing a quality control check."

He rolled his eyes.

"Let's hear it then," he said, pulling up a chair at the table.

Claudette had perked up a little, and was eyeing me hungrily. As I retrieved a bag of fresh boiled shrimp from the refrigerator and added them to the salads, I gave a quick rundown of the discussion of the ship's bell — and the race to identify the boat — as well as the book and photo I'd found in Audrey's room.

"If it was a crime of passion, why would Audrey kill him at the wreck site and scuttle the boat?" John asked.

"We don't know what happened to the *Lorelei,*" I said, finishing the last plate and popping a torn piece of shrimp into my mouth. "And maybe they went out for some late-night research, and she confronted him then and there."

"It's possible," he said. "But why wouldn't she just bring the *Lorelei* back here? And how did she get back to land if the boat sank?"

"I don't know," I said. "Maybe she used the *Lorelei*'s skiff, and then just let it go when she reached land."

"To my mind, the loss of the boat points to the folks from the university," he said.

"I don't think we can completely discount

184

Audrey," I said, "but based on what I heard today about the race to identify the ship-wreck, the loss of the *Lorelei* and Illiad's main partner gives the university a real advantage."

"And if Carl did find the cutlass, he could have used it and ditched the murder weapon to implicate Eli."

"But what about the fingerprints?" John asked. "Eli's were the only ones on it."

Claudette whimpered.

"Maybe Carl knew what he was planning to do and used gloves," I suggested.

"Maybe he followed the *Lorelei* out there in the *Ira B,* angry because he thought Carl was disturbing the site, or trying to beat him to the punch. He boarded the *Lorelei,* killed Gerald, scuttled the boat, and then got back on his own vessel and headed back to the inn."

"But Eli didn't see anything other than the body," Charlene said.

"Maybe it happened a half hour before he arrived." I looked at John. "Would one person be enough to crew either the *Lorelei* or the *Ira B*?"

"Tying up would be a challenge, but I suppose you could manage it in a pinch."

"But the *Lorelei* never tied up," I pointed out. "Or if it did, it was somewhere far away

185

from here." I thought of Ingrid's son, Evan. "No word from Sorenson Jr. yet?"

"None that I've heard," Charlene said, glancing at the clock. "It's six-thirty, Nat. Isn't that the dinner hour?"

"Need a hand?" John asked.

"All I've got to do is get everyone drinks and a salad, and then fill the bread bowls and serve the chowder," I said. "If you'll take care of everyone in here and then slice the pie for the dessert plates, that would be great."

"I'm on it," he said as I slipped through the kitchen door into the dining room.

The atmosphere was hushed; as usual, the Iliad crew sat at one end of the dining room, and the university duo was at the other, with the *Times* writer seated at a window-side table in between. She looked up as I approached.

"What's for dinner tonight?"

"A salad with chilled shrimp and creamy French dressing, New England clam chowder in a sourdough bread bowl, followed by blueberry or raspberry pie."

"Perfect fare for an autumn evening," she said, and I smiled, relieved. "Do you happen to have a Chardonnay to go with that?"

"I'll get you a glass," I said, glad I'd thought to tuck a few bottles into the fridge

186

that morning.

"Wonderful," she said. Then she gave me a grin. "I hear you're in the middle of a political maelstrom."

"What do you mean?" I asked. What had she heard about the murder investigation?

"The bake-off, of course," she said. "I walked down to the store today and overheard a few conversations. All the talk is of the shipwreck and the bake-off. You wouldn't believe what people are saying!"

"What are they saying?" I asked.

"Oh, the usual," she said. "That you'll be biased, of course. That people are buying you off with free lobster."

"They've tried," I said.

"I believe it. I can't tell you the number of things I've been offered for favorable reviews. Trips to the Caribbean, free spa weekends . . ."

"I'm afraid all I can come up with is seconds on pie," I said.

She laughed. "No need," she said. "This is a delightful little inn you've created. I think you'll be very pleased with the review."

"Thank you so much," I said, glad there was some good news this week. Although with Eli alone in a jail cell and his wife sobbing behind the kitchen door, the feeling of pleasure was muted. If only Adam hadn't pulled up that timber . . .

"I'll be back with your Chardonnay in a minute," I said. "If you need anything else, please don't hesitate to let me know."

I checked in with the other two tables, letting them know what tonight's menu was and writing down drink orders. Audrey's eyes were red-rimmed, and Frank seemed distracted, his hands fidgeting with the napkin in his lap. Carl was taut as a bowstring when I asked him if he'd like a beer or a glass of wine.

"Just water, please."

"Did you make any progress with the concretions?" I asked politely.

"Nothing identifiable," he said. "When we get back to the lab, we may have a better chance of softening them up and seeing what's in them. We'll be able to X-ray them, too. I wish we had the *Sea Vixen* here!"

"How do you manage to pull artifacts up?" I asked.

"Well, when the winch is working, we use that," he said. "Otherwise, we use inflatable lift bags."

"How much can they carry?"

"They come in a variety of sizes, but we usually use the 100-pound bags," he said. "You hook the artifact to the bag; then the bag inflates and floats to the surface of the water. The only worry is that they can move up too quickly and drop an artifact. You have to be very, very careful — but Molly's an expert with them."

"Clever," I said, aware of Molly's eyes on me. So the lift bag under her bed was the right size after all. Something told me she hadn't forgotten about it.

"We should have another batch of bags coming in tomorrow; I've arranged to pick them up early tomorrow on Mount Desert Island."

"I hope they get here on time," I said, and returned to the kitchen, where John was ladling chowder into bowls.

"You want one?" he asked.

"After I'm done serving, I'd love one." I retrieved a bottle of California Chardonnay from the fridge and dug in a drawer for the wine opener. "I realized I forgot to tell you something."

"What?" Charlene asked, looking up from her compact; she had been touching up her mascara. At my questioning look, she said, "I've decided to help you with the serving."

I grinned, knowing her intent had little to do with helping me and a lot to do with checking out the archaeologists.

"You were going to tell us something, remember?" John prompted me.

"Oh, right. Anyway, you know those lift bags they use to pull up artifacts?"

"The inflatable ones?" John asked.

I lined up three wine glasses and nodded. "Carl said they were out of them, and needed to wait for a shipment to arrive tomorrow morning, but I saw one under Molly's bed today."

"That doesn't make sense," Charlene said.

"Unless she's doing something else with those lift bags," John said.

I told them about the other things I had seen in Molly's bathroom.

"Why wouldn't she store those things on the boat?" Charlene asked.

"That's what I wondered. And Carl was complaining about the site being disturbed the other night, too." I poured the wine, admiring the golden glow of it in the crystal glasses. "Do you think maybe she's doing her own archaeology on the side?" I asked.

"You didn't find any artifacts in her room," John said. "Maybe the lift bag was defective — or she forgot she had it."

"What about the plastic tubs and the car battery?" I asked.

He shrugged. "I have no idea what they use when they're doing an excavation. Why don't you ask?"

"I can't," I said, blushing slightly as I

retrieved a bottle of beer from the fridge.

"Why not?" John asked.

"There was a 'Do Not Disturb' sign on her door," I confessed.

John sighed. "And you went in anyway?"

"Gotta run," I said, putting the drinks on the tray and disappearing through the door to the dining room.

John gave me a stern look when I returned to the kitchen. "I thought you said you weren't going to do anything illegal," he said.

"Who said it was illegal? I was just trying to help a friend," I said, nodding toward Claudette. "Besides, I'm supposed to go into the rooms. I'm the innkeeper."

John rolled his eyes, but I ignored it.

"I wonder what all that stuff was for?" Charlene asked as she applied a new coat of lipstick.

"Car battery, jug of clear liquid . . . who knows?"

"Maybe I could ask one of the Iliad archaeologists," I said.

"You're going to tell them you found all that stuff in Molly's room?" Claudette asked.

"Of course not," I said. "I'll be subtle. I'm good at subtle."

Charlene gave a little cough that I chose

to ignore and stood up, smoothing down her soft purple top. "Everyone gets salads, right?"

"Right."

"Who's sitting where?" she asked.

I gave her the rundown and sent her out with the salads. "Be extra nice to the woman by the window," I said. "She's a food writer for the *Times*."

"You're kidding me," Charlene said. "Really?"

"That's great, Nat!" John said, his face breaking into a smile for the first time in days.

I nodded, then gave Charlene a stern look. "Just try not to spill shrimp on her, okay?"

With Charlene in charge of serving, I poured myself a small glass of wine, ladled out a small bowl of chowder and sat down between Claudette and John. The creamy chowder was velvety on my tongue, and the oaky, slightly sweet Chardonnay was a perfect combination. I dipped in a leftover crust of sourdough bread and chewed it.

Claudette's bowl sat before her, untouched. "Eat," I said. "You need your strength."

"I can't," she said miserably.

"What about a piece of pie?" I asked.

She turned to look at me. "Is there sugar in it?"

I gave up, defeated.

The rest of dinner went well, at least according to Charlene. "That writer of yours gushed over the chowder," she said, "so you should be in good shape."

"See anything you like out there?" John teased Charlene as he rinsed the last salad plate and tucked it into the dishwasher.

"Well, the university guy is good-looking, in a weather-beaten kind of way," she said, taking a sip of wine, "but he seems a bit uptight."

"He's got anger management problems, too," I said. "Plus, he'd be out of town all the time."

"A challenge, but not insurmountable," she said, spooning up a bite of raspberry pie and chewing it thoughtfully. "It's good, but yours is better."

"Thanks," I said. "I just wish I could have gotten Claudette to eat some of it."

"She's not wasting away yet," Charlene said. Claudette did have an ample build, but I was still worried. We had tried to get her to stay in the kitchen with us, but she had excused herself and gone up to her room. I was planning to check on her in a little bit.

"Not having an oven has been kind of convenient today," I said. As much as I loved baking, a day away had been a nice break. "But I'm still hoping to be back in the baking business soon."

"If that repairman isn't here by 11," John growled, "I'll go get him myself."

"You may have to wait a bit if the weather doesn't improve," Charlene said, glancing at the rain-glazed windows. "Speaking of which, have you heard from Gwen?"

"Not yet," I said, glancing at my watch; it was coming up on eight.

"She and Adam were headed over to Mount Desert Island today. Adam was going to ask around about Evan," Charlene said.

The wind howled, rattling the windowpanes. "I hope they made it back before the weather got bad."

"Why don't you call and see if they're at his place?"

"Excellent idea," I said, dialing Adam's number. The phone rang four times before his pleasant tenor voice kicked in, inviting me to leave a message. I hung up, feeling a flutter of fear in my stomach. "No answer," I said.

Charlene sighed. "Most of the time, I love

it that cell phones don't work here, but sometimes it's a pain."

"If anything has happened, it'll likely be on the VHF," John suggested.

"Good thinking!" Charlene said. After donning raincoats, the three of us trooped down to the carriage house.

The storm really had kicked up. The rain was flying almost horizontally, and our jackets flapped as a strong gust of wind buffeted us. I was glad it was only a short walk to the carriage house — and prayed that Adam and Gwen were safely on land tonight.

As Charlene and I peeled off our raincoats and perched on the oatmeal-colored couch, John turned on the radio. Despite the circumstances, I found myself admiring once again the simplicity of the décor; the simple lines and the calm, neutral beiges and blues were at once masculine and serene. Not too unlike John, I thought. The crackling sound, along with the radio's eerie, high-pitched buzz, sent shivers down my back. I reached to touch the back of the driftwood seal sculpture on the coffee table, but the smooth wood did nothing to comfort me.

John tuned the radio to channel 9 and spoke into the transmitter. "*Carpe Diem,*

Carpe Diem, Carpe Diem. This is *Moon-catcher.* Over." *Carpe Diem* was the name of Adam's lobster boat; *Mooncatcher* was John's skiff.

I clutched the arm of the couch, hoping to hear Adam's voice, but there was no reply.

"They could still be over on Mount Desert," Charlene murmured as John repeated the call. No response. After he repeated it a third time, another voice responded. "*Mooncatcher,* this is *Rusty Nail.*" I knew that was Mac Barefoot's boat. "Haven't seen or heard from the *Diem* all day."

"Roger that and thanks, *Rusty Nail.* Over."

John looked up at us. "At least we know Mac hasn't heard anything bad. Let's check the distress channel, just in case," he said. He tuned it to channel 16. He didn't repeat his call on this channel — it was best to keep it clear for vessels in trouble — but after fifteen minutes, the channel remained silent.

"Doesn't sound like he's in trouble," John said.

"I hope not," I said as another gust of wind buffeted the carriage house, but I wasn't convinced.

John looked at me. "Why don't I take the radio up to the inn, so we can keep tabs on it? That way, if Gwen calls, we won't miss it."

As much as I didn't relish the thought of hours listening to the ghostly whine and crackle of the VHF radio, I knew it was the right thing to do.

"I'm so glad I moved to Cranberry Island to enjoy the peaceful life," I said as we hurried back up the walkway to the inn. The wind whipped my face as Charlene pulled open the kitchen door.

"At least you can't say you're bored," Charlene said as we hurried back into my warm kitchen and John shut the night out behind us.

It was almost ten o'clock before we heard from Gwen.

When the phone rang, all three of us jumped; I picked it up and dispensed with my normal "Gray Whale Inn" greeting. "Hello?" I barked into the receiver

"Aunt Nat, it's Gwen." My niece sounded like she was crying.

"What's wrong?" I asked, clutching the receiver. John switched off the VHF, and both he and Charlene looked at me with concern.

"It's Adam," she said. "He's in the hospital."

TWELVE

"Oh, no," I said, clutching the phone. Poor Adam . . . and poor Gwen. "What happened? Is he going to be okay?"

"I think so . . . oh, I don't know. Somebody attacked him, beat him up badly." I could hear Gwen's voice quavering. "He's unconscious right now. The doctors think he'll be okay, but they won't know for sure until he wakes up."

"Oh, Gwen . . . how did this happen?"

"I don't know. We went into Bar Harbor this afternoon. I went shopping for art supplies, and Adam told me he was going to ask around and see if he could find out anything about Evan." The words tumbled out in a rush. "He was supposed to come and meet me back by the dock, but he never showed up. I waited an hour, and then I went everywhere, asking for him. I finally called the hospital — I didn't know who else to ask — and they told me he was there."

"Who took him to the hospital?" I asked.

"One of the guys who works at the pizza place on Cottage Street found him," she said, her voice hoarse. "Someone propped him up against the back of a building. I can't believe this could happen . . . and here, of all places!" She sniffed again, and I could picture her wiping away tears.

Poor Adam. "What do the doctors say?"

"He's got a broken arm and ribs, and his face looks awful," she said. "But they're mainly worried about his head. They did a CAT scan, and he looks okay, but we won't know anything for sure until he wakes up. I'm praying he's okay."

I felt a swell of anger at the thought of Adam, unconscious from a head injury. Who had done this to him? "Did Adam tell you who he was going to talk to?"

"No," she said, sounding miserable.

"Oh, Gwen, I wish I were there," I said. I ached to be at the hospital with her, but with the storm outside, there was no way we could cross the water in our skiffs safely. As much as I loved living on an island, there were times when the isolation was a real hindrance — and this was one of them.

"It's not safe — not with the storm," she

said. "I'll be okay. Adam's mom and dad are driving up tonight."

"Thank God," I said. I was glad she'd have company — and crossed my fingers that they were able to support each other. It was going to be tough on all of them. "Please let them know Adam — and all of you — are in our prayers, Gwen. I wish I could be there with you."

"I know, Aunt Nat. But I'll be all right."

And I knew she would. As different as Gwen and Bridget were, My niece had inherited my sister's strength. "Call me as soon as you hear anything, okay? Any time of night."

"I will," she said.

"I love you, honey."

"I love you too, Aunt Nat."

I hung up and relayed what Gwen had told me to John and Charlene. "And she has no idea who Adam was going to talk to?" John asked.

"None at all," I said.

"Evan must have been in deep trouble," John said. "I heard he'd gotten into gambling, but he must have been in debt to some dangerous people."

"Do you think that's why he skipped town?" Charlene asked.

"I'm hoping he got a chance to skip

town," John said.

I shivered. Had Evan, too, fallen victim to a murderer? "Poor Evan."

"Poor Adam," Charlene said. "It was his generosity that got him mixed up with Evan in the first place."

"Adam's a kind-hearted man," I said. "That's a big part of the reason Gwen loves him so much."

"I know — it's just a shame."

"Before we throw anyone else into danger, I think we need to talk to Ingrid, and find out what she knows," I said.

Charlene snorted. "Get her to tell you anything negative about her precious boy? Good luck with that."

"If it means helping find her son, she might open up," I said.

"Anything's possible, I guess."

John leaned back and stretched. "I'm ready to hit the sack," he said.

"You're welcome to stay here if you want," I said to Charlene.

"I'd love to, but I've got to open early." She gave me a hug. "Call me if you hear anything, okay?"

I promised her I would, and after watching Charlene's one tail light recede up the drive, John put his arms around me and kissed me. Then, together, as lightning

201

forked in the sky outside and the wind howled around the eaves, we climbed the darkened stairs to the bedroom.

The storm had dissipated when I woke to darkness the next morning. As I stumbled down to the kitchen, I was glad I'd planned an easy breakfast; I was still half-asleep and worried about Adam. It was a good thing the oven wasn't working. Normally baking was a refuge for me, but this morning, I wouldn't have been surprised if I accidentally substituted salt for sugar.

I had just started the coffee when the phone rang. I almost dropped the basket of muffins in my hurry to get to the phone.

"Gray Whale Inn," I blurted into the receiver.

"He's awake!"

"Thank God," I said, slumping against the wall. "Is he okay?"

"He can't remember a thing that happened," Gwen said, her voice jubilant, "but other than that he's just fine."

"Oh, Gwen. I'm so glad. Are his mom and dad okay?"

"It was a tense night, but everyone's fine now," she said. "Of course, his face looks like hamburger meat, and they'll have to straighten his nose out, but he's going to be

202

just fine."

"How long will he have to stay in the hospital?"

"They want him there for at least another twenty-four hours before they'll let him go. His mom and dad have reserved two hotel rooms, so we're going to stay in town until he's ready to go."

"Don't let him drive the *Diem* yet, okay? I want you both back on the mail boat — or if it's not running, call me and I'll arrange something."

"Sheesh. Now I've got two moms."

"Three, if you count Adam's mother," I teased her. "Give him a hug for us, okay?"

"Will do, Aunt Nat."

I hung up feeling about a million times better, and called Charlene. Then I ran upstairs to pass the news on to John, who was still dozing.

"Wake up, sleepyhead," I called.

"Who called?" he asked, his sandy blond hair appealingly tousled.

"That was Gwen. Adam woke up, and he's going to be okay."

He fell back onto the bed. "Thank God."

"My thoughts exactly." I gave him a quick kiss. "If you want muffins, you'd better hurry and get downstairs."

He looked at his watch. "I'll be down in a

203

few minutes. Is there coffee?"

"Lots. I'll pour you a cup."

As I trotted back downstairs, the phone rang a second time. I answered it on the first ring. "Gray Whale Inn."

"May I speak with Franklin Goertz, please?"

It was barely eight o'clock; a bit early for a casual call. "I'll see if he's up," I said. "Can I tell him who's calling?"

"Sarah Marks," said the woman on the line. "Of Marks, Gravenstein, and Pousson."

"I'll see if I can get him," I said.

Frank was up and dressed in jeans and a flannel shirt when I knocked on his door and informed him he had a phone call. "You can take it at the front desk if you'd like," I said.

"I will," he said, following me to the desk. I hurried back to the kitchen and hesitated before hanging up the phone; I could hear their voices from the receiver. I was dying to listen in. Instead, I slipped through the kitchen door and crept to the far side of the dining room, straining my ears.

"He didn't sign it?" Frank asked. There was a pause; after a few minutes, he let out a whoosh of air. "So she's not in the picture, and everything's still the way it was when we set it up," he said. He was quiet for a moment. "Well, it's horrible what happened, but at least the timing worked out. Now we don't have to wrangle over an IPO, and the shares stay with the original partners." After a moment he spoke again. "Will the money from the insurance settlement automatically be used to buy the remaining shares?" There was silence again. "Okay. We've found a bigger R/V, and it's coming in today. We should have this site identified in a day or two, and then I'll be back in the office. Unless it's urgent, just send any paperwork that needs to be signed to my office address, and I'll take care of it when I get back." There was silence for a moment, and then he spoke again. "Thanks for calling — I've been on pins and needles this last couple of days."

As he hung up, I scurried back to the kitchen. Unless I was mistaken, I had just found one more person who benefited from Gerald McIntire's death.

John was sitting at the kitchen table, his hair gleaming in the morning sun.

"Who was that?" he asked.

"I think it was Frank Goertz's attorney," I said.

"What makes you say that?"

I told him what I'd overheard.

"Overheard, eh?" He shook his head, grinning. "You can't help yourself, can you?" he

205

teased. "You're as bad as the natives. I'll have to buy you a pair of binoculars for Christmas, so you can officially join the island's traditional sport."

I tried to look innocent. "Birdwatching?"

"No. Snooping," he said. "It does have its uses, though. Do you think that 'she' was Gerald's fiancée?"

"That's the only thing I can think of," I said. "It sounds like Gerald was altering the partnership agreement now that his marital status was changing. I'm guessing Frank didn't want the shares to revert to anyone other than him."

"But if it's a partnership, wouldn't both partners have to agree on something like that?" John asked.

"Not necessarily, if one is the majority partner. It depends on how the contract was written. He mentioned using an insurance settlement. Sounds like he had a policy on Gerald — that's what he's using to buy out the rest of the company."

"It was probably pretty substantial, then."

"Looks like we've got another motive," I said.

"Maybe," he said. "It would be stronger if he knew the papers hadn't been signed yet. Murdering your partner is a big risk to take if you're not sure of the payoff."

"You're right," I said, feeling my hopes deflate a little bit. Would we ever be able to get Eleazer out of jail?

"Still," John said. "If there was an argument over the IPO, it might have been worth his while to get rid of his partner." He leaned forward. "The new agreement might still have made him majority partner in the event of a death — and having Gerald out of the way could make it easier to forestall an IPO. And unless they were canceling the insurance policy, he still stood to make a bundle."

"So he still has a strong motive," I said.

"I'd say so." John grinned at me. "Excellent detective work. I think you're officially ready for a pair of binoculars."

"Thank you ever so much," I said. "See if you get muffins with *that* attitude."

He stood and bowed. "I deeply, humbly apologize, fair maiden and keeper of the baked goods."

"Oh, all right." I tossed him a fat muffin; he caught it handily and set to work peeling back the wrapper. I turned on my big griddle and put bacon on to cook, then poured two cups of coffee and brought them to the table. Within moments, the aroma of bacon permeated the room. I took a sip of coffee, still thinking about the conversation I'd overheard. "It's just too bad he's sending the paperwork to his office."

"You know that opening mail is a federal offense," he said.

"Perhaps," I said. "But coming across opened mail while dusting is still perfectly legal, as far as I know."

"Incorrigible," John said, chuckling.

"That's what makes me so irresistible," I said.

He leaned over to kiss me, but our embrace was interrupted by the creak of the kitchen door.

It was Claudette, looking more haggard than ever. "Come sit down," I said, getting up to help her to a chair. She hadn't eaten in at least twenty-four hours, and seemed to have aged ten years in the last couple of days. I was really starting to worry about her. "Let me get you some tea." I hurried to put a kettle on. "Are you hungry? I've got fabulous blueberry muffins from Little Notch."

"No, thanks," she said.

"Why don't you have just one — to keep up your strength."

"Okay," she said, but just stared at the muffin when I put it in front of her. "I heard the phone ring. Is there any news?"

John and I filled her in on what had happened to Adam.

"Thank goodness he's going to be okay," she said. "He's such a nice boy."

"He is," I agreed.

"Do you think what happened to poor Adam has anything to do with Gerald's death?"

"I don't know," I said. "It could. I'm going to see if I can talk to Ingrid today."

"Poor Adam," she said, shaking her head. "He's like Eli — good-hearted." She sighed. "I should go down to the house and check on the cats and the goats today."

I got up to turn the bacon and glanced out the window; the rain was lessening, but it was still coming down. "I'd wait until it clears up a bit," I said, opening the fridge and taking out a dozen eggs.

"It's supposed to be sunny by noon," John said.

"Maybe we can finally get the oven fixed, then," I said. I'd already planned to make sautéed chicken cutlets and steamed veggies for tonight — with a side of rice instead of bread — but it would be nice to know when I could start cooking normally again.

"Speaking of baking, isn't the bake-off this weekend?" John asked.

"Don't remind me," I said darkly, and

cracked an egg into a bowl with vigor.

By the time the first guests came down to breakfast, my kitchen was empty again. Claudette had borrowed a raincoat and headed out to check on her animals, and John had returned to the carriage house to call the repair company. The dining room was bathed in watery morning light; already a few rays of sun were escaping the thick cloud cover. Cherry sat in her customary table by the window, cheerful as usual despite the cloudy morning, and the Iliad duo sat a few tables away. There was no sign of Carl and Molly.

Frank looked more relaxed than I'd ever seen him as I poured coffee and informed him of what was on the menu. Even Audrey looked slightly less depressed than usual.

"You look like you've gotten some good news," I said as I finished my recital of the breakfast offerings and topped off Audrey's coffee cup.

"We got a line on a big R/V with a submersible," Frank said happily.

"What's an R/V?" I asked.

"Short for research vessel," he said with a smile. For a man who had lost his partner only two days earlier, he looked remarkably chipper. After what I'd overheard this morning, I guessed the R/V wasn't the only thing brightening his day. "It'll be here this afternoon," he added.

I topped off Frank's coffee cup and stepped back. "I thought all of your big research vessels were in the Caribbean right now."

"They are," he said. "My staff tracked this one down yesterday; it's in Portland, and we're leasing it for a few days. That'll allow us to do a sonar map of the area and pull up a cannon — should make identifying the wreck a whole lot easier."

"Congratulations," I said. "I've been meaning to ask, by the way — I know Evan Sorenson contacted you initially about the wreck. Did you enter into any kind of agreement with him?"

His smile faded. "I'm afraid I'm not at liberty to talk about that," he said.

"You do know that Evan has disappeared, don't you?"

"I'd heard something about that," he said, taking a sip of his coffee. "He's a young man — probably went to visit a girlfriend or something. You know how college-age kids are."

"Speaking of disappearing, any word yet on the *Lorelei*?" I asked.

"Not yet, unfortunately," he said. "If it

211

went down at the site, though, the sonar on the new vessel should pick it up, and we'll find out if we can salvage it."

"I hope it was insured," I said.

"Everything's insured at Iliad," he said, leaning back in his chair. "We like to cover all of our bases."

Including murdered partners, I thought as I drifted back to the kitchen.

Twenty minutes went by, and still Molly and Carl didn't come down. Where could they be? They were usually the first ones at breakfast. I peered out the window at the water below the inn, and was surprised to see that both of the mooring lines were vacant. They must have headed out early, determined to take advantage of the lull in the storm. Had Molly remembered the lift bag she'd stashed in her suitcase?

As I set down the basket of muffins, I replayed in my head the phone conversation I'd overheard that morning — and my brief chat with Frank. He seemed awfully cavalier about Evan's disappearance. Was Iliad somehow involved in it? That didn't explain what had happened to Adam in Bar Harbor yesterday, though.

There were too many unanswered questions, I thought as I refilled the carafe with coffee, and no way of knowing if any of them were linked to Gerald McIntire's death.

One thing was certain, though. If Carl had killed Gerald to buy the university time to identify the wreck, it was quickly running out.

THIRTEEN

By the time I finished loading the breakfast dishes into the dishwasher, the sun was breaking through the clouds, and it was shaping up to be a gorgeous fall day. John had kindly offered to stick around and wait for the repairman to come, and since none of the guests would be at the inn for lunch (Cherry was checking out the cafés on Mount Desert Island, and Molly had left a note on the front desk saying they'd be out until dinner), I had a luxurious few hours of freedom.

When my yellow kitchen was clean and sparkling, I slipped my windbreaker and sneakers on, retrieved a Tupperware container full of my oatmeal chocolate chippers I'd dug out of the back of the freezer — I would have baked fresh, but it's tough to make cookies without an oven — and headed out the door, enjoying the fresh, cold breeze against my cheeks.

After all of the stress of the last few days, the unsullied beauty of the island was a balm to my soul. The world looked washed clean, and although the wind and rain had torn enough leaves from the red maples to create a brilliant red carpet, there were still several clinging to the branches, glowing in the morning sun. Droplets of water glistened where they had caught in the russet leaves of a blueberry bush, and the low rush of waves hitting rocks and the cry of seagulls in the distance were a soothing counterpoint to the rustle of the pine trees. The island was like a jewel box — and I was reminded once again why I'd fallen in love with it in the first place.

When I reached the top of the hill, I turned back and looked down at the inn. It looked like it had always been a part of the landscape — and I realized what a big part of me the sprawling old house had become. It was hard to imagine it belonging to Captain Jonah Selfridge, who had built it to house his wife. She had wanted to live far enough from the dock so her delicate nose wasn't offended by the smell of fish. Time had marched on, but in many ways, Cranberry Island had changed little since the time of Captain Selfridge — or even of the famed pirate Davey Blue.

My eyes strayed from the gray-shingled inn with its Provençal-blue window boxes to the water beyond. Had Captain Selfridge met his end mere miles from his home, and lain deep under the blue water for almost two hundred years? Or had Davey Blue and his doomed seventeen-year-old love gone down centuries earlier?

And who had stabbed Gerald and left him drifting on Deadman's Shoal?

I turned away from the inn and headed down the hill toward Ingrid Sorenson's house, trying to recapture the feeling of peace I'd had so briefly a few minutes earlier. All I could think of was Eli's twinkling eyes, his wry sense of humor — and the hole in my heart since he was taken away. The trees still whispered, and the gulls still called, but the moment was gone. As I trudged down the ribbon of asphalt toward Ingrid's house, I found myself wishing the wreck had never been found.

Despite the anguish I knew she must be experiencing, Ingrid's house, like always, looked like it belonged on the cover of *Cottage Living*. The only sign that there might be any distress was the wilted pansies in the pots flanking the door, thirsty for a drink. It was a wonder, really, that they'd escaped

Claudette's goats. As I stood on the covered front porch, I couldn't help glancing at Claudette and Eli's house, just down the road, and despite the circumstances, I found myself smiling. Those boat parts stranded in the overgrown side yard must drive Ingrid nuts.

To my surprise, Ingrid opened the door just seconds after I knocked.

Her appearance was shocking. Her usually coiffed hair was a wild halo around her drawn face, and she wore a stained sweatshirt and sweatpants that hung loose on her thin frame.

"What do you want?" she asked, her voice hoarse.

"I heard about Evan," I said. "I know you've got to be going through a difficult time." I proffered the cookies. "I was hoping maybe I could help."

"Come in." She spoke in a monotone, then turned away without taking the cookies and walked deeper into the house's dark interior. I followed uncertainly.

The house was usually sunny and sparkling, smelling of potpourri and lemon Pledge. I could pick up a hint of potpourri today, but the house had an uncharacteristically stuffy and unpleasant odor. Ingrid walked through the dark living room into the kitchen, and I could see why. Dirty dishes were stacked beside the normally spotless sink, and the trashcan was overflowing, a blackened banana peel spilling over the side.

Poor Ingrid.

"Sit down and let me get you a cup of tea," I said. The circles under her eyes looked like bruises. She said nothing, which I took as assent, and stared blankly while I filled the kettle with water and busied myself clearing the table.

"You don't have to do that," she said.

"I want to," I told her. I opened the dishwasher and began dealing with the stacks of soiled plates and bowls. Ingrid protested again, weakly, but I waved her away. I decided to ask Marge to stop by and do a more thorough cleaning later. If I had the time, I'd join her.

By the time the tea was done steeping, I had taken the trash outside and wiped down the counters; now, I took a clean plate from the cupboard and loaded half a dozen cookies onto it before popping it into the microwave. I'd cracked the kitchen window open a few minutes ago. In addition to the streaks of afternoon sunlight, the smell of warm cookies, tea, and fresh autumn air lightened the room.

With the chaos relegated to the dish-washer, I retrieved the plate of cookies from the microwave and poured two cups of tea. I sat down across from Ingrid and slid a cup over toward her.

"Where's your husband?" I asked.

"He's over on the mainland, working with a private investigator," she said. "He's been gone for days."

"And you've been here all alone?" I asked.

"Yes," she said. "I haven't wanted to leave in case the phone rings. I've called the hospital, but Evan's not there." Tears filled her eyes. "He was doing so well, Natalie. He'd just gotten back from rehab, and seemed so excited about trying out lobster-ing. I thought we'd finally gotten him back on track."

"What happened?" I asked softly.

"I should have been more suspicious," she said. "All that time out on Mount Desert Island — and he didn't come back some nights. I wanted to talk to him about it, but my husband told me I was being overprotec-tive, and I backed off."

"Do you know who he stayed with when he wasn't here?"

"I wish I did," she said. "He talked about a guy named Pete — he was another lobs-terman, out of Southwest Harbor. I thought

219

he was just learning the ropes, but now . . ."

"Do you know Pete's last name?"

She shook her head. "I should have asked," she moaned.

I made a mental note to ask Tom Lockhart about lobstermen named Pete. There couldn't be too many lobstermen with that name fishing out of Southwest Harbor. "What happened the day he disappeared?" I asked.

"He got up early — ever since he'd gotten back from the . . . the medical center, he'd been an early riser." She sighed. "He was so excited about that wreck he and Adam found. He told me he'd gotten in touch with a company that did salvage work, and that if there was bullion, he'd get a finder's fee."

"Do you know if he signed any contracts with anyone?"

She shook her head. "He never said, and I haven't found anything. I've been through his room again and again. Nothing on the shipwreck, nothing about anyone named Pete . . ." She dropped her head to her hands. "We'd finally gotten him back, and now, this. I don't know what to do, Natalie."

"Tell me more about the last day you saw him," I said.

Ingrid looked up at me, wiping at her eyes,

trying to get herself together. "I've gone over it in my mind a thousand times, wishing I'd stopped him, wishing I'd done something different . . ."

I reached across the table to squeeze her hand.

She took a few deep, shuddery breaths before continuing. "He went over to Mount Desert Island on the early mail boat. He'd been on cloud nine since the discovery, but something had upset him. He was surly when he came back for dinner the night before. He wouldn't tell us why."

"Why didn't he go to the mainland with Adam?"

Ingrid shrugged. "They were arguing. Something to do with the shipwreck; I think Adam was upset that Evan had called the salvage company. I thought that might be why he was in such a bad mood."

"Adam got into some trouble last night," I told her.

"What do you mean?"

"He and Gwen went over to the mainland. I think Adam was looking for Evan — or anyone who knew him. Someone beat Adam up — he's still in the hospital."

"It wasn't Evan," Ingrid said vehemently. "He never would have done a thing like that!"

The passion of her response startled me. "I didn't say he did," I said. "I was just wondering if the two incidents were related."

"I'm sorry," she said, her face crumpling. "I'm overreacting to everything these days. Poor Adam. Is he going to be all right?"

"He is," I said.

Suddenly she gripped the arms of her chair. Her knuckles were white. "Oh my God. Do you think . . . do you think whoever did that to Adam might have done something to Evan, too?"

"I hope not," I said. "I was hoping you could suggest where to look, though."

She raked her hand through her hair again. "Oh, Evan . . . what did you get yourself into this time?"

"Did Evan say where he was going that morning?"

"Just to see his friend Pete," she said. "He promised he'd be back in time for dinner. I was making shrimp scampi, his favorite . . ." Sobs wracked her thin frame.

"Have you told all this to the police?" I asked.

"Everything," she said. "They're supposedly doing an investigation, but every time I call, they tell me they don't have any leads. I think the police think Evan stole the

Lorelei."

"They did disappear at the same time," I said.

Ingrid drew herself up. "He would never do a thing like that."

"I wasn't implying he did," I said quickly. "Just that the police are looking for a suspect, and the timing is convenient. Would Evan know how to drive a boat like that?"

She nodded. "He grew up around boats," she said. "But he had no reason to steal the *Lorelei.* He'd never do a thing like that. There was no reason to!"

"Ingrid," I said. "I hate to ask you this, but did your son ever play cards?"

"What do you mean?"

I told her about the rumor I'd heard down at the lobster co-op.

"Gambling?" she said, looking shocked. "He's never been a gambler. He's had other problems, of course. But never gambling."

"Would he have told you if he did?" I asked.

She slumped again, running a hand through her unkempt gray-blond hair. "I don't know," she said, her face more drawn than ever. She seemed to have aged a decade in the past week. "I just don't know anything anymore."

"Maybe we could look through his room

again, together," I suggested, not sure how she'd respond. "Maybe there will be something that might tell us what happened."

"I've looked through it a million times," she said.

"I'm sure," I said. "But sometimes two sets of eyes are better than one."

When I got back to the inn, sick at heart over Ingrid and her missing son, my kitchen was in pieces — or at least my oven was.

"You found someone!" I said, giving John a big hug.

"I did indeed," he said. "And it's an easy fix, too; just a loose connection."

"You should be up and running in an hour," said the repairman, poking his head out of the oven.

"We'll leave you in peace," John told him, taking my arm. "You can't do anything in here right now — let's go down to the carriage house for a bit. Just come down and knock if you need us, okay?" he said to the repairman.

"Will do," he said, and John opened the door and ushered me through.

As we stepped out onto the back porch, John put his arm around me. "I heard you were over at Ingrid's," he said once the door was closed behind us. "Any word on Evan from that end?"

I grimaced. "Ingrid's a mess. I told her about the rumor I'd heard — that Evan was into gambling — and she looked shocked."

"It was the same when she found out he was into drugs, too."

"She said he was spending nights out of the house," I said, "but her husband told her not to pry."

John shook his head. "With Evan's history? They're nuts not to pry. Has she gone through his things?"

I nodded. "She went through everything — and while I was there, we looked again — but there was nothing to find. Not a name, not a phone number — nothing."

"A dead end, then," he said, grimacing.

"Looks like it," I said. "I only found out one thing."

"That's something, at least."

"It's not much, though. She told me Evan was on the outs with Adam over the wreck, which we knew — but she did say that the night he disappeared, he was going to see a friend named Pete," I said as we walked down the well-trodden path to the carriage house. I glanced down at the water; the only boats there belonged to John and me. I hoped Carl and Molly were having luck getting the ship's bell up.

"Pete," John said as he opened the carriage house door. "Pretty common name, unfortunately. But it's something."

I crossed the small space and sank down on the couch. "She also told me he was looking for a big payoff from the wreck — and was upset about something the last day or two before he disappeared."

"Interesting," John said.

"That's what I thought. Do you think maybe Evan killed Gerald for reneging on the deal?"

"And took the boat?"

"Maybe," John said. "But what would he do with it?"

"Escape to the Caribbean and sell it?" I said. "I don't know."

"It's possible," John said. "But if he did, how did the cutlass end up in the bushes by the pier?"

I sank back into the couch cushions. "That is a problem, isn't it?"

"And it still doesn't explain what happened to Adam," he said.

"Coincidence?" I said, knowing I was reaching.

"Too bad we can't ask Adam," he said.

"That's right. He's got amnesia."

"Does he at least remember who he was going to see?" John asked.

"Gwen didn't say," I said, feeling a glimmer of hope. "I've been meaning to call and check on Adam anyway; why don't I see if I can find out?"

"It's better than nothing," John said. "I'll call and see if there's any change in the murder investigation."

"Iliad is getting a sonar rig," I said, "so if the *Lorelei* is anywhere near the wreck, we'll know."

"That would be one mystery solved, at least," he said.

"Unfortunately, it doesn't help Eleazer."

"Or Evan — if he's aboard," John pointed out.

I shivered at the thought.

The rest of the afternoon and evening were taken up by dinner preparations and clean-up. With Gwen off the island, the work fell to John and me. Everyone was cordial at dinner — the Iliad crowd looked quite cheerful despite the demise of their leader, and I was guessing it was due to the impending arrival of a new research vessel. Even Audrey was looking a little less morose. Was she a killer? I wondered as I refilled water glasses.

I wondered the same of Carl. "Any lift bags?" I asked as I picked up his salad plate.

227

"Not yet," Carl said. "I can't believe the shipment didn't arrive. They sent a duplicate order out today, though; should be here first thing tomorrow."

I was tempted to tell them Iliad's news, but decided against it; I had enough trouble without stirring up more.

The *Times* writer was dining on the mainland tonight, so it was a small group for dinner. Charlene had called to tell me Claudette was staying home to keep her cats company, so once the guests went to their rooms, John lit a fire in the carriage house fireplace and the two of us snuggled in front of it, each with a glass of red wine.

As I leaned into him, he toyed with a strand of my hair. "We probably need to set a date, you know."

"I know," I said. "It's just been so busy lately."

"It should slow down soon," he said, stroking my arm. "What do you think of a February wedding?"

"Cold," I said.

"True," he said. "But the inn will be dead — and the island will be a winter wonderland."

"We'd have time to take a honeymoon," I said.

"Maybe the Caribbean?" he said.

As much as I loved Maine, the Texas girl in me still longed for the sun in the dark months of winter. "If we can afford it," I said.

"We may have a bit more income soon," he said.

I sat up and turned to look at him. "What do you mean?"

"Apparently someone who's big in the New York art world saw one of my sculptures at a friend's house in Blue Nose," he said. "She wants to see a portfolio."

"John, that's wonderful! Your work might be in a New York gallery?"

"Looks like it," he said. "The gallery owner called me a couple of days ago. I told her I'd send her my portfolio next week."

"Why didn't you tell me?" I asked.

"With everything going on with Eleazer . . . the time just never seemed right," he said, shrugging.

"When will you know?"

"I've got to get her the portfolio first, Nat," he said.

"So you might be able to devote all your time to sculpture."

"And the inn," he said, running his calloused fingers down my cheek and turning my face toward him. "And you."

A February wedding, an opportunity for

John to do the work he loved . . . two bright spots in the clouds. John's lips were warm on mine, and we sank back into the couch together, the fire crackling at our feet, our arms around each other, the worries we carried left outside — at least for a little while.

It was dark when I woke up. I was disoriented for a moment, then realized we were in the carriage house, John stretched out beside me, breathing evenly. A sliver of moon peeped through the window, and I was about to turn over and go back to sleep when I realized I had forgotten to take the bacon and cranberry bread out of the freezer.

An innkeeper's work is never done.

I dragged myself out of bed and dressed quickly, borrowing one of John's coats from the hook by the door before hurrying up the walk to the inn. I filled the sink with cold water and dropped in the bacon, then pulled my last loaf of cranberry nut bread from the freezer and set it on the counter. Then I turned off the light and headed for the kitchen door.

As I pulled the door shut behind me, a light flashed on the water near the shore, and the low purr of a motor reached my ears. I paused, curious who would be out in the middle of the night. The light grew closer as I stood on the porch step, and the little boat — I couldn't tell what it was — came right up to the inn's dock.

I made my way down the pathway as the engine cut off; I could hear the clunk of the boat against the bumpers. The slender beam of a flashlight illuminated little; I could make out a dark form crouched near the boat, tying it up to the dock. I was only a few yards away now, squinting to make out who was paying the inn a middle-of-the-night visit. Goosebumps crawled up my arms. I glanced up at the carriage house, wishing John was with me, and took another blind step forward, right into a hole.

The breath whooshed out of me as I fell, hitting the ground with a grunt. The flashlight bounced toward me; I heard a muttered oath, and then something hard crashed into my skull.

A stray thought flashed through my mind — *I need to invest in a helmet.* Then the sliver of moon dissolved into darkness, and everything went black.

Fourteen

It was the shaking that woke me.

I sat up slowly, my head throbbing, my whole body shivering violently. The sky was slate-colored, with a milky rim over the mountains on the mainland — the moon was long gone.

And so were the boat and the flashlight.

I staggered to my feet, struggling to control the spasms in my muscles, and grabbed with numb fingers at the lapels of John's coat. The short path up to the carriage house seemed to last for miles; when I finally got to the door, my fingers wouldn't close around the knob. After the fourth try, I got the door open. By the time I pushed it shut, John was in the bedroom doorway.

"Natalie!" He closed the distance between us in a heartbeat. "What happened?" He touched my face. "You're ice cold."

"I saw a boat," I rasped, my body still vibrating with shivers. "Someone hit me. I blacked out."

He quickly inspected my head and peered into my eyes. I was shaking so badly I couldn't keep my head steady.

"We've got to get you warm," he said. Pulling the coat even tighter around me, he led me to the bathroom, where he turned the hot water tap on full. As the bathtub filled, he grabbed the comforter from his bed and wrapped it around me, hugging my body to his to warm me. When the tub was finally full, he peeled off my clothes — my numb fingers couldn't manage the buttons and snaps — and helped me in.

The hot water felt like fire on my feet and legs.

"I can't do it," I said, trying to step out of the tub.

"It'll get better," he said. "We need to get the circulation going. You've got hypothermia."

I sat down gingerly, trying not to scream. It felt like my body was covered in third-degree burns, with needles just under the skin. After what seemed like an eternity, the tingling, burning sensation faded, and I began to feel the ache of the cold in my bones.

"How long were you out there?" he asked.

"I don't know," I said. "It was dark, and

the moon was still high."

"It's just now beginning to dawn," he said. "There's no telling how many hours you were out there." He touched my head, and I flinched. "Where does it hurt?"

"All over," I said, but pointed to what seemed to be the source of the throbbing. He grazed it lightly, and I cringed.

"It's a bad bump," he said, peering into my eyes again. "I don't think you have a concussion. Do you have any idea who hit you?"

"I don't know. It was someone tying up a small boat to the dock. I tripped and fell, and then whoever it was whacked me on the top of the head."

He shook his head. "If you keep getting clobbered like this, I'm not going to let you out of my sight." Another shiver pulsed through me, and he ran a bit more hot water into the tub. "What were you doing out there, anyway?"

"Defrosting bacon," I said.

"Out at the dock?"

I laughed, which made my head hurt. "No," I said when the pain subsided. "I woke up and remembered I hadn't taken the bacon out to thaw. I was on my way back down to the carriage house when I saw a light (so I went) down to the dock to see who it was."

"Well, whoever it was didn't want to be seen," he said. "Next time you see something strange in the middle of the night, come get me before you go investigating, okay?"

"We live on a small island. It's supposed to be safe."

"Well, lately, the opposite seems to be the case. Lucky for you you didn't fall in the water. You'd be down in Davey Jones' Locker," he said.

"Like Gerald McIntire," I said.

"Like Gerald McIntire," he said gravely, leaning down to kiss me on the forehead. "And that I couldn't bear."

John insisted on taking care of breakfast while I huddled in bed under several blankets and waited for the Motrin to kick in. It wasn't until ten o'clock that he returned to the carriage house.

"Did everything go all right?" I asked.

"Just fine," he said. "They were a little surprised when I served them raw steak instead of bacon, but other than that, no problems."

"Oh, no! I defrosted the wrong meat?" I thought of the *Times* writer. "What did Cherry think?"

"Relax," he said, leaning down to kiss me. "I was kidding. Everything went great, and Ms. Price was very happy. What's on tap for the rest of the day?"

"I've got a grocery order coming in this morning," I said, and outlined the menu for the rest of the day. "I should be able to manage, though. The headache seems to be fading."

"You are ordered to take it easy," he said. "I went down by the dock, by the way; no sign of a boat. No sign of anything, in fact."

"I'm not surprised," I said.

"I keep trying to figure out who it could have been."

"Practically everyone on the island has a skiff. And the *Ira B* crew ties up their dinghy at the dock every night."

"Do you remember where the skiff — or the dinghy — was tied up?"

"It was too dark to tell," I said.

"You probably couldn't tell if the *Ira B* was moored there, either."

I shook my head. "It was too dark to see anything other than the flashlight. But if it was the dinghy, it didn't come in directly from the *Ira B*," I said.

"So either someone took the *Ira B*'s dinghy out and then came back, or it was someone else's boat." John shook his head. "But why tie up at the dock in the middle of the night? And why knock you out?"

"Maybe I scared him. Or her. Or whoever it was. I don't think there was more than one person."

"I scared you just the other day when I opened the kitchen door and you were chopping onions. You didn't throw a French chef's knife at me."

"I'm not a murderer, though," I pointed out. "Other than dispatching the occasional lobster, that is."

He smiled, but his tone was serious. "Do you think what happened last night might be connected to Gerald McIntire's death?"

"Whoever attacked me didn't want me knowing what they were up to. So maybe it was — although I can't think how." I glanced out the window at the dark blue water. It looked so peaceful and serene this morning — but had seemed so sinister just hours ago. "On the other hand, they didn't kill me, so maybe not."

"Thank God for that," John said, and lapsed into silence, thinking. His weathered face seemed more lined than usual, and I longed to kiss away his cares. But I couldn't kiss away Gerald McIntire's death — or Eleazer's imprisonment.

"But there was no *need* to kill you," he

finally said, slowly. "They just needed to make sure you didn't know who they were."

"The facts just aren't fitting together," I said.

"What facts?"

"Oh, just . . . everything," I said.

I told him about the "Rules" book and the torn-up photograph I'd found on Audrey's nightstand.

"Did you dig through the rooms *again?*" he asked.

"No, just the once," I said. "I just forgot to tell you about Audrey's room."

"Interesting," he said. "She doesn't strike me as the Southern Belle type."

"Me neither," I said. "Maybe she was desperate, though." I'd used a few embarrassing self-help guides myself in the past. *The Smart Woman's Guide to Finding Mr. Right,* which I'd bought after my former fiancé cheated on me, had been my bible for a few months, so I understood the impulse.

"But I don't see what it has to do with Gerald McIntire's murder."

"I don't know. It certainly provides a motive. How would you feel if someone you thought was in love with you suddenly got engaged to someone else?"

"I'd be upset," he said, and there was an uncomfortable moment. Both of us were thinking of my former fiancé's visit to Cranberry Island — and his attempts to woo me back to Austin. "But I don't think it would drive me to murder."

"I should hope not," I said. "But it did look like a crime of passion," I pointed out.

"The idea has some merit," he said. "But unless whoever did it was already in possession of the cutlass, that would imply premeditation, not passion."

"I wish there were some way to prove that Eleazer wasn't in possession of that stupid cutlass," I said.

"He claims he left it at the inn for the archaeologist," John said.

"I know," I said. Then I had a thought. "When did he drop it off?"

John shrugged. "That's all they told me."

"A time would help narrow things down, at least."

"How?" John asked. "If he left it here with a note on it, anyone could have picked it up."

I sighed. "Another dead end, then."

John reached out and rubbed my shoulders. "So you found a self-help book and a ripped-up photo in Audrey's room," he said. "Anything else you forgot to mention?"

"Actually, yes," I said. "And it was much stranger than a photo." I told him about the plastic tubs and the car battery I'd seen in Molly's room.

"I don't see what's strange about that. She's a marine archaeologist. Why wouldn't she have scientific equipment?" he asked.

"That part makes sense," I said. "But why keep it in your room instead of in the boat? I don't remember her unloading any of that stuff when she checked in."

"Have you asked?"

"Of course not," I said. "I wasn't supposed to be in there. There was a 'Do Not Disturb' sign on the door."

I glanced over my shoulder at him; he cocked an eyebrow at me, but I ignored it and continued. "But besides that, the car battery seems weird. So do the jugs of liquid. Plus, they've been delayed two days waiting for a lift bag — but she's got one under her bed."

"Did she forget about it, maybe?" He continued to knead my shoulders as he spoke — I had no idea they were so tense.

"I doubt it," I said. "It's not like they're tiny or inconspicuous. And she must have put it there just a couple of days ago."

"Why wouldn't she bring it out, then? From what I understand, it's a race against time to identify the boat."

I nodded. "And they think they may have

found the ship's bell, which usually has the vessel's name on it."

"You're right," he said. "It doesn't make sense."

"Maybe she's double-crossing Carl," I suggested. "I thought she had a connection with Gerald — turns out they used to work together. Do you think maybe she was sabotaging the university?"

"If so, it doesn't explain Gerald's death."

I leaned forward as he worked his strong, warm hands down my back. As wonderful as the massage felt, I was still frustrated. "Carl and Audrey obviously had motives, but it doesn't explain everything else that's happened. And the only other person I can think who might have murdered him was Frank."

"Monetary gain, right?"

"If Gerald was going to restructure his will and the business once he got married, it would be to Frank's benefit if Gerald died before that could happen. He certainly seemed relieved that Gerald hadn't signed some papers before he died."

"But Frank didn't know whether or not Gerald had signed them?"

"Didn't sound like it."

"Weakens the motive, but it's still interest-

241

ing," he said. "It's certainly worth looking into."

"The police aren't going to be interested, are they?"

He gave me a sad smile. "I don't know. But even if they're not, it might provide something for Eleazer's defense attorney to chase down."

"We're missing something," I said. "I'm going to talk with everyone again, see if I can figure it out. I can sense it, just beneath the surface."

"First we'd better get you well — and check up on Adam."

"Adam!" I couldn't believe I'd forgotten. "Where's the phone?"

"I already called, my sweet. He still doesn't remember anything about the beating, but he's doing better. They'll probably release him later today."

"Thank goodness," I said. "But the puzzle is still missing a big piece."

"On the plus side, it sounds like Adam's parents have really taken to Gwen."

"Let's just hope Gwen's parents take to Adam." As John continued to rub my back, my mind strayed to thoughts of our wedding — and the potential disaster if my sister came to the island. "Maybe we should just elope and tell everyone after the fact."

He laughed and kissed me. "Your sister is the least of your worries right now, my dear. You have enough on your plate; don't go looking for trouble."

"I don't have to look for it. It seems to find me on its own."

"I can't argue with that," he said, gently touching the bump on my head.

FIFTEEN

We had no guests for lunch, so I had the inn to myself for the afternoon — and an oven that was finally in working order. What I really wanted to do was talk some more to Carl and Molly, but since they were out at the wreck site, that wasn't an option. I called Charlene to see if she'd heard anything on Evan, but she was uncharacteristically unhelpful.

"Nobody knows anything," she said. "Lots of rumors, of course. None of them particularly pleasant."

"Have you seen Ingrid?"

"Neither hide nor hair," she said. "You?"

"I stopped by to see her yesterday. She's a wreck."

"Poor thing. I'll swing by today and check in on her. How's Adam?"

"He's going to be okay, thankfully. He'll probably be out today."

"Well, that's good news, at least." I heard

voices in the background. "Half the island just turned up; can I call you back?"

"Keep me posted," I said, and hung up, feeling at loose ends. I had three hours before dinner, and nobody to question. On the other hand, my freezer was empty of back-up baked goods, I had a kitchen full of fresh groceries, and a folder full of recipes I'd been meaning to try out. Thanks to the painkillers, my headache had faded, and my energy was high, so I decided to spend a few hours immersed in one of my favorite creative activities.

I grabbed the folder I kept tucked in at the end of my cookbook stack and leafed through it, wondering what to try first.

The recipe for caramel dumplings caught my eye first, but while they looked appealing, I needed something that would freeze well — and work for breakfast. Normally I would choose something with cranberries in it, but with all the "treats" I'd received recently, I was uncharacteristically cranberried-out.

I flipped through the pages, glad to be absorbed in the comforting — and pleasantly anticipatory — task of selecting which delicious concoction I was going to try next. I lingered briefly over a decadent-looking recipe for sticky pecan cinnamon rolls, but cinnamon rolls always tasted best fresh, so that recipe was best saved for a morning when I felt like getting up extra-early. Besides, I was low on pecans. I finally settled on a lemon-berry Bundt cake that would use the bag of organic lemons John had picked up for me — and an apple streusel muffin recipe that made my mouth water. If I doubled both, I could have one batch to serve and one to freeze. Perfect.

I started with the lemon Bundt cake, since it had the longer baking time. I zested a few more lemons than the recipe called for — you can never have too much lemon, in my opinion — and squeezed several of them. Within minutes, the scent of fresh lemons floated through the kitchen, lightening my spirits as I creamed the butter and sugar together and added eggs. The recipe was far from sugarless — Claudette would never approve — but already my mouth was watering. In no time at all, I was sliding the filled pan into the oven, and the smell of baking mixed with the citrus aroma to turn my kitchen into heaven.

There was a knock at my door just as I was selecting apples to chop into chunks for the apple muffins. I set down the Granny Smiths I had chosen and opened the door to let Matilda Jenkins in. She was dressed in a green boiled wool coat with a cherry red scarf, and looked like Christmas, even though it was only October. In her arms was a stack of books.

"Hi, Matilda. Come in!" I said. "You're looking merry today."

She laughed as she set the books on the table and unwound her scarf. "I guess I do look a little festive. But it feels like Christmas with all the discoveries they're making out there, doesn't it?"

I thought of Eli's imprisonment, Adam's trip to the hospital, and Evan's disappearance — not to mention the murder victim found floating near the wreck a few days earlier — and found it hard to agree. Instead, I directed her attention to the stack of tomes she had deposited on the table. "What have you got there?"

"All the information I could find on the two ships," she said. "I promised Carl I'd see what I could get from my friend down at the maritime museum in Portland." She stopped and sniffed the air. "What is that heavenly smell?"

"Lemon Bundt cake in the oven," I said, retrieving an apple and a cutting board. "Mind if I peel while you tell me about what you found?"

"Not at all," she said.

"I can put the kettle on, too. Care for a cup of tea? It's chilly out there."

"That would be lovely, thanks." She glanced at her watch. "I'm supposed to meet Molly. Do you mind if I go and see if she's there?"

"Not at all," I said. I glanced out the window to where the *Ira B* usually moored. "Doesn't look like they're here, though."

"Hmm," she said. "She said she was going to take me out to the wreck site this afternoon, too."

"I'll get the tea going while you go and check her room. She's in the Seaglass Room, on the second floor."

"I'll be right back," she said.

She returned a few minutes later, looking disappointed. "She told me she'd meet me here, but she's not in her room. She was going to take me out to the wreck site, and I was going to show her Smuggler's Cove. What do you think happened?"

"They're racing to bring up the ship's bell," I said, pouring her a cup of tea. "And Iliad's supposed to have a big research vessel coming in today. They may just be trying to pull it up as quickly as possible, to make sure they have a chance to claim the wreck."

"I suppose," she said, taking a sip of tea

248

and reaching for the top book. "And of course it would be much better for the university to claim the wreck than a treasure hunter."

That seemed to be the opinion of most people I'd talked to. "Why don't you tell me what you've found?" I said as I peeled the first Granny Smith apple.

"You really want to know?" she asked.

"Of course," I said. "The ship could belong to one of the most illustrious pirates of the Maine coast — or to the man who built my house."

"I don't know which one to hope for," Matilda said.

"How will they be able to tell the difference?" I asked.

"Well, the ship's bell would be pretty definitive. And if there's bullion, the dates on the coins will be a dead giveaway. The two ships went down in two different centuries."

"Assuming they both went down."

"That's true," she said. "It's never been confirmed."

"What else could identify it?"

"Oh, any number of things. Tools, shoes — but you'd have to have exhaustive knowledge of the items manufactured in a particular time period. One of the easiest ways is to count the cannons."

"I'd heard something about that, but I thought it mainly had to do with identifying them."

She nodded, eyes bright. "It's wonderful to be able to identify them, but just the number they find can be a clue. Both ships had them. But the *Black Marguerite* had ten — he was a pirate, after all, so he needed them — and the *Myra Barton* only had six."

"I'm confused. Even if they do find the cannons, couldn't they belong to another ship?"

"They could," she said. "But it's unlikely. The only two ships unaccounted for in this area — the only two we could find records of, anyway — were the *Black Marguerite* and the *Myra Barton*."

"How do you count cannons, anyway? I imagine it's pretty dark down there."

"It's amazing what they can do these days. My friend in Portland told me they can do sonar scans of the bottom that look almost like photographs."

"Hmm. That's what Iliad's planning to do," I said. "They've got a big ship coming in with a sonar rig."

A wrinkle appeared in Matilda's brow. "Do they know about the number of cannons?"

"I'm guessing so," I said. "But I wouldn't volunteer it."

Matilda closed the top book and pulled it to her chest. "Mum's the word," she said.

I finished grating the apples and added a bit of lemon juice to the bowl to keep them from browning. "Are you going to have a chance to show the archaeologists Smuggler's Cove?" I asked.

"I'm hoping so," she said. "It depends on the tides." She glanced at her watch. "And what time they get here. What's taking them so long?"

"I don't know, but you're welcome to keep me company till they get back."

"Thanks," she said. "I will."

As I creamed butter and sugar together for the muffins, I glanced up at Matilda. "Did you find anything else out about Eleanor Kean?"

She shook her head. "Nothing, I'm afraid. We're lucky to have the documentation we have. For letters to survive for so many years intact is really rare."

"There are a lot of mysteries on this island, aren't there?"

She nodded. "That's what makes history so fascinating. You never know when the missing key will turn up."

"Tell me more about Jonah Selfridge," I

said as I opened the pantry in search of a bag of walnuts.

"He was a very successful man," she said. "He started out by shipping local fish to Boston and selling it. Before long, though, he'd expanded to international trade, and kept buying bigger and bigger ships."

"He managed to marry well, didn't he?" I asked. "I understand Mrs. Selfridge was quite a catch."

"Yes," she said. "Her name was Myra Barton, and she originally came from a wealthy, upper-class family."

"That's why he built the house here," I said, "instead of right by the pier, like most of the others."

"That's right," Matilda said. "Her delicate nose couldn't tolerate the smell of fish."

Having smelled the salted herring down by the pier, I couldn't argue with her logic.

"He must have loved her, if he named a ship after her. Where was she from?" I asked.

"He met her in Boston, apparently. It was a most unusual pairing for the time. Despite the fact that he was a prosperous captain, I can't imagine the match was one her family approved of."

"Particularly once they got to know him," I said. From what I knew of him, he wasn't a very nice man. Not at all. "And I can imagine Cranberry Island was a bit of a change for her."

"I imagine it was. There were only a few families living here then, and once the winter began, there was no going ashore unless it was an emergency."

"Ashore — you mean to Mount Desert Island?"

She nodded. "And despite her husband's income, life must have been very hard for Myra. Although by then, at least, there were coal-fired stoves — and a store. A few decades earlier, she would have spent her summer canning fruit and vegetables, and chopping wood."

"Delightful," I said. "Well, at least she had a good supply of lobster."

Matilda laughed. "Actually, believe it or not, nobody fished for lobster back then. It wasn't considered a delicacy; in fact, it was the opposite. Servants used to write into their contracts that they couldn't be served lobster more than once a week."

"Times sure do change, don't they?"

"Yes they do," she said. "But some things don't."

"What do you mean?" I asked.

"People seem to always do crazy things for love," she said. "Eleanor Kean, running off with a pirate captain, only to go down with his ship. And then, two hundred years later, another young woman, leaving Boston to marry a sea captain, moving to a tiny island off the coast of Maine — and losing him at sea a few years later."

From what I knew of Captain Jonah Selfridge — who had murdered a maid in his house — I thought his wife might have been better off without him. Still, Matilda was right; both relationships ended in tragedy. "It didn't go well for either couple, did it?"

Matilda shook her head. "Not at all," she said.

I looked down at the bowl in my hands — listening to the historian, I'd forgotten all about my recipe in progress. As I dug the wooden spoon into the creamy batter, I couldn't help thinking of Gerald, who had died mere days ago — and the carefully reconstructed photo in Audrey's room. Had love brought Gerald McIntire to an early death, too?

"Is that them?" Matilda said, pointing out the window. The *Ira B* was coming into the dock.

"Sure looks like it," I said.

"I'm going to go and let them know I'm here," said Matilda, slipping out the kitchen door and hurrying down to the dock. By the time I finished sprinkling streusel on top of the batter and sliding the muffin pan into the oven, Molly was trotting up the path toward the inn with Matilda. I quickly washed my hands and walked out to meet them.

"Any luck?" I asked as I closed the kitchen door behind me. The air was tangy with salt, pine resin, and a hint of wood smoke from somewhere on the island. I could tell from the spring in the archaeologist's step that their outing had likely been a success.

"The lift bags came in this morning," said Molly, eyes bright, "and we did manage to bring something up. But I'll only tell you if you'll promise to keep it under your hat."

"I promise," I said.

Molly turned to Matilda and me. "Do you have a minute?"

"Of course!" said Matilda. "And if you have time, it'll be low tide in an hour; we could go check out Smuggler's Cove!"

"I almost forgot!" Molly said. "That sounds great. And the water's calm today, so that should make it easier to get in. I can't wait to see it!"

"Unfortunately, I'm afraid it will be a bit disappointing."

"Why?"

"It's simply a cave that formed at the base

of the cliff, and it's got a few subterranean rooms," Matilda said with a shrug. "Anything that used to be kept there is gone, but there are some old iron rings buried in the stone, for tying up boats. I've tried to date them, but I haven't had any luck. I was hoping you might be able to help me."

"You never know — maybe with a close examination, something will turn up," Molly said, her voice cheerful. "Do you think the cove earned its name?" she asked.

"It's common knowledge that the cove was used for smuggling liquor during Prohibition. But legend has it pirates also used to use it as a hideout — and perhaps even a place to hide their treasure." Matilda glanced at her watch. "We've got a little bit of time. Why don't we take a look at what we pulled up first?"

"I've got some muffins in the oven, but I'll ask John to take them out when the timer buzzes," I said.

Once I'd enlisted John's assistance with the muffins, we followed Molly down to the dock and climbed into the dinghy after her. The face of her enormous watch caught the sunlight as she reached to pull the cord to the motor.

"That is the biggest watch I've ever seen," said Matilda, echoing my thoughts. "It must weigh a ton."

Molly held up her arm. "It's much more than a watch, actually — it's my dive computer. It keeps track of my time down, my oxygen, the time and duration of all my dives . . . it's like my second brain. It keeps me safe."

"Handy," I said.

"I never dive without it," she said, yanking at the starter. The motor started on the first try. We crossed the short stretch of water in less than a minute, and soon were boarding the *Ira B.*

"It's kind of Spartan," she said, and I had to agree with her. The *Ira B* was a small vessel, and the wheelhouse, which was the only 'room' on the boat, was cluttered with gear, including scuba tanks, big plastic tubs, and bright orange lift bags. Carl was standing at a worktable, bent over a large, rusty object and carefully chipping away at it with a chisel. He looked up and frowned when he saw me. "What are they doing here?"

"I wanted to show them what we found," said Molly.

"Are you sure that's wise?" asked Carl, eyeing me with suspicion. He hadn't forgotten that I'd mentioned his death threat to the investigators. I felt my cheeks getting warm, and looked away from him. My gaze was drawn to the lift bags. They looked exactly like the one I'd seen under Molly's bed.

"Everyone's going to know soon enough anyway," Molly said. "And Iliad already has the R/V with the submersible and the sonar here. What do we have to lose?"

He sighed. "You're right, I suppose."

"Well, then. You have to promise not to tell anyone from Iliad, but we finally managed to bring up the ship's bell."

"Wow," I said, looking more closely at the thing Carl was chipping away at. I hadn't been able to see it at first, but now that I knew what it was, it was obvious.

"That's wonderful," Matilda said. "Any sign of a name yet?"

"Not yet," said Carl. "But I'm optimistic."

"Ideally we'd use electrolysis to get the concretion off," Molly said, "but we're a little short on time."

The rough surface of the bell was dotted here and there with barnacles and strings of seaweed. "Hard to believe that was shiny once, isn't it?" Molly remarked.

"Isn't it?" Matilda agreed. "It's amazing what a couple of centuries at the bottom of the ocean will do."

I looked around the wheelhouse. The wall was lined with plastic tubs, all filled with water and chunks of what looked like debris. No car batteries or jugs of clear liquid, though. And even though the wheelhouse was crowded, it wasn't overflowing. I didn't know why Molly had extra equipment in her room, but it wasn't due to lack of space on the *Ira B.* "What's all this?" I asked, walking over to the line of tubs.

"Artifacts we brought up from the bottom," Molly said. "We won't know what they are until we have a chance to X-ray them back at the lab. If it's anything worthwhile, we'll chip them out."

"Why are they in water?" I asked, looking into the closest tub. The contents looked a bit like a chunk of solidified mud, with a couple of barnacles attached.

"If they're left exposed to air, metal artifacts will decay and crumble to nothing. We have to use electrolysis to change the chemistry and make them able to survive in dry conditions. That process can take awhile, though."

No wonder they wanted to pull up the ship's bell. I turned my attention back to Carl, who was painstakingly chipping off flakes of what looked like rust. "Are you sure there are letters on there somewhere?" I asked, peering at the rough surface of the object. All I saw was thick, pitted rust.

"There's no way to know if they survived, but we're hoping so," Carl said. "If I can get enough of this off to see even a few letters, we'll have enough to claim the wreck."

"Which ship are you hoping it'll be?"

"Either one would be fascinating," Carl said. "The *Black Marguerite* would be more historic, but also more controversial. If it's the *Myra Barton,* we should be able to proceed without interference."

"What about the Selfridges?" I asked. "Won't they want to stake a claim?"

"I don't foresee that being a problem," said Carl.

"You haven't met Murray Selfridge then," I said.

Carl gave me a cryptic look, then returned to his work.

As Carl and Molly bent over the bell, I walked over to a small stack of lift bags. "How do these work?" Matilda asked.

She picked up the bag, which was an inverted triangle, and pointed to the strap on the bottom. "You attach this to the object you want to lift," she said, "and then you fill the bag with air from one of your hoses, and it floats the object to the top of the water."

"Clever," Matilda said.

"It's actually tough to get it just right,"

she said. "Like Carl said the other day, If you put too much air into it, it goes up too fast, and can drop the artifact. That's what he was worried about with the bell, but we made it work." She grinned.

"Amazing," Matilda said, then glanced at her watch. "I'd love to stay and see more, but if we're going to make low tide, we'd better get going."

"Do you want to head out to Smuggler's Cove with us, too?" Molly asked me.

I suppressed a shiver. My memories of that dark, dank place weren't particularly pleasant. On the other hand, it would be fascinating to be on hand if Molly found something relevant. "I think I can make it," I said. "Can we make a quick stop back at the inn, first?"

"If we hurry," Matilda said.

"What about you?" Molly asked Carl.

"I'll trust you to make the first run. I've got to keep working until I find something," he said, barely looking up from his work.

"We're off then," she said, and leaving Carl to his chisel, we clambered back down into the dinghy.

SIXTEEN

Within five minutes, we were back at the inn dock. "Let me just make sure the cake and muffins are out of the oven and I'll be right back down," I said to Molly and Matilda.

John was taking the muffins out of the oven when I hurried into the kitchen. Thankfully, they looked perfect — golden brown on top, with crannies where the butter had melted into the batter — and the kitchen smelled divine.

"Back so soon?" he asked.

"The university team brought up the ship's bell today," I said. "I went over to take a look at it, and now we're going to show Molly Smuggler's Cove."

"Who's we?" he asked.

"Matilda and I. Want to come?"

"Last time you and I were there, things didn't go so well," he said. He was remembering a time not long after I moved to the island, when I'd been cornered in the cove by a murderer and had almost drowned trying to get out.

I shivered thinking about it, but shooed the memory away. "It was touch-and-go," I admitted, "but thanks to you, it turned out just fine," I said, remembering how John had gotten there just in time to haul me out of the water. "Thanks to you, I'm still here."

He looked hesitant. "I was going to work on my portfolio, but I'm not comfortable with you going out there by yourself."

"I'm not by myself. I'll be with Molly and Matilda. Do you really think either of them is the murderer?"

"The only one with a motive is Molly, and she doesn't seem half as concerned with the wreck identification as her partner," he confessed. "I'll tell you what. I'll walk down with you so they know I know where you're going," he said. "And if you're not back in forty minutes, I'll come find you."

"You're really that worried?" I asked.

"Better safe than sorry," he said. "And you draw trouble like a magnet."

I glanced at the Bundt cake pan. "If you're going to be here, could you take the cake out of the pan and cool it on a rack in about twenty minutes? I'll glaze it when I get back."

"My pleasure," he said. "I'll even sample a slice."

I laughed. "You're so self-sacrificing. But it'll be better if I've glazed it before you try it."

"I suppose I can wait a little bit longer, then," he said, grinning. He proffered an arm. "Shall we?"

"With pleasure," I said, and together we walked down the path to the dock, where the *Ira B*'s dinghy was waiting for us.

It was a calm, beautiful day, with only a slight breeze off the water, but I was still apprehensive about the approach to the cove. We passed by the beach where the black-chinned terns nested every year. It was the only sand beach on the island, but virtually unreachable except by boat; I'd fallen and gotten stuck on a cliff ledge trying to climb down once, and had never been brave enough to try it since. John occasionally took *Mooncatcher* over after a storm, to pick up any driftwood that washed up on the beach, but it was not a popular destination. The terns' nesting season was over now, and the sandy beach looked deserted. As we passed it by, however, I noticed something like a black plastic garbage bag peeking out from behind one of the rocks.

"Look at that," I said, pointing it out to Matilda.

She sighed. "I hate litter. Usually this beach is safe from it, but so many of the kids have skiffs these days, they sometimes come here and have picnics, and then don't bother to pick up after themselves."

"A little late in the year for a picnic on the beach," I said, zipping my jacket up. The wind was light, but it was still a crisp day.

"Who knows how long it's been there?" she said. "Could be someone who doesn't want to pay to have their trash hauled, too. You never know."

"Where's the cove?" Molly asked, focusing on the stretch of blue water ahead of us. I looked down at the water, catching a glimpse of a ghostly moon jelly as the dinghy cut through the waves.

"Right up ahead on the left," Matilda directed her. "It's a bit of a tight entrance, though — and there are lots of rocks just under the water. I'll go up to the bow and keep an eye out," she said.

"Good idea. Wouldn't want to damage a fine boat like this one," she said, winking. We all laughed; the dinghy, whose sides were splintered and dented in a number of places, had obviously seen a lot of rough use.

Just the sight of Smuggler's Cove unnerved me. As we puttered closer to the dark hole in the cliffs, surrounded by rocks that jutted through the water like sharp teeth, I found myself clutching the edge of the boat, bracing myself for another dangerous entry.

"Not an easy approach, is it?" Molly asked.

"Not at all," I said. "I almost drowned trying to get out of there once," I said.

Molly glanced at me, surprised.

"It's a long story," I said.

Molly was a better boatswoman than I, though. With Matilda at the bow, she deftly maneuvered us through the gap, only once grazing a submerged rock. "Another beauty mark," she said as we passed out of the sunny afternoon into darkness.

"Kind of spooky in here, isn't it?" Molly's voice echoed off the close, damp walls. I could hear the slap of the waves against the stone.

"Let there be light," Matilda said, and snapped on the flashlight she had brought. "There are the rings I was telling you about," she said, training the beam on first one rusty iron loop, then the other.

"Interesting," Molly said. "Let's tie up the boat, and then I'll take a closer look."

266

Matilda and Molly quickly secured the dinghy to the iron rings, and the three of us hoisted ourselves onto the rocky shelf.

"Can I borrow the flashlight for a moment?" Molly asked, and when Matilda handed it to her, she knelt to examine the iron loops. "These aren't that old," she said. "Probably less than a hundred years."

"Oh," said Matilda, disappointed.

"But that doesn't mean they didn't replace an earlier set that corroded away," she said, standing up and playing the light across the cave walls. "Not much in here," she said.

"The entrance to the cave is toward the back," Matilda told her, and the beam soon located the gap at the end of the rocky shelf we stood on.

"Is that it?" Molly asked.

"Yes it is," I said. "Careful, though — the floor is really uneven."

The three of us carefully made our way back, away from the bit of light from the cave's entrance, and I found myself grateful that John would come out to look for us if we didn't make it back in time.

"There's obviously some wear here," Molly said, training the light on the rocky floor. "See how those rocks are worn down? There's been a lot of foot traffic over the years." Something glinted in the beam of the light, and she bent down to examine it.

"What is it?" asked Matilda.

"A shard of glass," Molly said, holding it up. "I'll take it back and see if I can date it."

"Could be from Prohibition times," Matilda suggested, excitement in her voice. "A piece of a broken bottle belonging to one of the smugglers."

"Good chance of it," said Molly, pocketing the shard. "Might even be some residue of the contents."

We followed her deeper into the subterranean cavern. Molly was nothing if not thorough; she ran her flashlight over every inch of the walls and floors, touching rocks, peering into crevices. She picked up a few odds and ends; a bullet casing, a penny minted in 1938, and a few more shards of glass, but nothing that would tie the cave to Davey Blue. As she pored over every inch of the cave, I was keenly aware that the slap of the waves was growing louder. The tide was starting to come in; the longer we tarried, the harder it would be to slip through the narrow opening. Molly seemed unperturbed, but I found myself wiping my sweating hands on my jeans. Smuggler's Cove had bad memories for me; I didn't relish the thought of spending ten hours in it, waiting for the tide to drop again.

"I think we've got to call it a day," I said finally. "Tide's coming in. And if we don't get back to the inn in the next fifteen minutes, John is going to come after us."

"Give me just five more minutes," Molly said, sounding utterly engrossed in her search of the cavern room. I waited patiently as she continued her examination of the deepest part of the dark cave. I was about to tell her five minutes were up when she said, "Hello. What's this?"

Matilda bent closer, peering at the wall. "It looks like letters," she said. "Carved into the rock."

"What does it say?" I asked.

"I can't tell," Molly said, moving the light closer. "Looks like initials . . ." She laughed suddenly. "It's love graffiti!"

"What?" I asked.

"You know. John loves Sally — like the things teenagers spray paint on bridges, or carve into trees. I think it's two sets of initials."

"One of them is E.K. — could be Eleanor Kean!" Molly said, excitement in her voice.

"That doesn't explain the other one, though," Matilda said, pulling a digital camera out of her pocket and snapping a few pictures. "Who the heck is AT?"

"Good question," I said. "Kind of shoots down the Davey Blue theory."

"Unless there was someone else on board his ship that she fell in love with," Matilda suggested.

"It's too bad there's no easy way to tell how long ago this was done," Molly said. "Could be last year, could be five hundred years ago. If we could tell what tool was used . . ." she trailed off.

"Looks like whoever did it had some time on their hands," Matilda said, rapping her knuckles against the cave wall. "This rock is hard stuff."

"Maybe they got trapped in here waiting for low tide," I said, only half in jest. As I spoke, a particularly strong wave slammed into the rock walls, then retreated with an eerie sucking sound. "We really have to go," I said. "If we don't get out of here soon, we'll have plenty of time to do our own rock carving."

"She's right," Matilda said. "We can come back tomorrow if you'd like."

Molly sighed. "I suppose you're right — but I hate to leave so soon."

"If we're going to go, let's do it now," I said, resisting the urge to grab Molly's sleeve and drag her to the boat. Finally, she turned and sauntered back toward where the dinghy was tied up. She stopped in surprise when she saw that the opening to the cove had already shrunk.

"I didn't realize the tide came in so fast!" she said.

"It does, and it's still coming," I said, feeling dread rise in my throat. The three of us hurried into the boat.

"Shoot," said Molly. "I forgot to snap a picture of this area."

"We can do it tomorrow," I said. "Let's get out of here while we still can."

I had the ropes untied in record time, and waited with bated breath for Molly to start the motor. She pulled it twice, and it didn't catch. She was about to pull the cord a third time when a huge wave pounded into the cove, filling two-thirds of the opening. The boat yawed drunkenly, slamming against the stone shelf, and Molly's flashlight clattered to the bottom of the boat. The cove was darkening by the second.

She pulled the cord three more times, to no avail, and I began looking in vain for oars. Then, finally, the motor caught.

"Wait until the next wave," she said. "When I give the word, let go of the ropes, and we'll make a run for it."

We didn't have to wait long. Seconds later, another big wave almost eclipsed the cave entrance. I held tight to the ropes as the boat strained to break free. The wave had barely subsided when Molly barked, "Now!"

SEVENTEEN

I let the ropes drop and Molly gunned the motor, hurling the little boat toward the small entrance. We were at the narrowest part, just before the opening, when a rogue wave pushed us sideways, right into the wall. Molly swore and swung the rudder around, but there was a cracking, grating sound as the side of the boat scraped against the rough rocks. Then she gunned it again and we shot out of the cove into bright daylight, right ahead of another breaker.

I'd never been so thankful to see the sun before.

"That was a close one!" Matilda said, inspecting the side of the boat for damage.

"How bad is it?" Molly asked.

"It's caved in a little," Matilda said, "but it should hold. You'll probably want to replace some of the wood before you take her out again."

I looked down at the jagged hole in the

side of the boat, and thought what a shame it was that Eli wasn't on the island; he'd get her fixed up in no time. The hole was high up, so water only sloshed in when there was a wave, but there was enough water accumulating in the bottom of the boat that I reached for the bailing bucket. The recycled bleach bottle bottom was sitting on top of a plastic lid that looked just like the lids on the tubs I'd seen in Molly's bathroom.

"What are these for?" I asked, picking up a lid and showing it to Molly.

"Oh, that's just a lid to the tubs we keep the artifacts in," she said after a quick glance.

"But the tubs in the *Ira B* were bigger than this," I said, watching her closely.

She shrugged. "Maybe it's left over from the last researchers. We have to share the boats, unfortunately — and people leave all kinds of things behind. There are a couple of lockers down there that people forget to clean out. Once I found a huge dried squid someone had left below decks. It reeked like you would not believe!"

"I'll bet the smell lasted for weeks," Matilda said, wrinkling her nose.

"It did," she said. "Sometimes I still think I smell it. Kind of put me off calamari."

I set the lid down and began bailing, still

not convinced it was a leftover from a previous user. "Do you ever dive from the dinghy?" I asked.

Her eyes darted to me; I sensed the question made her uncomfortable. "Why would I dive from the dinghy when I have the *Ira B*?" she asked. "Many times, we don't even have the dinghy with us; we only towed it along because we figured the dock would be too short for the *Ira B* to tie up."

I shrugged. "I don't know. Just wondering."

"You could, though, couldn't you?" asked Matilda.

"I guess so," she said. "But I never have." Her eyes didn't meet mine; they were focused instead on the water in front of us. Another skiff was headed toward us: John. I waved to him, and he hailed me back. His teeth shone white as he smiled.

"He was coming out to find us, wasn't he?" said Molly, who was less concerned than I was by the water level in the bottom of the boat.

"Looks like it," I said, emptying another jug of water over the side.

"You two are a wonderful couple," Matilda said, smiling at me. "Have you picked a date yet?"

"We're thinking February," I said.

"Your sister in California might have a hard time making it out here if the roads are bad," Matilda said.

"Exactly," I said, and winked at her.

"You make it out okay?" John called over the thrum of the motors.

"More or less," I yelled back, brandishing the bailing bucket.

"Find anything?"

"Just some initials carved into the wall," I called back. "Did you remember the cake?"

"I'm just headed back to do it now," he said, looking a bit sheepish.

He'd forgotten, in other words. Matilda and I exchanged a knowing glance. "Thanks," I called to him. "See you shortly!"

He waved, then turned *Mooncatcher* back toward the inn.

"It's like you're married already," said Matilda.

I laughed.

Fortunately, the dinghy made it back to the inn without springing any more leaks, and I climbed out onto the dock, thankful to be back on land, then reached back to help Matilda out of the boat. "What are you going to do about that hole?" I asked Molly, who was inspecting it with a frown.

"It doesn't look too bad. I'll nail some

wood over it for now," she said.

"We've got scrap wood in John's workshop if you need it," I said. "Why don't I send him down to help you find some that will work?"

"Thanks," she said, smiling. "That would be great."

As I walked back up to the inn with Matilda, I glanced back at Molly, who was watching us as we climbed the path. She shaded her eyes from the sun, and the sunlight glanced off the face of her watch.

There was something she didn't want us to know. And I was sure it was connected with that plastic lid — and the strange equipment I'd seen in her room.

It took fifteen minutes for me to get Matilda on her way home. John was down at the dock with Molly, helping her nail a patch on the hole in the dinghy. I hurried to the front desk and grabbed the skeleton key, then took the stairs two at a time. I wanted one more look at Molly's bathroom.

The "Do Not Disturb" sign no longer hung on the door — curious, I thought. I quickly slipped the key into the lock and stepped into the room, closing the door quietly behind me.

The stack of books still lay scattered on

the desk, and I did a quick scan of the room, looking for anything unusual. Everything appeared as I had last seen it. I crossed the room to the bathroom — and that's where I found my surprise.

All of the equipment I had seen just a few days ago was gone.

I rocked back on my heels, confused. Where was the car battery, the jugs of liquid, the tubs?

Then I remembered the lid on the bottom of the dinghy. It hadn't been left by a previous researcher; it had been left by her as she moved her equipment. But where had she moved it to? The *Ira B*?

I quickly checked the closet, just to be sure, and even looked under the bed. The lift bag was gone from her suitcase, and everything appeared to be in order. Then I hurried out into the hallway, locked the door, and headed out to join John and Molly at the dock.

John had just finished hammering a chunk of plywood into the hull of the boat, and stood up as I jogged down to where the dinghy was tied up.

"Looks like you got that fixed up," I said.

"Thanks," Molly said, smiling up at him. "I should probably go and see how Carl is progressing."

"Mind if we come along?" I asked. "I'd love to show John the bell you brought up."

"I heard you managed to pull it up," John said.

"The lift bags finally came in," she said. "It was touch and go with the currents, but we got it up safely."

"Carl is chipping away to see if he can find the name," I said. "You really should see it."

"It sounds amazing," he said. "Why don't we follow you over in *Mooncatcher.*"

"Okay," she said, smiling up at John. "Thanks a million for your help, by the way. Hard to bail and steer the boat at the same time."

I joined John in *Mooncatcher,* and together we motored over to the R/V. We both followed Molly up to the wheel room, where Carl was still chipping away at the bell.

"Any luck so far?" Molly asked.

"I got a T," he said, his voice excited.

John peered over his shoulder. "You're right — I can see it there. That's amazing!"

"I can't make out the letter next to it — hoping it isn't too corroded to read."

"All we need is a letter or two more, and we should be able to ID it," Molly said.

"I just hope we find it in time," Carl murmured.

"Um . . . I hate to ask, but can I use the head?" I asked.

"Sure," Molly said. "It's right there," she said, pointing toward a door at the front of the wheelhouse.

"Thanks," I said, disappointed. I was hoping for an excuse to nose around the boat. I was dying to know if she'd moved the equipment to one of the storage cabinets.

Carl was still chipping miniscule piece after miniscule piece when I stepped out of the head a few minutes later. John was peering into the tubs of water. "What are these?" he asked.

"Those are concretions," Molly said, and I took advantage of the distraction to saunter out of the back of the wheelhouse and head down the short flight of steps to the belly of the boat. I was determined to find out where Molly had stashed all of the equipment.

Below decks it was dim, and smelled like motor oil, gasoline, and fish. The wall beside me was lined with a row of what looked like storage lockers. I opened the first one and peeked inside; it was stuffed with life jackets. The second was filled with ropes, and the third housed something that reminded me of an old desktop computer.

"That's a salinometer," said Molly quietly.

I jumped at the sound of her voice, and turned to look at her. She was framed in the doorway, blocking out most of the light. "We wondered where you'd gone. Can I help you find something?"

"I was just looking around," I said, closing the locker behind me. There was one more to open; I was dying to look inside. I glanced at Molly, then decided to go for it. "What's in here?" I asked, pulling the latch and opening the door. A red cylinder rolled out, squashing my toes. I yelped in pain and stepped back.

"A fire extinguisher," she said, moving forward to pick up the offending cylinder and stow it back into the locker. She closed the door firmly and looked at me. "Shall we go back up?" she asked.

"Sure," I said.

"After you," she said.

"Thanks," I muttered, and hurried back up the steps and into the wheelhouse.

John and Carl didn't appear to have noticed my absence. Both were peering at the ship's bell.

"I think it may be an L," John said.

"I just can't tell . . . could also be an I, or an E."

"Or maybe even an N," John said, peering at it. "It's so hard to tell!"

"I hate to drag you away from the bell," I said, "but we really should be getting back."

"Thanks for letting us come and see what you've been working on," said John, stepping away from the bell and putting his arm around my waist. "Let us know if you figure it out, okay?"

"Of course," said Carl, looking happy for the first time since I'd met him. He was sure he would have an identification soon. I just hoped he got it in time.

"Thanks for your help with the boat," Molly said to John.

"Any time," he said, and after a few more pleasantries, we left the *Ira B* and took *Mooncatcher* back to the inn.

"She's hiding something," I announced to John as we walked back up the path to the inn.

"Who? Molly?"

"Yes," I said. "Remember all that paraphernalia I saw in her room? It's gone."

"So that's what you were looking for on the boat," he said.

I grinned. "You *did* notice I was gone. Molly did, too. She came to find me."

"Did you find anything?"

"I found plenty of places to store the equipment — she didn't move it off the boat for lack of storage space — but it wasn't there."

"Then where do you think she put it?" John asked.

"I don't know," I said. "And the other question is — *why* did she move it out of her room?"

John cocked an eyebrow at me. "Maybe because she knew the innkeeper was nosy?"

I thought of the "Do Not Disturb" sign I'd knocked off her door. "It's a possibility," I confessed. "I found one of the lids in the dinghy. She must have loaded it up to move it." I thought about it. "Maybe she was the one who attacked me the other night. That would explain why she left the lid behind; it was dark."

"Whatever she's doing, she doesn't seem to want Carl to know about it."

"She must be doing something to the wreck she's not supposed to."

"Maybe she's secretly pulling up artifacts and selling them on the side," he suggested.

"Who would buy them?"

"I'm sure there's a market," he said.

"It still doesn't explain the car battery," I said as John opened the door to my kitchen. The inn still smelled of baking, and I sniffed appreciatively.

"Too bad you can't put that cake in the

bake-off," he said.

I groaned. "Thanks for reminding me." I glanced at the calendar, and realized with a sick feeling that the big day was tomorrow. I also realized today was Marge's day off. Which gave me a bona fide opportunity to check out the rooms, but also meant I was way behind on the day's work. "I forgot Marge isn't here today," I said. "Can you take care of dinner tonight, by the way?"

"What's on the menu?"

"Steak, which is easy," I said. "I can't believe I got the days mixed up!" With all of the excitement of the last week, my schedule had been thrown off. And with both Gwen and Marge gone, I was on my own. Except, thankfully, for John.

"No problem," he said, kissing me on the forehead. "I'll do setup and clean-up, too, if you'll take care of the serving."

"Thanks a million," I said.

"My pleasure. I've got a new salad dressing recipe I've wanted to try, anyway."

"Just don't make it too crazy," I said as I headed to the laundry room to pick up a basket of cleaning supplies. "Remember — we've got a *Times* food writer staying at the inn."

"No pressure," he said with a grin.

I laughed, and after a last, quick kiss,

headed upstairs to tidy the rooms.

To my disappointment, there was very little of interest in the rooms — unless you count a bunch of dirty towels. The archaeologists — and Cherry — were all relatively tidy, and since half of them made their own beds out of habit, it was a breeze getting in and out.

Audrey's laptop wasn't in her room, so I couldn't snoop there, and if Frank had any papers pertaining to the partnership, unfortunately, he didn't have them with him. I finished my cleaning with no new information. On the plus side, at least I had time to spare.

After stowing my cleaning supplies and starting a load of towels, I checked on John, who was whisking together a delicious garlic vinaigrette.

"Need any help?" I asked.

"I need you to relax, my dear. I've got it covered."

"What about dessert?"

"Chocolate pudding cake," he said.

I felt my mouth start to water. "I hope you're making a double batch."

"Only if you go and take it easy for a few minutes," he said. He shooed me out of the kitchen, and I retreated to the front desk to tidy the stacks and pay some bills. The answering machine light was blinking; there were two new reservation requests, both for next summer, which I promptly called back and confirmed. There was also a message from Gwen; she and Adam would be returning to the island tomorrow, and he was doing much, much better. I smiled, making a mental note to bake some cookies to welcome him home. One more reservation request waited for me in my e-mail box, also for the following summer. I had practically nothing booked for the next several weeks, and as I leaned back in my chair, I found myself grateful for the recent business. As stressful as the discovery of the wreck had been, it certainly had helped the inn's bottom line. It was nice paying the electric bill without breaking a sweat.

Although I'd still rather have Eli safe at home with Claudette.

As I licked the last stamp and affixed it to an envelope, I realized I had forgotten to replace the dirty towels with fresh ones. I stacked the outgoing mail and headed to the laundry room, breathing in the heavenly garlic smell in the kitchen.

"Will there be enough for me?" I asked as John washed a head of lettuce.

"I'll make a little extra," he said.

"Can't wait," I said, and pushed through the kitchen door into the dining room, then hurried back up the stairs. It was great having someone else around to do the cooking — particularly someone as talented as John.

I replaced the towels in the first four rooms, and then let myself into Audrey's room. After slipping a new bath towel onto the towel rack, I stepped back into the bedroom, doing a final check before going downstairs. The "Rules" book was no longer on her night table; she had either taken it with her or tucked it into a drawer. There were no personal effects anywhere in the main room; if I hadn't known she was staying here, I would have guessed the room was unoccupied. The blue and white counterpane was neatly arranged on the bed, the crisp white curtains were open, and the floor was polished and gleaming. I nodded in approval and started to walk to the door when I noticed something sticking out from beneath the end of the bed.

I walked over and nudged it out with my foot, drawing in my breath when I saw it.

It was the missing scabbard.

EIGHTEEN

"Come look what I found," I said breath-lessly when I burst into the kitchen a minute later.

"What is it?" John asked, putting down the whisk.

"Just come and look," I said, grabbing him by the sleeve and pulling him after me. A minute later, we both stood in Audrey's room, staring at the scabbard.

"Is that what I think it is?" John asked.

I nodded.

A look of relief spread across John's face. "So Eli wasn't lying, after all. And it looks like Gerald McIntire's death might have been a crime of passion after all. Wait until I tell the investigators about this."

"What do we do with it for now?" I asked.

"I'd like to get a picture of it," he said.

"My camera's in the kitchen."

"I'll stay here; you run and get it," he said. I raced down to the kitchen and back, short of breath. He took a few shots and then untucked his shirt, using the fabric to pick it up off the floor.

"Making sure we don't mess with the fingerprints?" I asked.

"Exactly," he said.

"What do we do with it?" I asked.

"We put it where nobody can relocate it," he said. "I'll call the investigators tonight. And tomorrow, I'll take it over to the mainland to check for fingerprints."

"One thing bothers me," I said.

"What?"

"This wasn't here the other day."

"How do you know?"

"I looked under all the beds."

John looked at me, the scabbard dangling from his hand. "Are you saying someone might have planted it here?"

"It's happened before," I said, thinking not for the first time that I needed to do a better job hiding the skeleton key. "It would be interesting to see whose fingerprints are on it."

John nodded. "It will be interesting. Even if nothing turns up, though, at least we have something that points in a direction other than Eli."

"Hard to plant a scabbard from jail, isn't it?"

"And Claudette hasn't been here, either," I said.

For the first time in days, I found myself feeling hopeful.

It was a full house at dinner that night, and despite the tragedy earlier in the week, the mood was optimistic. Including mine; I couldn't wait to hear what the investigators found on that scabbard.

"How did it go today?" I asked Audrey as I served her a plate of salad loaded with baby greens, spring onions, yellow grape tomatoes and tangy garlic dressing. Had she noticed that the scabbard was missing? I wondered. Or did she even know the scabbard was in her room?

She glanced toward the doorway, where Carl had just disappeared. "We mapped two of the cannons," she said in a low voice. "And Frank got confirmation that the company now belongs to him."

"The whole thing?"

"He certainly made a killing," she said sardonically, stabbing a grape tomato with her salad fork. "If they hadn't already arrested someone, I'd have to wonder."

"Really?" I asked, watching as Frank sauntered back into the room, a smile on his usually worried face. Had he picked up the cutlass from the front desk and used it to eliminate his partner, then planted the scabbard in his employee's room? The timing certainly was right. But if he did kill his partner, how did he get the body to the wreck site — and how did he make it back to the inn without a boat?

Every theory I came up with kept circling back to that same problem.

On the other hand, maybe nobody had planted that scabbard at all. Maybe Gerald's death was a crime of passion — and Audrey just hadn't had a good opportunity to get rid of the rest of the evidence. The only thing I couldn't figure out was why she hadn't ditched the scabbard when she got rid of the cutlass.

"Did you have a good day today?" I asked Frank as I set his salad plate down in front of him.

"Excellent, thank you," he said. "The Sea Vixen arrived safely and is already mapping the site."

"So I've heard," I said. "And I understand you're now in charge of Iliad?"

He lifted his eyebrows and glanced at Audrey, who busied herself with her salad. "I didn't realize that was public knowledge."

"Oh, was that confidential?" I said, glancing at Audrey, who looked uncomfortable.

"I was just guessing, actually. I figured that since your partner was gone . . ."

The irritated look softened. "Ah," he said. "Well, it was up in the air for a bit, and it's still not been made completely official, but yes — it looks like ownership of Iliad reverts to me."

"It looks like things are turning out well after all — except, of course, for the loss of your partner."

"A terrible tragedy," he said, shaking his head. "Who would have thought that tiny old man had it in him?"

"Some people still aren't sure he did," I said, watching Audrey. Her expression didn't change.

"I'm sure the police will sort it all out," he said, waving the issue aside. "But as for the arrival of the rig, I've been meaning to talk to you. I'm afraid it means this will be our last night at the inn."

"I understand, but I'm sorry to see you go," I said.

"I'll be sorry to say goodbye to your excellent cooking," he said, putting his napkin on his lap and picking up a fork.

"I'll pass your compliments to the chef," I said, and as he seemed more interested now in eating than talking, I drifted away from the table.

Cherry, too, was delighted by John's artfully plated salad, and I found myself wondering how she had survived so many years in the cutthroat New York restaurant world, yet still seemed unjaded. "Where did you learn to cook?" she asked as she finished her first bite.

"Actually, I can't claim responsibility for tonight's dinner. My fiancé John is the chef this evening."

"Well, tell him I want the recipe for this dressing."

"He'll be honored to give it to you," I said, smiling at her before moving on to the next table. The Iliad crew might be checking out, but with a good review in the *New York Times,* I was hopeful that the rest of the winter season would be profitable.

Carl obviously believed he was hours away from uncovering the name on the ship's bell. He dug into the salad as soon as it arrived, anxious to finish and get back to his work.

Molly gave me a speculative look as I set her salad plate down. "Any luck on the bell yet?" I asked Carl, ignoring Molly's stare. The bubbly woman I had first met had somehow disappeared this afternoon, and I was more convinced than ever that Molly was up to something she didn't want me to know about.

"We're close," Carl said, oblivious to his colleague's change in demeanor. "Should have it by morning, with any luck."

"They're mapping the site," I said in a low voice. "They've already found two cannons." He might be a murderer, but I'd still rather the university lay claim to the wreck than a treasure-hunting company.

"Well, then," he said, spearing two tomatoes and glancing over toward the table where Frank and Audrey sat. "We'd better get cracking."

When the dishes were done and the kitchen clean, John poured us two glasses of wine, and together we walked out onto the back porch overlooking the water. The night sky was awash in stars, and the crescent moon was rising, casting a pale reflection on the black water. The lights were burning in the *Ira B*'s wheelhouse, where I was sure Carl was still chipping away at the bell.

"I hope the university identifies it first," I said.

"Me too," John said.

I took a sip of wine and snuggled closer to John. The evening had gone from crisp to cold, and the warmth of his body was comforting. "Do you think Audrey killed

Gerald?" I asked.

"I don't know," he said.

"I found something else tonight," I said.

"What?"

"Remember how Audrey said she found out about Gerald's engagement after his death?"

"What about it?"

"She lied," I said.

"How do you know that?" I'm glad it was dark so I couldn't read the expression on his face.

"I slipped upstairs during the main course and checked her email," I said.

He coughed. "Not exactly something I can share with the investigators," he said. "But if they suspect her, I'm sure they'll confiscate her computer and find out on their own. When did she find out?"

"The day before he was killed," I said.

"Who told her?"

"Her sister forwarded the announcement to her," I said.

John was quiet for a long time. "It still doesn't explain how she got out there, killed him, hid the cutlass in the bushes and made it back to the inn," he said eventually. "Or what happened to the *Lorelei*."

"We can't explain that for any suspect," I said.

"Except Eli," John said.

I stared out at the humps of the mountains on the mainland, barely visible in the faint light of the moon. "Maybe Gerald took a skiff out there with someone."

"Why would he do that?"

"I don't know," I said. "Maybe it was a romantic outing with Audrey."

"Could be," John said, not sounding convinced.

"It would explain how somebody got out there, killed him, dropped the cutlass by the pier and got back." A cold breeze swept off the water, and I snuggled in closer to John.

"It's a possibility," he said. "But what about the *Lorelei*?" he asked.

"Maybe Evan stole it."

"On the same night?"

I shrugged. "It's a theory. Speaking of theories, is there any confirmation that Eli's cutlass was the murder weapon?"

"It's suspected, but there's no confirmation. The blade was clean, and the wound was damaged — nibbled at by fish — after death."

"So it could have been something else," I said.

"If it was, why get rid of the cutlass?"

"To throw suspicion on Eli. He'd threatened Gerald with it that afternoon, remember?"

"It's a thought," he said. We stood together in silence for a few minutes, both lost in thought. I was starting to get chilled and was about to suggest we go back inside when I noticed a flashlight on the *Ira B*. Someone was getting into the dinghy.

"What's going on?" I asked, pointing toward the light.

The motor hummed to life, and a moment later, the dinghy was headed out, away from the *Ira B* — and the inn.

"Let's follow her," I said.

"Her? How do you know it's Molly and not Carl?" John asked.

"Do you think he's going to leave his ship's bell? Come on," I said, and abandoning our wine glasses, we ran down the path to the dock.

Mooncatcher's motor caught immediately, and John quickly cast off and turned the little skiff in the direction the dinghy had gone. It was colder still on the water, and I hugged myself, wishing I'd taken a moment to grab a jacket.

The faint light of the moon was enough to illuminate the wake of the dinghy; I could also see the beam of the flashlight searching the rocky cliff. John kept the motor low and the *Mooncatcher* at a good distance; close enough that we wouldn't easily lose her, but not so close that we were obvious. Suddenly, the dinghy turned toward shore. John cut the engine, and we drifted, the waves splashing against the sides of the skiff.

"Is that the beach?" I whispered.

"Looks like it," he said. We followed the beam of the flashlight. It was hurrying away from the water's edge. After a moment, it disappeared. "What's she doing?" he asked, still in a whisper.

"I don't know," I said. "Maybe that's where she hid the equipment. Matilda and I saw something sticking out from behind a rock earlier today. We thought it was trash, but it could be something else."

"Should we wait, or keep going?" he asked.

"I don't know. Do you think this is her only stop?"

"Hard to know," he said. "If we don't move and she comes back this way, she may see us.

"Is there anywhere to hide?"

"We could either go in close to the rocks, or row out until we're a little farther out from shore," he said.

"Which do you think is the better choice?"

I asked, watching the beach for the flash-light.

"I think we should go out," he said, reaching for the oars.

"I'll do it," I said. "It'll keep me warm. You keep an eye on the beach."

I had been rowing for five minutes when the light appeared again, jouncing along the beach.

"Are we far enough?" I asked.

"I'll take a turn," he said, trading places with me. The light returned to the edge of the water; a moment later, I could hear the dinghy's motor revving, and the light flashed in our direction.

"Do you have a fishing rod in here?" I asked.

"I think so," he said. "It should be on the floor."

I fumbled around until my hand closed on the rod.

"What are you doing?" he asked as I pulled it up and felt for the hook. The dinghy — and the beam of the flashlight — were growing closer.

"Pretending," I said, as the hook pierced my finger. I winced and released the hook, then dropped the line into the water. "Come up here and put your arm around me, so it looks like we're out having a romantic evening."

"A romantic fishing trip at eight o'clock at night in October?" he asked, but did as I asked him to, pulling me close. "Maybe we should do this more often," he murmured into my ear as the dinghy came closer.

"Think we're far enough out?" I asked, leaning into him.

"We'll see," he said.

I held my breath as the motor puttered behind us. It had almost passed by when the light swept past us, then doubled back, glaring right into my eyes.

NINETEEN

I smiled and waved; John did the same. The motor slowed as the light flicked from my face to his, then back to mine. Then the driver gunned the motor, and the light — and the dinghy — slid away from us, back toward the direction of the inn.

"Do you think she bought it?" I asked.

"I don't know," John said. "But if you want to find out what's on that beach, I think tonight's the night."

"Shoot. We didn't stop for a flashlight."

"Let's run back and get one then," he said.

"What if she sees us?"

"She already has," he pointed out, and I couldn't argue with him.

I pulled up the line, and after waiting a few minutes, John gunned the motor and we headed for home. The dinghy was back in its place at the back of the *Ira B,* but I noticed a figure sitting on the back of the vessel, watching us in silence.

I felt a chill that had nothing to do with the weather.

She didn't follow us back to the beach — at least not immediately — but I felt a low buzz of fear at the thought of her following us. I had brought jackets for both of us, and as the temperature continued to drop, I was glad for the extra layer.

"Why am I so worried about her?" I asked John as we pulled *Mooncatcher* up onto the beach. The water lapped against the crescent of sand, and the stars were like tiny diamonds above us. It would have been an enchanted spot — if the temperature were forty degrees warmer and we weren't secretly looking for hidden contraband, that is.

"Maybe because she's got a secret she doesn't want you to know about — and you don't know what she'll do if you find out about it?"

"I think you pegged it," I said as we walked away from the water, our flashlights scanning the sand. "We saw something over there, behind one of the big rocks," I said, pointing my flashlight to the left.

We searched the beach for only a few minutes before John's flashlight found footprints in the sand.

"That makes it easy," I said. We followed them until they stopped behind a group of boulders. Tucked behind them were the plastic buckets I had seen in Molly's room — alongside a big, lidded plastic tub with wires poking out of it. It was attached to a big black garbage bag.

"Is this what you saw?" John asked, pointing to the bag, which was nestled behind a rock.

"Yup," I said.

"Looks like a car battery to me," he said, feeling the contours of the bag's contents.

"Wonder what's in the tub?" I asked.

He lifted up the lid and shone the flashlight inside. On the bottom of the tub was the wire mesh I had seen in Molly's bathroom. On top of it were a few muddy-looking lumps I recognized as concretions. I opened the lid of another one of the buckets; there were more concretions in it.

"So she was raiding the site," I said. "What's this contraption, though?"

"I think she's trying to get rid of the concretions," John said.

"With a car battery?"

He nodded. "It's a rudimentary electrolysis setup. The liquid in those jugs must have been an electrolytic solution — something like sodium hydroxide."

"I don't understand. They didn't find anything of real value at the site. Why steal from it?"

John trained his flashlight on the contents of the tub. "Iliad didn't find anything of value, but it looks like Molly did."

I followed the beam of the flashlight — and swallowed hard. Inside the concretion, I could make out what looked like a pile of gray poker chips. "Holy moly. Those are coins!" I said.

"A whole lot of coins, from the look of it," John said.

"No wonder Carl said it looked like someone had disturbed the site and taken things. Someone had!"

"Only it was Molly, not Iliad," he said.

"So she's been selling stuff on the side?" I asked.

"I don't know if she has in the past," John said, "but I'm guessing she's not doing this for scientific posterity."

"She's had the key to the ship's identity all along, then."

"If these coins have dates, she has," he said.

"What do we do now?"

"We should probably tell Carl," he said.

"Should we tell the police, too?" I asked.

"I don't know if it's illegal or not. Ownership hasn't been determined." He was quiet for a moment, thinking; I could make out the silhouette of his face against the weak light of the moon.

I sighed. "Well, we've solved one mystery, but we're still no closer to getting Eli out of jail."

"Unless," John said slowly, "this is somehow related."

"To Gerald's death? How?"

"I don't know," he said, shrugging. "Maybe he found out about it, and threatened to blow her cover."

"But if what she's doing isn't illegal, why would she kill Gerald to keep it quiet?" I asked. "Besides, we found the scabbard in Audrey's room, not Molly's."

"True," he admitted.

I glanced back toward the dark water with apprehension. Ever since we'd landed, I had half-expected to hear the sound of the dinghy's motor approaching. "Let's look around one more time, make sure we haven't missed anything. Then we can go tell Carl."

"We should probably take something with us," he said.

"See if you can find a small concretion," I said. "I'll search the area, see if there's anything else." As John sifted through the chunks of coins in the tubs, I walked around the area, which was cleverly located to be invisible from the cliffs above, yet safe from the tide — and hard to see from the water. I found only one more thing; another garbage bag. It was filled with diving paraphernalia, including a lift bag — probably the one I'd seen under her bed — a coil of rope, a dive knife, some glow sticks, a waterproof flashlight, and a gold watch that would be a much better fit on her arm than her bulky diving computer.

"Found a good one," John said, training the flashlight on the small concretion he held in his left hand. "How about you? Anything interesting?"

"Just some diving gear," I said, showing him the contents of the bag. "She must have been doing surreptitious dives late at night, when Carl was back at the inn. No wonder she changed the subject quickly when I asked if she'd dived from the dinghy before."

"You don't think she took the R/V?"

"It's possible," I said, "but I would take the dinghy. It would be missed less easily, and easier to refuel."

"Good point," he said. "Ready to head back?"

"Ready when you are," I said — although I was dreading a potential confrontation with Molly.

I steeled myself as we drew closer to the inn, thankful that I wouldn't have to face Molly and Carl alone. But by the time we got back to the inn, the *Ira B* was gone.

John idled the engine, and we looked at the buoy where the R/V had been. "Where did it go?" he asked.

"Look," I said, pointing to the dock. "The dinghy's still here."

"What the heck is going on? Do we have two disappearing boats?"

"I don't know," I said, "but I'm betting someone in the inn can tell us."

Molly was sitting in the parlor, curled up on the couch with a book, her red hair loosely caught up in a clip. She looked up with a strained smile as we entered.

"Where's the *Ira B*?" John asked.

"Carl took her down to Portland," she said.

John's eyebrows went up in surprise. "Tonight?"

She nodded. "He wanted to file papers first thing tomorrow," she said.

"He identified the bell then," John said.

Molly nodded, smiling. "It belonged to the *Myra Barton,*" she said. "Iliad probably isn't interested — there's likely to be nothing of value aboard — but Carl isn't taking any chances."

Nothing of value *anymore,* I amended silently. From what I could see, Molly had already made off with everything worth selling. "So, Davey Blue's ship is still lost to posterity," I said. "Along with his girlfriend and his fabled treasure."

"For now, anyway," Molly said.

At least the archaeologists had located the late Jonah Selfridge's long-missing ship. Another ghost laid to rest.

"And Carl will get his funding," I said.

"I can't think why he wouldn't. I saw you in your skiff, by the way," she added, and something in her tone made me squirm. "You two out for a late-night fishing run?"

I nodded.

"Catch anything?" she asked, and I couldn't help but hear a double meaning.

"Not a thing," John lied smoothly. "Mac Barefoot told me the cod were running, but we didn't even get a nibble."

"Shame," Molly said, still looking at me.

"All that fresh air tired me out, though," John said, stretching his back. "Not to mention the seating — no cushions. What do you say we hit the sack, Natalie?" he asked, putting an arm around me.

"Sounds like a good idea," I said, feigning

a yawn. "I'll just do a little breakfast prep and then head to bed." I smiled at Molly. "See you in the morning."

"Why didn't you ask her about the stuff on the beach?" I asked when we were safely in the kitchen. I had grabbed a pot from the drawer and was mixing butter, brown sugar, and corn syrup in it for overnight French toast. The recipe was scrumptious, and just the thing for an easy breakfast; toss the pan in the oven first thing in the morning, then cut up a fruit salad and cook some sausage while it baked, and you had a delicious yet quick meal.

"I was hoping she'll leave it there another day if she thinks we haven't found it," John said. "I want to be able to show Carl exactly what we found. I'll call the university and get in touch with him tomorrow morning."

"Should we have moved it?" I asked.

"To where?" he asked. "If I get a chance, I'll head over and snap some photos tomorrow. If what she's doing is illegal, and if there's some way they can press charges, moving it would be tampering with evidence."

"That's true," I said, reaching for a loaf of French bread and a knife. "Speaking of evidence, let's take another look at those coins, now that we've got light."

John dug in his pocket and pulled out the fist-sized concretion. I watched as he turned the clump over and over in the light.

"Do you think they're gold? Or silver?" I asked.

"I don't know," he said. "It's impossible to tell." The coins were identifiable by their shape, but too crusted over to make anything out. "Can you believe these have been sitting on the bottom of the ocean for more than a hundred and fifty years?"

"I always wonder about the people who went down with the ship," I said. "It's morbid, I know, but I still think about it. What happens to their bones?"

"If they haven't degraded, I imagine they're still down there," he said. "The bottom is probably littered with them."

I shuddered, thinking of the lives lost mere miles from my home. Then again, one of the men who went down had caused another life to be lost — in my own house. He'd paid the price, but he'd taken others with him. I laid the slices of bread on the cutting board to dry and gave the syrup a stir; it was almost ready to pour into the baking pan, still thinking about Jonah Selfridge, whose descendant, Murray Selfridge, still lived on the island.

"I'd better put this concretion in water,"

John said, breaking me out of my reverie. "So it doesn't degrade."

As he filled a bowl with water, I whisked eggs and milk together for the custard component of the French toast. Then I poured the hot syrup into the pan, layered it over with slices of bread, and topped it all with the creamy egg and milk mixture, making sure the bread soaked up the liquid. I put plastic wrap over the pan and tucked it into the fridge, and then John and I climbed the stairs to my room,

I lay awake in John's arms an hour later, thankful not to be alone — and, particularly with a potential murderer staying in the inn, thankful that there was a lock on my bedroom door. As John slept beside me, I kept running through what we'd found at the beach. Something about it was nagging at me, and I kept running what I'd seen over and over again, trying to figure out what it was.

Finally, I drifted off, still not sure what it was that was bothering me.

Frank and Audrey were the first ones down to breakfast the following morning — their last at the inn — and both looked grim. I couldn't help but wonder why. Frank, normally a healthy eater, was picking at his

French toast, and Audrey was only toying with her fruit salad. Did they know Carl had identified the ship's bell — and that the wreck was the *Myra Barton,* not the *Black Marguerite*?

"Everything okay?" I asked as I refilled Frank's coffee.

Frank and Audrey exchanged a look, and he nodded. "We found the *Lorelei,*" he said.

My heart leapt. Did that mean they'd found Evan, too? "Where is it?" I asked.

Frank grimaced. "On the bottom of the ocean, not far from the wreck site," he said. "We picked it up when we were doing the sonar scan of the area."

"What happened to it?" I asked.

Frank sighed. "It appears to have hit a rock; there's a gaping hole in the hull."

I swallowed, my hopes dashed. "Were there . . . was there anyone aboard?"

He shook his head. "We haven't found anyone yet," he said. "But we'll take a better look with the submersible today," he said.

I closed my eyes and said a silent prayer that Evan hadn't gone down with the *Lorelei.* Who had been driving it? I wondered. Gerald? Or whoever murdered him?

And had the murderer made it back to shore, or been sucked under with the boat?

"Will you be able to salvage it, do you think?" I asked.

"We'll see," he said. "At least now that we have it, the insurance has a better shot at coming through with some money," he said.

"Any luck identifying the big shipwreck?" I asked.

"Not yet," Frank said, "but we should finish mapping the area today." He sighed. "This operation has been a nightmare from the beginning. First Gerald, and now this . . ."

I glanced at Audrey, wondering if she'd noticed the scabbard was gone from under her bed, but her face was unreadable.

"And if this wrecked ship turns out to be nothing," he continued, "we've spent tens of thousands of dollars to rent this research vessel, only to come up empty-handed."

"I'm sorry to hear that," I said. "It's a risky business, isn't it?"

"You bet," he said, taking a swig of coffee and looking sidelong at Audrey. "Look at what happened to poor Gerald."

Audrey's eyes filled with tears, and she looked away quickly. After topping off their coffee cups, I returned to the kitchen, pretending not to have noticed. I checked the clock when I got back to the kitchen; it was almost nine o'clock, and I hadn't seen

Molly yet, which was unusual. I glanced out the window and felt a pit open in my stomach. The dinghy was gone.

TWENTY

The rest of breakfast seemed to go by in slow motion. John had gone to the mainland with the scabbard early, so I couldn't ask him to go and check the beach with me, but with Gwen still with Adam on Mount Desert Island, I couldn't go myself until breakfast was over. When Cherry finally finished her breakfast — I had to force myself to smile and make polite conversation — I tossed the last of the dishes into the sink, grabbed my jacket, and ran down to my skiff, the *Little Marian.*

The sky was leaden, and the wind howled out of the north, reminding me that winter wasn't far off. I huddled in the back of the skiff, bracing myself as the little boat rode a big wave and then slammed back down into the water.

What am I doing out here? I asked myself as I fought the choppy water and made for the little strip of beach. I wasn't sure what I expected to accomplish by finding Molly at the scene of the crime — which I was more than likely to do.

My body tensed as I rounded the turn before the beach. The dinghy was nowhere to be seen, and I wasn't sure whether to be frustrated or relieved.

I made my way in to shore, almost swamping the little skiff twice in my inept maneuvering — and pulled the skiff up onto the sand, making sure the outboard motor didn't get ground into the beach. When I was sure the skiff was far enough away from the water — the last thing I wanted to do was to have to climb the cliff to get out of here — I hurried back to where we had found the concretions the night before.

As I guessed, Molly had been hard at work relocating her stash. All but one of the tubs were gone, along with the car battery. I peered into the remaining tub — it contained two medium-sized coin concretions — and then opened the trash bag I had sorted through the night before.

Everything was as I had left it — the lift bag, the rope, the dive knife, the glow sticks, and the flashlight. And the watch, which was in a Ziploc bag.

I picked up the small bag and examined it, wondering why the watch was here instead of in her room. The face was blue, with all kinds of dials on it — a compass, a little circle that showed the phases of the moon — even a miniature map of the constellations. It didn't look very feminine, but then again, neither did the massive dive computer I'd seen on her wrist since I'd met her.

Using the hem of my T-shirt, to avoid leaving my fingerprints or smudging Molly's, I turned the watch over to put it back into its baggie, and then froze. There were initials engraved on the back.

But they weren't Molly's.

I stuffed the watch back into the baggie and shoved it into the trash bag, heart pounding. Then an awful thought occurred to me. I carefully dug through the bag until I found the dive knife. I unsheathed it slowly, holding it up to the light. At the base of the knife, where the blade met the hilt, there was a rust-colored stain.

I quickly slid the blade back into the sheath and dropped it into the bag, wiping my hands on my jeans.

Unless I was very much mistaken, Molly had murdered Gerald with her dive knife, and then planted Eli's cutlass — the one he had threatened Gerald with hours before —

near the dock as a decoy.

The only thing I couldn't figure out was why.

I bit my lip, trying to decide what to do next. If I didn't take the bag with me, Molly would soon return and hide it where I'd never find it. With no motive and no evidence, there would be no way I could prove to the police that Eli was innocent.

If I took it with me, though, I'd be tampering with evidence — even if I did have another witness to verify where I'd found it. And I still couldn't figure out why Molly had killed Gerald. From everything I'd learned, unclaimed treasure was just that — unclaimed treasure. Even if Gerald knew what she was up to, the only leverage he had was telling her colleague what she was doing. It might damage her career, but it didn't seem sufficient reason to commit murder.

Was Molly covering for someone else? Had Gerald done something else to merit her anger? Or was she just a psychotic person who enjoyed stabbing people in the back? From the mood change I'd sensed in her over the last day, I wasn't about to dismiss that as a possibility.

I would have to take the bag with me, I decided. If I left the evidence here, it would be gone by the time I got back, and then Eli would likely rot in jail while Molly roamed free — and free to kill again. I grabbed the bag and slung it over my shoulder, shuddering to think of its contents. Then I ran across the beach, racing to get to the *Little Marian* before Molly returned.

Unfortunately, I wasn't fast enough.

I heard the roar of the dinghy's motor when I was only halfway across the beach. There was nowhere to hide — the skiff was out in plain sight, and in moments, I would be, too. I ran as hard as I could, my feet sliding in the sand, and reached the *Little Marian* just as the dinghy came into view. I tossed the bag into the skiff, ran to the back, and had just heaved the little skiff into the water when there was a terrible cracking sound. The *Little Marian* juddered to a halt, throwing me forward, into the bow of the boat.

Icy water was flowing in through the hole in the side of the boat as I pushed myself up off the boards. My jacket and the front of my jeans were soaked. A hard gust of wind slammed into me, and I gasped at the cold.

Molly's cheery expression was gone, and the flatness in her eyes terrified me. "You figured it out," she said.

"That you were stealing artifacts?" I said, trying to sound confident and unconcerned, even though I was sitting out here in a wrecked skiff talking to a murderer. No one even knew I was here, I realized. John would figure it out — but by the time he got back, it would be too late. "I guessed it, yes."

"That's not what I'm talking about," she said, "and you know it."

"I don't know what you mean," I lied.

"Then what are you doing with that?" she asked, jabbing a finger at the black bag, which was already half submerged in the leaking boat.

I shrugged.

Quick as a flash, she grabbed the bag. I reached for it, trying to pull it from her hands, but she was too fast for me. She dumped the contents on the beach and grabbed the dive knife, knocking me to the ground with her sharp shoulder as I struggled to shake it out of her hand.

"Damn," she said, reaching down to scoop up the watch with the hand that wasn't gripping the now unsheathed knife. I hadn't closed the bag, and a bit of water had seeped in. "I was hoping not to get this wet."

"What do you want it for?" I asked. "A keepsake?"

"Awfully expensive keepsake," she said.

"Don't you know? It's a Tour de l'Ile — worth at least half a million. Maybe more."

A watch worth a half-million dollars? I could see why she wasn't willing to let it go down with its owner. "You were planning to sell it along with the artifacts," I said.

"Once I got rid of the engraving, of course. I was a little worried about the serial number, but that can be changed, too." She shook the watch and peered at it. "Should be waterproof, but you never know." She pocketed it and focused on me again. "You were right after all. It wasn't your friend who did Gerald in. It wasn't his money-grubbing partner, even though I know Frank's glad I did the dirty work for him. And it wasn't that pathetic little Audrey, either — although I'm sure she thought about it, once she found out he was using her."

"Why *did* you do it?" I asked.

She blinked at me. "You don't know?"

"I know you killed him, and used the cutlass as a decoy. And even put the scabbard in Audrey's room — nice touch." I glanced over at the *Little Marian;* to my dismay, the little craft was drifting out to sea. I started toward it, but Molly shook her head sharply, and I had to let her go.

"Idiot left her door unlocked," she said.

"Of course I took advantage of it."

"But what happened that night?" I said. "That's what I can't figure out."

"I was doing a nighttime dive," she said. "That's how I got the coins; I spotted them during the daytime dives, tagged them with glow sticks, and then went back for them at night."

"So you did dive off the dinghy," I said.

She nodded. "The only problem was, when I came up, guess who was waiting for me?"

"Gerald," I said. "On the *Lorelei.*"

She nodded. "He invited me aboard, of course, and then told me he knew all about my activities — and the other artifacts I'd fenced. He knew I'd been raiding the university's finds for years."

"So this wasn't the first time," I said, shivering as another cold gust sliced through my wet clothes. The light glanced off Molly's knife as she shifted position. How was I going to disarm her?

"He threatened to turn me in unless I paid him," she said. "It was either hundreds of thousands of dollars a year, or twenty years in jail. What choice did I have?"

"So when he turned his back . . ."

"Do you know what made him turn his back?" Molly asked. She was enjoying the audience, I realized.

"The rocks," I said. "The boat hit the rocks."

"Bingo," she said.

"So you stabbed him as he tried to save the *Lorelei.*"

"Yes, and it would have been perfect if he weren't so chunky."

"Why?" I asked, and then realized what she meant. "Oh. The body floated instead of sinking, didn't it?"

"And it was just my luck that your friend was nosing around that night. It was convenient that your friend left his cutlass on your front desk. I took it and ditched it near the dock as a precaution. With divers out there, there was a chance he'd be found — but I never expected he'd be out of the water so quickly."

"Are you the one who hit me the other night, too?"

"You're always where you shouldn't be, aren't you?" she said. "I was just coming back in from a dive to retrieve the last of the bullion. It's too bad I didn't hit you harder — I wouldn't have to take care of you now."

I glanced down at the *Little Marian,* which was several yards away from the beach now. Then I scanned the water behind her, hoping to see a boat — someone I could flag down.

"Don't even think about it," Molly said, reading my intentions. She pushed a ringlet of red hair out of her face, and I found myself wondering how I ever could have found her likeable. "You've made things difficult for both of us, you know. I have to get rid of you quietly, or they'll link your disappearance to Gerald's, and I don't want that to happen."

I swallowed hard, looking at the knife. "A stab wound would be a clear similarity," I said.

"There's always drowning," she said, stealing a glance at the *Little Marian.* "The boat's already got a hole in it."

"If you were going to drop me off the side of your boat, though, someone's bound to see you," I said. "It's a small island, and there are a lot of boats out on the water."

"You're right," she said. "That is an inconvenience. But not an insurmountable one." She dug through the bag and pulled out the hank of rope. "I'll just have to come back for you this evening," she said. "It'll look like an accident — only this time, the body will turn up much, much later."

"But I'll have rope burn," I said as she jerked me around and laid the blade against my throat. The metal was cold and the rough rope grated against my skin as she bound my wrists together.

"By the time they find you, they'll have a hard time figuring out who you were," she said in a voice that made me shudder. "The crabs will have you picked clean."

She yanked the rope tight and tied it quickly, then grabbed me by the arm and started marching me to the back of the beach. I started to feel some hope — if John came looking for me when he got back, I had a chance of getting out of this alive.

Evidently, Molly had the same thought at the same time.

"Never mind," she said. "It's too risky." She jerked me around and pushed me toward the dinghy.

"Where are we going?" I asked.

She checked her dive computer. "You'll see." She pushed me into the dinghy. "Lie down," she ordered, and I curled up in the bow of the boat, the fishy water on the bottom sloshing up into my face. I felt a wave of nausea, and swallowed down bile. I listened hard for the sound of a boat motor — if we came across Tom Lockhart, or another one of the lobstermen, they'd be sure to see me, and I'd be free.

The ride wasn't a long one. Only a few

minutes had passed before she idled the engine. I lifted my head to see where we were, but she pushed it down with her foot. "You'll see where we're going soon enough."

She idled a minute or two more, then gunned the motor and drove the boat forward. The side of the boat smacked into a rock with a grating sound, and my heart juddered in my chest. Then the light dimmed, and the familiar sucking sound filled me with dread.

"Smuggler's Cove," I said.

She didn't bother answering, but I knew I was right.

She was an expert boatswoman, I'll give her that. She had the dinghy tied up in no time flat, and her bulky flashlight wedged under one arm. When the boat was secure, she yanked me to my feet and pushed me up the short walkway toward the cave. "Let's go," she said brusquely when I resisted, giving me a sharp poke in the back with the tip of her knife. I gasped, feeling a warm spurt of blood. "Give the sharks something to get excited about," she said, then ordered me to sit on the floor.

She bound my feet expertly. "I'll be back tonight," she said. "I'm sure we'll find the dinghy this afternoon, and I'll volunteer to help out with the search and rescue."

"Do you really want more blood on your hands?" I asked weakly, my back still smarting from where she had jabbed me.

"In for a penny, in for a pound," she said. "See you tonight."

Then she retreated toward the dinghy, taking the flashlight with her.

TWENTY-ONE

I don't know how long I lay in the darkness on the cold rock in my damp clothes, but slowly, the sucking sound diminished, the faint hint of light at the mouth of the cave faltered, and then I knew the cove's entrance was completely submerged. I worked at my bonds, wriggling around on the bumpy floor and trying to saw through them by rubbing the rope against a sharp rock, but all I managed to do was bloody my wrists.

It was the second time I had found myself confronted by a murderer in Smuggler's Cove, I thought to myself as I lay like a beached fish on the rocky floor. I'd escaped — barely — the first time, but I was afraid Molly was too smart for me to hope I'd get lucky a second time. The next low tide was well after midnight — and after finding my skiff in the water, no one would think to look for me here. John might suspect Molly was involved in my disappearance, but what would he be able to do? The evidence was gone, and no one had seen Molly and me together. And even if I did get free of my ropes, what then? If I managed to swim out of the cove, the current was strong and the rocks jagged. If I did manage not to be smashed against the side of the cliff, it was still a long swim to a place where I could haul myself out of the water. I would likely die of hypothermia before I was found.

Unfortunately, I couldn't think of a plan B, so despite the less than rosy prognosis of plan A, I went back to trying to cut through the ropes with a dull rock. If nothing else, the movement kept me slightly less frozen, the effort passed the time — and the pain in my raw wrists distracted me from the terror.

As the hours passed with no discernable change in the condition of the ropes binding my wrists, the eerie sucking sound of the waves against the rocks returned, and I knew the tide was going out. When I gauged the tide to be halfway out, I wriggled toward the mouth of the cave and started yelling. It was likely that the pounding waves drowned out my voice, but I called out until I was hoarse, then took a break and started yelling again.

It seemed like an eternity that I lay there,

shivering in my damp clothes, back and shoulders aching from my efforts to saw through the ropes, praying for someone other than Molly to come back and discover me. When I heard the sound of a motor, I renewed my yelling, and felt a surge of hope when the motor grew closer. But when the boat entered the cove and no one responded to my call, I knew with a sickening certainty that it was Molly, not John, who had come to retrieve me.

All too soon, the flashlight appeared at the opening, and Molly was yanking me to my feet.

"You can't do this," I said, my voice hoarse from yelling.

"Let's go," she said, slicing through the ropes that bound my feet and pushing me toward the dinghy.

My feet were numb from being bound tightly for so long, and I stumbled, but Molly's grip was like steel. I reeled against her once, hoping to knock her down, but she quickly evaded the move. I crashed into the floor on my side, grazing the side of my head on a rock.

Mercilessly, she hauled me up again and shoved me down into the dinghy. Then she climbed after me, still brandishing the knife. "Shut up and stay down," she hissed. The motor started on the first try. She set the flashlight on the bench seat and untied the ropes, but left them looped around the iron rings until a big wave filled the cave. As the water receded, she released the ropes and gunned the engine, and a moment later, I left the cove for the last time.

There were no stars in the sky. I couldn't see anything — Molly had doused the flashlight — but from the moisture in the air, I was guessing there was fog. My already low hopes dropped even further.

I don't know how far we went, but with every moment, I felt more frustrated, hopeless, and angry — both at Molly and at myself. Why had I gone to the beach without telling anyone where I was going? Why hadn't I brought something to defend myself with? I'd dealt with murderers before. Why had I not had more common sense?

The fog seemed to thicken as we went, lightless, into the night. How did she know where she was going? I wondered. She was confident — or reckless — to be moving so fast at night, in fog. I saw a bluish glow in the stern of the boat, and realized she was trying to pull something up on her Blackberry. Navigation charts, maybe? Although with no landmarks to steer by, how was she going to figure out how to get home?

I took a deep breath, and smelled a new, sharp odor in the mist. Molly must have smelled it too, because the boat slowed with a jerk, and a moment later, she cut the motor.

The gasoline smell of the motor wafted over me — but so too did the other smell. Tar, I realized — and something else. Something foul. The waves lapped at the side of the dinghy, and I could hear the sides of the little boat creak. Only I'd never heard the dinghy creak before. I raised my head slightly; there was a glow in the mist, like a flickering flame. I opened my mouth to call out, and at the same moment, Molly delivered a vicious kick and a short, sharp, "Sshh."

"Help," I called in a hoarse voice. At this point, I had nothing to lose — my life was forfeit anyway. Molly kicked me again, and I yelped in pain, but called again — louder, this time. "Help!"

Molly scuttled to where I was and jammed her hand over my mouth. I bit it, hard, and she swore, pulling her hand back. I struggled to sit up. "Help!" I called again.

She hit me across the face with the back of her hand, then jammed a foul-tasting rag into my mouth.

The flickering light grew closer, but the taste and smell of gasoline and fishy water eliminated the smell of tar. I thought I could hear footsteps, the faint flutter of a sail. Whoever it was was close. I tossed my head this way and that, trying to lose the rag, but she clamped it firmly to my face.

Slowly, the flickering light retreated, and the sound of footsteps faded. Molly loosened her grip on me, and I felt tears spring to my eyes; I'd missed my last chance to be saved. She sat down at the stern of the boat and revved the motor again — but now, there was another light in the fog. She veered away from it, pushing the little dinghy hard and recklessly into the darkness. I was searching my brain, trying to come up with a plan — kick her with my bound feet? Try to push her off the back of the boat? — when the dinghy bucked to a halt with a loud scraping sound. The motor whined like an angry bee for a moment, then when silent.

Molly cursed quietly. Icy water licked my cheek. Despite the fear that welled in me — fear of being sucked under into cold, dark, nothingness, to molder at the bottom of the ocean for eternity — I realized that Molly and I were now quite literally in the same boat. The water seeped into my nose, and I turned my head, sick with dread. The death she had intended for me was seeping into the little dinghy, intent on taking not one of us, but two.

Molly was not unaware of her situation.

"Out," she said, heaving at me. "Get out."

"I can't," I mumbled through the rag. "I'm tied up."

With what seemed like superhuman strength, she pulled me to a sitting position and then started heaving me over the side. For the first time in my life, I found myself glad of my addiction to sweets; not only did it make it harder for the slight woman to lever me out of the boat, but my extra padding would keep me floating — and alive — for at least a few minutes longer. I could hear the low thrum of a boat motor nearby. Would I stay afloat long enough to be found? Surely John must have everyone combing the water for me by now.

I fought her as long as I could, but eventually she gave a mighty push and sent me headlong into the water.

The water was like ice, and I gasped involuntarily, sucking in a mouthful of cold water. My body bobbed to the surface, and I twisted my head to get a mouthful of air, choking and coughing.

Molly had already lit her flashlight and was waving it in the air, calling for help. I tried to stay near the boat, but with my arms tied, it was all I could do to stay near the top of the water and grab a mouthful of air. I relaxed and tried to float on my back, but with my arms close to my body, the waves kept rolling me over, and the icy water was numbing my already chilled limbs. I was floating farther and farther from the dinghy, feeling hope gutter like a dying candle.

I gasped for air as a wave rolled my body over again, and noticed a bright white light — and the smaller red and green lights of a boat's bow — approaching. They were zeroing in on Molly's dinghy — and I was drifting farther away, my sodden clothes swaddling me like a lead blanket.

A wave submerged me, pushing me deep under the water, and I fought to get back to the surface. I kicked my legs and propelled myself upward, sucking in as much air as I could when my head broke through the surface. The boat was closing in on Molly now; I could see her silhouetted in the light.

With a mighty effort, I pointed my head in the direction of the boat and kicked with all my might, trying to close the distance. The wet, heavy clothes dragged on me, pulling me down. On the third kick I strained my neck to see if I was still on course, and glimpsed Molly reaching for a life preserver. I yelled at the top of my lungs, only to find myself sinking into the water again. I fought to right myself, then sucked another lungful of air and drove my body forward again, toward the other boat. I couldn't feel anything anymore — not the cold water, not the air ripping through my lungs, not the bonds on my hands. My entire being was focused on closing the distance before my only hope of rescue floated away.

I lifted my head for another mouthful of air; Molly was no longer in the dinghy, but the smell of tar and decay was in the air again. The searchlight was moving again, but I couldn't tell in what direction before I was underwater again, kicking as hard as I could in the direction of the light.

The next time I broke through the surface, the light was closer. I stopped kicking for a moment, flipped to my back, and struggled to stay afloat, praying they would see me. My clothes tugged at me, pulling me into the deep, but I wriggled my body like a fish, fighting to stay afloat — and praying the light would glance across me. The tar smell was strong again, and the light growing closer. I kicked harder, too out of breath to call for help. My only hope was that I would be seen.

My body was about to give out, my numb, tired limbs no longer responding to my brain's commands, when the light glanced across me.

Something hit my face; a moment later, there was a big splash beside me, and someone was pushing me up toward the surface.

I relaxed and let the arms push me toward the boat. More hands were there, lifting me over the side. I glimpsed the flicker of a lantern, the ghostly flutter of a sail, and then John was there, face white in the bright light, hugging me to him. "Thank God you're alive," he said.

Twenty-Two

"I believe in ghosts now," John declared as I huddled beside the inn's fireplace, a mug of hot chocolate cradled in my hands and two down comforters wrapped around me. I'd taken a hot bath and was swaddled in twenty pounds of goose feathers, but I was still chilled.

"You saw the ghost ship too, then?" I asked.

"We were about to give up when one of the crew spotted the lantern," he said. "I could almost make out the shape of it — but I could definitely smell it."

"What were you doing out there in the first place?" I asked.

"When we found your skiff, we knew something terrible had happened — and I was still suspicious of Molly. When she headed out to Smuggler's Cove at low tide, I followed in *Mooncatcher,* but after she came out, I lost her in the fog."

338

"You followed her?" I asked.

"Of course," he said. "It was too much of a coincidence — the day after we find her stash, you disappear and your skiff winds up wrecked. I was afraid I was too late, and she'd already done something horrible to you, but I had to try."

"I didn't hear your boat when we left the cove," I said.

"The stupid motor wouldn't start," he said. "By the time I got it going, she was gone. I got her bearing and radioed the Coast Guard. They picked me up, then used their radar to track her down."

"That was terrifying," I said. "I thought no one knew where I was."

"Well, believe it or not, the legendary ghost ship saved you," he said. "We saw something flickering in the fog, about a hundred yards off the bow of the boat. If we hadn't shone the lights on it, trying to figure out what it was, we never would have found you."

"I saw it too," I said. "And smelled it — the tar smell. And something else too — something rotten."

"Eerie, wasn't it? But I'm so glad it turned out to be true." John squeezed my hand.

"Maybe Captain Selfridge redeemed himself," I said.

"I don't care who or what it was," John said. "I'm just glad you're alive."

"You and me both," I said. "And now Eli's off the hook."

He didn't respond.

"What?" I asked.

"The problem is, the evidence is gone," he said.

"But what about me?"

"You're a witness, to be sure," he said. "And Molly's been arrested for attempted murder. But without the evidence . . ."

"His watch was in the bag, too, you know. Gerald McIntire's watch — it's worth half a million dollars. And she used the dive knife to kill him — not the cutlass. She was there when the *Lorelei* hit the rocks."

"I know," he said, stroking my damp hair. "I was there when you told the investigators."

"They have to let Eli free!" I said.

"I wish we had some scrap of real evidence," John said. "We may be able to get him out, but without something to put her at the scene of the crime — or a murder weapon — the case is still sketchy."

I felt the helplessness well up in me again — and the frustration that my dear friend was locked up for a crime that Molly had committed in cold blood. Then I remembered something. "The dive computer," I said, sitting upright. "The one on her wrist."

"What about it?"

"It logs her dives — all of them. Including the one she did the night Gerald died."

John's eyes gleamed. "So if we download the information, it will prove that she was diving just before he died."

"Exactly. If she hasn't cleared it, it should put her at the scene."

John stood up. "Why didn't I think of that? I'm calling the investigators now."

"Now?" I said. "It's two in the morning!"

"I don't care," he said, and disappeared into the kitchen.

When he returned a few minutes later, he was smiling. "They already downloaded the data; it's got the dive we were looking for. It's not as good as a smoking gun — or a bloody knife — but it's a solid piece of evidence."

"Do you think they'll find the bag with the knife and watch in it?"

"They're looking, but there are no guarantees. There's a good chance she dumped it all overboard somewhere, or hid it on one of the outlying islands. But with your testimony . . ."

"You mean Eli will go free?"

"The investigator said they would probably be dropping charges tomorrow," he said.

"Thank God," I said, sinking back into the loveseat. "Now if only we could find Evan, that would solve all of our problems."

"Actually, he turned up today," John said.

"What? Where?"

"In Portland, with a girl he's been seeing."

"So after all of that, he was just hanging out with a girlfriend?" I shook my head. "What about what happened to Adam? And who was that Pete guy?"

"It's all connected," John said. "Evan was behind on his debts, but when he went to Pete — the lobsterman who ran the poker game — to ask for more time, Pete beat him up and threatened to kill him if he didn't pay up. Then Pete and his buddies beat up Adam when he came around asking questions."

"Lovely," I said, shivering. "I had no idea that kind of thing went on in our part of the world. Is that why he went to Portland?"

"Exactly," John said. "He was bunking with a girl he'd dated in college — told her he just needed a place to crash for a few days. Only his girlfriend was suspicious — he was pretty beaten up when he got there, and seemed afraid to leave the house. She finally called Ingrid this afternoon and told her she thought Evan was in some kind of trouble and needed help."

"At least he's still alive," I said. "And he didn't head off to the Caribbean with the *Lorelei*. Still — it's not good. What's Ingrid going to do?"

"Right now I think she's just relieved he's not at the bottom of the ocean," John said. I shivered, thinking how close I'd come to that exact fate a few hours earlier, and John pulled me to him, hugging me hard. "Pete will be arrested for assault," he said, after kissing the top of my head, "but I'm guessing Ingrid will end up making good on Evan's debts — and keeping her son on a very short leash."

"I'll be surprised if she ever lets him out of her sight again," I said, feeling a wave of drowsiness wash over me. Molly was locked up, Eli would soon be back with Claudette, and Evan was okay. I could finally relax.

"Let's get you to bed," John said.

"But I haven't gotten breakfast ready . . ."

"I'll take care of breakfast," he said, leaning down to kiss me. Then he picked me up and carried me up the stairs to bed. I was asleep before my head hit the pillow.

"Natalie!" It was Charlene. "You scared us

yesterday — I heard John found you out by the wreck site. Thank God you're okay!"

"Thanks," I said. "And Eli's going to be back on Cranberry Island before we know it."

"That's great," she said. "There's only one problem."

"What?"

"Where the heck are you?"

I paused as I soaped a pot, shifting the receiver to the other ear. "I'm in my kitchen, washing dishes. Where else would I be?" John had taken care of breakfast, but when I woke up and discovered he hadn't slept at all the night before, I sent him to bed and insisted on doing the clean-up.

"Um, I don't know," Charlene said. "Maybe the Town Hall?"

I was about to ask why when suddenly it hit me. I almost dropped the pot. "Oh, no. It's the bake-off."

"That knock on the head did have some impact after all," she said, cheerily. "Too bad it wasn't a little bit harder, or you'd be in a hospital bed and they'd have to find someone else."

"If you only knew," I said darkly.

"Tell me about it when you get here. But you'd better get here fast. The natives are getting restless!"

I was turning off the sink and wiping my hands on a dishtowel, steeling myself for the inevitable, when an idea occurred to me. "It may take me just a bit longer."

"What?"

"I have an idea. Can you hold them off for a few minutes?"

"I'll do my best," she said. "But Florence Maxwell is already as red as Maude's cranberry chutney. You'd better get a move on it."

"I'll be there as soon as I can," I said, abandoning the pot, hurrying out the kitchen door, and praying my plan would work.

"You're late! The bake-off judging was supposed to start an hour ago!" Irene Dinsdale, the bake-off chairwoman, twittered at me forty minutes later. The town hall was filled with islanders, and the tension in the large, whitewashed room was almost palpable; Maude and Florence both smiled thinly at me, then turned away, whispering to one another. The tables at the back of the room were covered in bright red tablecloths and numbered plates of cranberry dishes. I spotted the gumdrops and the chutney and suppressed a shudder.

"I'm sorry I'm running behind this morning," I said.

"Well, you'd better hurry up. Meg White keeps complaining that if her pudding isn't consumed at the right temperature, the texture is ruined."

"Actually, before we begin, I'd like to propose a change."

"Natalie, the bake-off is already underway. We can't change the rules!"

"Not the rules, of course. There have been some issues of impartiality raised . . ."

"I haven't heard them," Irene said peremptorily.

"Well, I have. So, in the interest of fairness, I would like to substitute a different judge."

Irene was aghast. "But . . . who will I find on such short notice! You agreed to do it!" She put her hands on her ample hips. "You can't possibly back out now! There's no time!"

"I've already found an alternative. Irene, this is Cherry Price, food writer for the *New York Times*. She has graciously agreed to judge the contest in my stead."

Irene's eyes grew round behind her wire glasses. "The *New York Times*?"

"Will that be acceptable?"

"Why . . . of course." She clasped Cherry's hands between hers. "I'm so honored to meet you, Ms. Price. Thank you so much for honoring us with your presence. It's so hard to scrape up qualified judges here. We do what we can, but . . . to have a genuine professional is a real honor!"

Cherry smiled back and said something gracious.

I bit my tongue. It wouldn't have mattered what I said, anyway . . . Irene had completely forgotten about me, and was leading Cherry toward the tables. I watched her go, thankful I had dodged the bullet — and that I wouldn't be exposed to Maude's cranberry chutney a second time.

Charlene sidled over to me. "What was that all about?"

"You'll see," I said as Irene stood at the podium and fussed with the microphone.

"Ladies and gentlemen," she said — even though the only male in the room was Mr. Snuggles, Maude Peters' large, neutered brown tabby. He had a reputation for dropping in on town gatherings. "I want to thank you for your patience, and announce a change in the judging."

A murmur swept through the room, and several eyes flicked in my direction.

"How in the world did you pull that off?" Charlene asked.

I winked at her and whispered, "You'll see."

"Although Natalie Barnes was a fine choice, we've had the opportunity to engage the services of a judge with far more experience and qualifications," she said.

"Nice," said Charlene in a low voice beside me.

"I am pleased to announce that Ms. Cherry Price, food writer for the *New York Times*, has graciously agreed to judge our contest today."

There was a smattering of applause, and a hum of voices. Cherry gave the audience a wave, smiled and winked at me, and allowed Irene to guide her to the first table.

"You," Charlene said, poking me with a polished fingernail, "are the luckiest woman on earth."

"My reputation is safe," I said. "And I never have to have another spoonful of Maude Peters' cranberry pickled chutney again, as long as I live."

"I'll drink to that," Charlene took a swig of Cranapple juice from her plastic cup and winced. "I think I need a real drink."

"Once the judging's over, you can have one on me. With one condition."

"What's that?"

"That no matter what, you will never let

me volunteer for anything so stupid ever again."

She raised her cup. "Deal."

Emmeline's streusel cake won top honors, and although Florence was disappointed with her second place prize for her gum-drops (apparently they tasted better than they looked), she was still pleased. "It's not as nice as winning first place, but it's still a credential," she said, holding the empty plate to her chest. "Particularly with a *New York Times* food writer judging."

Once the bake-off was over, the tables were open to the public, and everything except the chutney disappeared fast. Maude finally swept up her bowl and marched out in a huff, with Mr. Snuggles trailing behind her. "That's the problem with these small towns," she said before departing. "Too provincial to appreciate sophisticated cuisine."

Irene walked over to where Charlene and I stood, observing the proceedings. "A very successful event," she said, preening. Cherry was being mobbed by a trio of island bakers, who were scribbling down baking tips and asking for advice. Irene smiled at her fondly, then turned back to me. "And the addition of Ms. Price really made it world-class. She's such a delightful woman. So kind of her to agree to judge."

"Maybe she'll come back next year," Charlene said.

"That would be lovely," she said. "But if not, we always have Natalie."

"Personally, I think it's nice to have an impartial judge," I said. "Someone who doesn't know anyone from the island."

Irene cocked her head slightly. "The idea may have merit. There have been some accusations of bias, I must confess . . ."

"Maybe," I suggested, "if you can't get a food writer from New York, you could find someone from Mount Desert Island to do it. Or maybe even the food writer from Bangor."

Irene's eyes lit up. "That's a brilliant idea, Natalie! It would certainly broaden our choices; you have no idea how hard it is to find someone with even *minimal* qualifications."

Charlene rolled her eyes at me, and I just grinned. She had a point. I might be an innkeeper, but my fifteen years in the Parks and Wildlife Department hardly qualified me to judge cooking contests.

"Well, then," I said. "That solves all of our problems, doesn't it?"

"What do you mean, all of our problems?"

Irene blinked rapidly. "I don't understand. Do you mean you didn't want to be this year's judge? It's such an honor . . ."

"Of course it's an honor! And I was honored to be asked," I said quickly. "It's just that it's such an important contest on the island; I didn't want to . . . well, you know. Disappoint anyone."

"Ah. I can see your point," Irene said, tapping her chin with one thin finger. She glanced over at the front of the room, where Florence and Emmeline were rolling up the tablecloths. "I must assist in the clean-up. All part of organizing; you're involved in every step of the process. I want to thank you again, though, for bringing Ms. Price."

"My pleasure," I said. "Why don't I give you a hand with those tablecloths? It's the least I can do."

"That would be wonderful," she said, and I joined my fellow islanders in cleaning up the town hall, thankful to be the clean-up crew instead of the judge and jury.

TWENTY-THREE

My head healed quickly, thankfully, and within a few days, things were largely back to normal. After searching the island for almost forty-eight hours, the police had found Molly's black bag in the woods not far from the inn, with the dive knife and Gerald's watch still in it. Along with the dive computer log, the evidence was enough to free Eli and charge Molly with murder — and attempted murder, for her efforts to eliminate me. Carl had been shocked and upset — but the recovery of the coins had helped buoy his spirits. It also helped that Murray Selfridge had not only released all claim to the *Myra Barton* to the University of Maine, but had offered to fund the research.

Matilda was over the moon when she came to visit me almost a week after Molly was arrested. I was on my own that morning, and with John searching for driftwood on the nearby islands and no one staying at the inn, it was the perfect day to catch up on my baking. "I told you Murray was a good man," she said as I invited her to have a cup of coffee in my kitchen. I was adding the sour cream to one of my favorite recipes — Wicked Blueberry Coffeecake — as she spoke.

"He has his moments," I confessed as I finished mixing the batter and pulled a bag of frozen blueberries from the freezer. I hadn't experienced the generous side of his nature before — he hadn't made millions in business by being generous — but I was happy to hear that he was supporting the excavation of his ancestor's ship.

"I'm hoping we can work with the university to put together a display on the island," she said.

"Any word on what those coins were from?" I said.

"Jonah Selfridge was a merchant, so it may have been from the sale of his cargo," she said. "They also found what looks like rum bottles down there; that might have been what he was trading at the time."

"I thought rum was from the Caribbean," I said, measuring out the berries and dredging them in a bit of flour to keep them from bleeding into the batter.

"The molasses for it was often from the West Indies," she said, "but they distilled it here in New England — it was a big business."

"Sounds like a great museum display," I said.

"That *would* be interesting! We could display a few of the rum bottles from the wreck, and talk about the history of the rum trade and Maine's involvement in it . . ." Her sharp face became dreamy for a moment. "And if we find Davey Blue's ship . . ."

"That would be a coup," I said.

"Wouldn't it, though? I'm hoping we can encourage Professor Morgenstern to do a more thorough survey of the waters near Cranberry Island." Her eyes sparkled, and even though we were alone in the sunny kitchen, she lowered her voice. "I think I may have found something that will spark some interest."

"Really? What's that?" I asked, folding blueberries into the batter.

She pushed up her glasses. "Remember those initials?"

"The ones in Smuggler's Cove?" I asked as I poured the berry-studded batter into a baking pan. I shuddered at the memory of the place.

She nodded. "Guess what Davey Blue's real name was?"

"What?" I asked.

"Archibald Tucker," she said.

"No wonder he changed it," I said as I retrieved the brown sugar canister from the pantry. "Archibald Tucker doesn't exactly inspire fear."

"That's not what I'm talking about," she said. "The carving said EK + AT."

"Oh," I said, finally making the connection. "You're saying he used his real name with Eleanor?"

She shrugged. "There's no way to really know, but it's a good theory," she said. "The rock is really hard, but if they got caught waiting for the tide to go out, they'd have plenty of time."

I shivered as I blended the brown sugar with a bit of flour. Yes, they *would* have had plenty of time if they were stuck waiting for the tide to go out. I knew that from personal experience — although I hadn't been in a position to do any carving. I glanced down at my wrists, which were still scabbed from my attempts to free myself.

"I'm going to tell Murray today," she said, almost bouncing with excitement on her chair. "I'm hoping he'll fund a broader search of the area."

"I assume you haven't mentioned it to Iliad?" I asked as I mashed butter into the brown sugar and flour with a fork. The streusel would make deep, buttery crannies in the coffee cake; I could almost taste them already.

"They left the moment the university won the claim to the *Myra Barton*."

"I know — but I'd still keep it quiet," I said as I finished the streusel and scattered it over the creamy batter.

"Good point," she said, finishing her coffee and standing up. "I'm off to the Selfridges," she said. "Assuming he's not out on the *Sea Vixen*."

Carl had checked out a few days ago, when he managed to commandeer the university's bigger research vessel, and had been literally living at the site the last few days, with Murray as his constant companion.

I slid the pan into the oven and set the timer. "You're going to be turning the Cranberry Island museum into a world-class historic education center, Matilda."

"I know — first the lighthouse, and now the Selfridge ship . . . it's amazing, isn't it?"

"Keep it up," I said. "It's great for business!" And it was — the Cranberry Point lighthouse had been making news over the last year, and I'd gotten a good number of bookings out of it. The gorgeous spread Cherry Price had put in the *Times* hadn't hurt, either; I was short on bookings at the moment, but my spring was rapidly filling up.

"Do you think maybe Murray would fund a separate building for the display?" she asked.

"It would be nice near the lighthouse," I said. "Kind of a one-stop shopping experience for tourists."

"That's brilliant!" she said. "I'm off to track down Murray — and I'm going to pass on your idea!"

"I'll keep my fingers crossed," I said. Matilda practically jogged up the hill; I found myself smiling as I watched her go. Some good had come from the discovery of Selfridge's ship.

And most importantly, we had Eli back on the island.

Claudette and Eli were my next visitors.

"We brought you a pie," Claudette said, looking happier than I'd ever seen her as I let them into the inn's kitchen. They'd come in Eli's skiff, and knocked on the back door.

"There's even sugar in it!" Eli said.

"What an honor," I said, grinning. "Thank

you — I'm looking forward to having it for dessert tonight!" It did look delicious, with a golden lattice crust and ruby-colored berries. She'd missed the bake-off this year, but if she tried next year, a bit of sugar might take her pie a long way — the one she had baked today was beautiful.

"I'm so glad to see you back on the island!" I said, putting the pie on the counter and giving Eli a big hug. "And good to see you looking like your old self," I said, giving Claudette's solid body a hug, too.

"I'm glad to be back," Eli said. "And I thank you for all you did to get me out of that place. John told me what all you did, and I won't forget it."

"That ghost ship of yours came in handy," I said.

"So I hear," he said. "Funny thing that, isn't it? But all's well, that ends well, as I always say. And I'm mighty glad to be home; I missed Claudie's cooking something fierce," he said, giving his wife an admiring glance. "Would you believe, she even made *me* a pie with sugar."

"Don't get used to it," Claudette said sternly.

Eli sighed. "I'll enjoy it while it lasts, I suppose. Anyway," he said, turning to me. "We just wanted to say thank you."

"It was my pleasure," I said. "Did you ever get your cutlass back, by the way?"

"We did," he said, "and I finally got Professor Morgenstern to take a look at it."

"What did he say?" I asked.

"He can't say if it's Davey Blue's, but it's the right time period," Eli said. "He'll keep researching it, though — and you never know what he'll find out!"

"Another mystery," I said. "We've got a lot of them, haven't we?"

"That's what happens when a place has history," Eli said. "Oh — and there's one more thing."

"What?" I asked.

"Come here," he said, taking me by the elbow and leading me out to the back porch. Claudette smiled at me as I followed him.

"What do you think?" he said, pointing down to the dock.

There, gleaming in the sunlight with the hole patched and a fresh coat of paint, was the *Little Marian.*

"It's the least I could do," he said quietly, as my heart swelled with love and gratitude.

"You'd better make it in February," Gwen said, as she walked into the kitchen that evening and plopped down her art bag. "Or at the very latest sometime before next fall."

"What should I make in February?" I asked, taking another sip of wine. John and I had just finished dinner — a lovely bowl of lobster bisque prepared by my future husband alongside a salad with his famous dressing — and I was thinking about a bowl of Blue Bell Homemade Vanilla for dessert.

"The wedding, silly!" she said, pulling up a chair next to John and me.

"Why?" I asked, glancing at John.

"I already told my mom. She wants to make plane reservations."

"You *what?*" I asked.

"Adam's accident made me do some thinking," she said, crossing her slender legs and leaning forward with her elbows on the table. "We're getting pretty serious."

"I thought so," I said. "And I'm glad of it — Adam is a wonderful man. Kind, funny, smart, and loyal."

"Sounds like someone else I know," Gwen said, winking at John.

"Thank you, ma'am," John said, putting an arm around me and giving me a squeeze.

"Anyway," Gwen said, "I figured it was time to let my mother know the truth."

"What did she say?" I asked, reaching for my wine. I'd led Bridget to believe Adam was a bigwig in shipping, and had been dreading her reaction when the truth came out.

"She said if I was happy, then she was happy for me," she said.

"You're kidding me. She actually *said* that?"

"Not immediately," she said, grinning. "First I had about forty minutes of the third degree — including my future prospects, his future prospects, limiting my options . . . you know."

"I can imagine," I said.

"But she finally came around — and is insisting on coming out to visit."

"How's Adam doing, by the way?"

"Back on the boat and doing great," she said, beaming. "And they think they've found the guy who beat him up — they've got a witness who saw him with Adam the day he got hurt."

"I'm glad he's doing better — and I'm glad they caught the man who did that to him," I said.

"You and me both," she said. "But at least this shake-up has made us think about things. We've been talking a lot about the future."

I raised an eyebrow. "Could there be a second wedding in the offing, then?"

"I think that's where we're headed," she

said, eyes sparkling. "But there are a few things I need to do first."

"Like what?" John asked, glancing at me and then at Gwen.

"I don't know how to say this," she said, taking a deep breath, "but I'm planning on going back to California for a year or two to finish my degree."

I swallowed. As much as I hated to lose Gwen — even if it was only for a while — I knew she was making the right decision. "I'm glad to hear it, Gwen," I said. "I'll miss you tons, and I expect you to visit and call all the time, and you're welcome back *any* time. But I'm proud of you for finishing what you started."

"Thanks, Aunt Nat," she said, pushing back her chair and hurrying over to hug me. "I'm planning on coming back, though," she said as I released her.

I blinked at her. "You're thinking of staying here?"

She nodded. "I've been talking to Fernand — if it's okay with you, I'll come back in the summer and help out at the inn, and continue working with him. When I'm done with my degree, I'll help him run his retreats — and he'll give me a studio space of my own."

"Sounds like a great plan," I said, relieved

362

her departure wasn't going to be permanent. As thrilled as I was for her, I couldn't help feeling a twinge of sadness. "What am I going to do without you? I feel like my daughter's leaving home!"

"I'm not leaving *now,*" she said. "I'm not starting back until next fall."

"Good — because I'm going to need your help this summer!" I said.

Gwen looked at John. "By the way, did you tell her your news yet?"

"What news?" I asked, looking at John. "Oh — is it the gallery?"

He nodded, smiling. "The show is planned for December," he said.

"That's wonderful!"

"And Gwen's right — we'd better set a date," he said, stroking my hair. "I'd recommend February 14."

"Valentine's Day? How romantic!" Gwen said.

"And convenient," he said, "because our plane leaves for the Virgin Islands February 15."

I turned and goggled at John. "What?"

He grinned. "I took the liberty of booking us a honeymoon at a resort on the beach in St. Thomas," he said. "Fourteen days of sun, sand, and absolutely no cooking."

"But the inn . . ."

"We'll close for two weeks. And if there's anyone we can't turn away, Charlene, Claudette, Emmeline, and Marge have it covered."

"What about the church?"

"Already booked it," he said, mischief in his green eyes. "And all the ladies on the island have offered to cater the reception for us. Emmeline's even making the cake. In fact," he said, grinning, "all you've got to do is find a dress and sign the marriage license, and I think we're done."

I sat there, speechless, staring at him. After a long moment, his grin faded. "If you're still interested, that is?"

"I can't think of anything I'd rather do," I said, and as he folded me into his arms, I inhaled his woodsy, masculine scent and thanked God once again that I'd found my way to Cranberry Island — and home.

RECIPES

Me-Maw's Gingersnaps

Rhonda Shield is not at all fictional, and is an amazing cook. This treasured family recipe belonged to her grandmother ("Me-Maw"), and was a finalist in the 2009 *Austin American-Statesman* cookie swap competition. Thanks, Rhonda, for letting me include it — and you — in the book!

2 cups flour
2 teaspoons baking soda
1 teaspoon cinnamon
1 teaspoon ground ginger
1/2 teaspoon ground black pepper (If possible, use a mill with a very fine grind)
1/4 teaspoon salt
1/2 cup butter, softened
1 cup white sugar
1 cup brown sugar
1 large egg

1/4 cup molasses
1 teaspoon vanilla

Sift all dry ingredients together in a medium bowl. In a large bowl, with electric mixer, cream butter and both sugars. Stir in the egg, the molasses, and the vanilla, Gradually add in the dry ingredients. The batter will be **very** stiff.

Form balls using a medium-size ice cream scoop. (Rhonda likes to warm hers in hot water and then dry it.) If you don't have an ice cream scoop, you can make the balls by hand — they should be about the size of a Ping-Pong ball. With slightly damp hands, roll the balls in white sugar.

Bake at 350°F for 13 minutes, then rotate halfway. The cookies will spread, so space them out a bit. Leave them on the cookie sheet until they firm up a bit, and then transfer the cookies to a wire rack.

This makes approximately 30 cookies.

DOWNEAST CLAM CHOWDER
6–7 pieces bacon
1 medium onion, chopped
10 ounces canned baby clams, with juice reserved
6–7 medium-sized potatoes, cubed (Natalie prefers Yukon Gold)

2 10 1/2 ounce cans cream of celery soup
1 cup heavy cream
1 cup milk
1 tablespoon butter
1/2 teaspoon dill (optional)

Dice the bacon, cook in a saucepan until crispy, then add onion and saute until translucent. Add clam juice and potatoes, then cook and cover the pan until potatoes are fork tender, about 15–20 minutes, stirring occasionally so the potatoes won't stick. Stir in clams, soup, cream, milk, and add dill if desired. Add the butter last, letting it melt into the chowder, and cook for about 30–45 minutes or until thickened, stirring occasionally. Natalie prefers to serve this in small, hollowed-out loaves of sourdough bread, but it's also wonderful in a bowl with bread or oyster crackers on the side.

Serves 4 for dinner, 6 for lunch.

TO-DIE-FOR GLAZED APPLE STREUSEL MUFFINS

Muffins

3 cups flour
1/2 cup sugar
4 teaspoons baking powder
1 teaspoon cinnamon
1/2 teaspoon salt

1/4 teaspoon nutmeg
2 cups tart apple, pared & shredded
1 cup milk
1/2 cup melted butter
2 eggs, beaten

Streusel
1 cup brown sugar
6 tablespoons flour
1 1/2 teaspoon cinnamon
6 tablespoons butter, softened
1 cup chopped walnuts

Glaze
1 cup confectioners' sugar, sifted
2 tablespoons milk
1/8 teaspoon vanilla

Preheat oven to 400°F, and prepare muffin tins (Natalie uses muffin cups). In a medium bowl, sift together the flour, sugar, baking powder, cinnamon, salt, and nutmeg. Stir in apple and set aside.

In small bowl combine the milk, butter, and eggs until blended. Add to dry ingredients, and stir just until moistened. Spoon half of batter into muffin cups.

To make the streusel, combine all of the ingredients until crumbly and well-mixed. Reserve a scant 3/4 cup, and sprinkle the remaining streusel on the muffins. Cover each muffin with the remaining half of the batter, and sprinkle the reserved streusel on top of muffins. Bake for 20 to 25 minutes, or until muffins spring back to the touch.

Glaze: in a medium bowl, whisk together the confectioners' sugar, milk, and vanilla until completely smooth. Immediately drizzle glaze over warm muffins.

Makes 24 muffins.

LUSCIOUS LEMON-BERRY BUNDT CAKE
Cake

2 3/4 cups flour
1 1/2 teaspoons baking powder
1/4 teaspoon baking soda
1/4 teaspoon salt
1 cup butter, softened
1 3/4 cups sugar
4 eggs
2 tablespoons fresh lemon juice
Zest of two lemons
1 teaspoon vanilla extract
1 cup buttermilk
1 1/4 cups blueberries, raspberries, and/or blackberries, tossed with 1 tablespoon flour (fresh or frozen is fine — you may need a touch more flour if frozen)

Glaze

1 1/2 cups confectioners' sugar
3–4 tablespoons fresh lemon juice
1 tablespoon light corn syrup
Lemon zest (optional)
Fresh berries (for garnishing — optional)

Heat oven to 350°F, and grease (or butter) a 12-cup Bundt pan. Stir together flour, baking powder, baking soda, and salt in a large bowl, and set aside. In another large bowl, beat butter until smooth, then add sugar and beat for 2 to 3 minutes, until fluffy. Beat in eggs, one at a time, beating well after each addition. Add lemon juice, lemon zest, and vanilla, and beat until combined. Alternately beat in the flour mixture and buttermilk, beginning and ending with the flour. Fold in berries and spoon into prepared pan. Bake for 50 minutes or until a toothpick inserted in center of cake comes out clean. Cool on a wire rack for 20 minutes, and run a sharp knife around edges of the pan. Turn out and cool completely.

Glaze: in a small bowl, mix together confectioners' sugar, lemon juice, and corn syrup until smooth. Drizzle over top of cake and let it roll down the sides, and garnish with a few fresh berries if you've got them.

CRANBERRY ISLAND COD CAKES WITH LEMON MAYONNAISE

Cod Cakes

4 cups milk

2 pounds cod fillets, cut into 2-inch pieces

1 cup panko (Japanese breadcrumbs), divided

1/4 cup minced chives

2 tablespoons grated onion

2 1/2 teaspoons lemon zest

1 1/2 teaspoons salt

1 teaspoon black pepper

3 eggs, lightly beaten

2 garlic cloves, minced

1/4 cup fresh lemon juice, divided

1/4 cup olive oil, divided

Lemon Mayonnaise

1/2 cup mayonnaise

2 tablespoons chopped fresh flat-leaf parsley (optional)

2 teaspoons Dijon mustard

2 teaspoons fresh lemon juice

1 teaspoon minced fresh garlic

1/2 teaspoon black pepper

Bring the milk to a simmer over medium heat in a large, heavy saucepan, and add the fish. Cover the pan and simmer for 5 minutes or until fish flakes easily when tested with a fork, and drain well. Combine cod, 1/2 cup panko, chives, onion, lemon zest, salt, pepper, eggs, and garlic, then stir in 2 tablespoons juice. Divide the fish mixture into 16 equal portions, shaping each into a 1/2-inch-thick patty (you may need to add a bit more panko if patties are too moist), and coat patties with the remaining 1/2 cup of panko. (Again, you may need more.)

Heat 1 tablespoon olive oil in a large nonstick skillet over medium-high heat. Add 4 patties to pan, and cook for 4 minutes on each side or until golden. Remove from pan, and drain on paper towels. Repeat procedure 3 more times with remaining olive oil and patties. Drizzle with remaining 2 tablespoons juice.

To prepare sauce, combine all ingredients in a bowl. Serve with cakes. (Natalie likes to garnish this with chopped chives — if you want, you can add some to the lemon mayonnaise as well.)

Serves 4.

EMMELINE'S AWARD-WINNING CRANBERRY STREUSEL CAKE

Cake

2 cups flour
1 teaspoon baking powder
1/2 teaspoon baking soda

1/2 teaspoon ground nutmeg
1/4 teaspoon table salt
1/2 cup butter, softened
1 1/3 cups sugar
1 teaspoon vanilla extract
3 eggs
1 cup sour cream
1/2 cup fresh cranberries, chopped

Streusel
1/4 cup brown sugar
2 tablespoons all-purpose flour
1/2 teaspoon ground cinnamon
2 tablespoons butter
1/4 cup chopped walnuts
1/4 cup cranberries, chopped

Heat the oven to 325°F, and lightly butter and flour a 9-inch-square baking pan. In a medium bowl, whisk the flour, baking powder, baking soda, nutmeg, and salt together. In a large bowl, beat the butter, sugar, and vanilla on medium speed until well blended. Reduce the speed to medium low and add the eggs one at a time, mixing until just incorporated. Alternately fold the flour mixture and the sour cream into the butter mixture, beginning and ending with the flour mixture. Add the chopped cranberries with the last addition of flour, then spoon the batter into the prepared pan. Tap the pan gently on the counter to release any air bubbles and bake for 40 minutes.

While the cake is baking, combine the brown sugar, flour, and cinnamon in a medium bowl. Add the butter and mix, using a fork, until the ingredients are well blended and form small crumbs. Stir in the walnuts and cranberries. After the cake has baked for 40 minutes, sprinkle the streusel evenly over the top of the cake. Continue baking until a pick inserted in the center comes out clean, another 10 to 15 minutes.

NATALIE'S CARAMELIZED OVERNIGHT FRENCH TOAST

This is my favorite holiday recipe; it goes together quickly the night before, and all you have to do is put it in the oven as soon as you get up. Before the kids are done unwrapping their presents (or finding their hidden eggs), you have a decadent, sweet, sticky pan of French toast on the table — and you haven't had to do a thing!

Ingredients
2 tablespoons corn syrup
1/2 cup butter
1 cup brown sugar, packed
12 slices French bread (preferably 1–2 day

old bread)
8 large eggs
2 cups half-and-half or milk
1 teaspoon vanilla extract
1/4 teaspoon salt

Butter a 13 × 9-inch baking pan. In a small saucepan combine the corn syrup, butter, and brown sugar over medium heat, stirring until sugar has dissolved and the mixture is syrupy. Pour the mixture over the bottom of a buttered baking pan, and lay 6 slices of bread over the brown sugar mixture.

In a bowl, whisk together the eggs with half and half cream or milk, vanilla, and salt. Pour half of the egg mixture over the bread slices in the pan, then layer the remaining 6 slices on top. Pour the remaining egg/milk mixture over the top (make sure that all the bread is covered with the mixture — Natalie often spoons some of the egg mixture from the bottom of the pan over the bread to make sure it is soaked). Cover the pan with plastic wrap and refrigerate overnight.

The next morning, remove plastic wrap and bake, uncovered, at 350°F degrees for 45 minutes.

Serves 6.

ABOUT THE AUTHOR

Although she currently lives in Texas with her husband and two children, Agatha-nominated author **Karen MacInerney** was born and bred in the Northeast, and she escapes there as often as possible. When she isn't in Maine eating lobster, she spends her time in Austin with her cookbooks, her family, her computer, and the local walking trail (not necessarily in that order).

In addition to writing the Gray Whale Inn mysteries, Karen is the author of the Tales of an Urban Werewolf series. You can visit her online at www.karenmacinerney.com.

We hope you have enjoyed this Large Print book. Other Thorndike, Wheeler, Kennebec, and Chivers Press Large Print books are available at your library or directly from the publishers.

For information about current and upcoming titles, please call or write, without obligation, to:

Publisher
Thorndike Press
295 Kennedy Memorial Drive
Waterville, ME 04901
Tel. (800) 223-1244

or visit our Web site at:

http://gale.cengage.com/thorndike

OR

Chivers Large Print
published by AudioGO Ltd
St James House, The Square
Lower Bristol Road
Bath BA2 3BH
England
Tel. +44(0) 800 136919
info@audiogo.co.uk
www.audiogo.co.uk

All our Large Print titles are designed for easy reading, and all our books are made to last.